KEEP YOUR
Witches
CLOSE

COLETTE RIVERA

Edited by May Peterson

www.maypetersonbooks.com

Cover design by Ink & Laurel Design Studio

www.inkandlaurel.com

ISBN

Print: 978-1-99-118791-8

Kindle: 978-1-99-118790-1

AUTHOR NOTE

Dear reader,

This book is intended for mature audiences.
The following are content guidance and trigger warnings: gaslighting, blackmail, magical mind control, characters being framed for a crime (ultimately unsuccessfully), kidnapping of side characters, victim blaming (challenged, and not in relation to SA), emotionally manipulative/abusive parental relationship, instance of on page magical violence, sexual content: intended for mature audiences only.

Happy Reading!

LOVE & MAGIC

GIVE A WITCH A CHANCE

KEEP YOUR WITCHES CLOSE

ONE WICKED NIGHT

WITCH BOYFRIEND WANTED

KEEP YOUR *Witches* CLOSE

COLETTE RIVERA

1

JULIET

No matter how hard I tried, I couldn't shake the nagging suspicion that disaster was on the horizon. Recent events did nothing to put me at ease, but it was more than that. The problem was Mea Dubois' imminent arrival. The woman was a walking annoyance.

"Juliet, I've already got you a coffee," my psychic assistant Aria Belmonte called to me from a nearby table as I stood, momentarily frozen in the doorway to the Coffee Cat Cafe.

Her innocuous words felt like a shock, startling me before I collected myself and made my way over to her. Coffee and pan dulce sat waiting on the table for me, and our expected guests. Aria and I, the two-Witch team comprising Herrera Investigations, had an important meeting with Mea today.

A few days ago, I'd stumbled across an urgent situation that was finally being addressed by the magical Authority. If they bothered to show up. I was late but the Authority Witches were later. Not that I was secretly pleased Mea's own tardiness outdid mine, that would be petty.

I sat down across from Aria and she handed me a macchiato. I checked the time. There was only a certain degree of lateness to be endured before wondering if something was wrong. I wasn't sure why, but my mind kept jumping straight to worry this week.

I fiddled with one of my crystal rings. "They haven't emailed, have they?"

Aria shook her head and unlocked her phone to check again. "I'm positive I said to meet here, not at the office."

"I just came from the office. They weren't there."

I'd chosen the cafe as a meeting place for a silly reason. Up until now, I hadn't doubted it. I didn't need Mea poking around my personal spaces on top of everything else, but now that the day wasn't going to plan, I wondered if I'd somehow messed up and caused the delay.

Aria and I drank our coffees in silence as we waited for the tardy officials. A small team was meant to arrive and discuss the disappearance of a local Witch, Sarah Arroyo, whose absence I came across by chance. Sarah was a regular contact of mine. I'd worked with her since moving to this beachside town in the late nineties. She'd missed an appointment for the first time in decades and while that was understandable, what had happened to her house wasn't.

As a private paranormal investigator, I had to pass on cases like this to the Authority. Missing persons and foul play were not in my wheelhouse and I wanted it to stay that way.

Mea wasn't my first choice of backup—or my second, if I was honest. However, she worked for the closest Authority branch in LA. It was nothing more than bad luck Mea picked up this particular case out of everyone, and avoiding her wasn't more important than figuring out what happened to Sarah.

"If Edwin were involved he wouldn't be late," I grumbled after another fifteen minutes in which our guests did not arrive.

The Authority's response had been slow from the start and my worry for Sarah left me increasingly anxious. I'd have more confidence in the situation if Edwin was looking into the problem, rather than Mea or any of the rest of the organization. For more than a few reasons.

Aria gave me a reassuring look. "Mr. Bickel has an unfair advantage, not having to deal with traffic. I'm sure they'll be here soon."

Edwin Bickel, my friend at the Authority, was whom I called about Sarah's disappearance in the first place. Unfortunately, he was engaged with another case and couldn't be assigned to this one too. I couldn't always work with Edwin, especially when he was based in a different judicial district, but the whole thing felt like a mess.

Aria's phone rang. She answered and made meaningful faces for my benefit as she spoke. "The Authority aren't meeting us here," Aria said once she hung up.

"What? How can they cancel?"

"They're not. I've got an address. We'll get an explanation when we arrive." Aria gave me an exasperated look, like she too thought this was overly mysterious.

We stood, gathering our coffees and half-eaten pan dulce in a hurry. Aria waved goodbye to her Mortal friend who worked the cafe's register and we were out the door.

Aria eyed me as I got in her car. "Is there anything I should know about these particular Authority Witches?" Maybe this was her tactful way of asking why I was frazzled.

"I used to know one of them. It's nothing more than that." Which was true, so why couldn't I act like it? I drummed my nails on the car door's armrest, glad I wasn't driving. My concentration was shot.

"Not a friend of yours?" Aria joked in her usual dry manner.

I snorted. "Considering she's not you or Edwin, then no, we're not friends."

We wound our way up to a section of town that overlooked

the ocean and came to a stop outside a house perilously close to falling off the cliff it was built on. A woman in a suit waited at the side gate of the gravity-defying house. She led us through to the backyard wordlessly.

The view was spectacular, nothing but ocean and distant islands with hardly enough fencing to keep you from toppling to your death. I couldn't detect a boundary spell, which seemed odd. Unless this wasn't a Witch's house—Mortals didn't know about magic—but then why would we be here?

Four Witches were gathered around the patio a safe distance from the cliff edge. Mea stuck out like a sore thumb, her hair a shocking shade of blue. As we approached, I fought an unreasonable amount of outrage that she'd dyed her usual sandy blond.

When did she decide to do that?

Mea looked over her shoulder as the other Witches acknowledged our arrival. She smiled and waved enthusiastically at me. Really. Was a wave necessary? It was impossible not to notice her.

"Juliet, it's so good to see you." The fact that I hadn't retuned Mea's wave didn't seem to faze her. She radiated nothing but genuine pleasure at the sight of me. "I wish we could have caught up under better circumstances. It's been too long."

"Truly," I mumbled, though five years was hardly long enough.

"Oh good, you know each other," said Grant Easton, a Witch I'd encountered at least once before and wasn't a fan of. He looked the same as ever, pale and smug.

"Juliet and I go way back." Mea beamed and placed a friendly hand on my shoulder. "We went to Investigators College together."

Mea's hand was gone half a moment later. Had she ever touched me this casually in the years between college and now?

I didn't think so. What inspired her to do so today? Had the woman gotten even more remiss with her professionalism than the last time I'd seen her? And why the *hell* was her hair blue?

As I pondered the mysteries of Mea, the other investigators fell into a conversation about which decades we'd all attended college. Due to Witches' magically impacted longevity, there was about eighty years in age differences within the group. Easton and his work partner Isabella Torres were slightly older and showed the first signs of graying hair, while Mea, her partner Terra Reyes, and I were only forty-eight, and looked about twenty-five—as the Mortal ages.

Aria, who was the youngest of us, joined in their conversation even though she'd never attended Investigators College. She had a real skill for fitting in and talking to people, possibly from a life lived mostly in Mortal society.

I had no desire to fit in with this particular crowd and let it show as the conversation dragged on. I never bothered with niceties around the Authority. They knew I didn't like the organization as a whole, as well as most of its individuals. So why pretend otherwise?

After a while Reyes turned to me. "Juliet, I'm surprised you didn't stay in New York after school."

I didn't know her personally and wasn't sure why anything I did was a surprise to her. Maybe she was just trying to rope me into the conversation. She seemed like that sort of friendly, inclusive person, but I thought I'd made it clear I didn't want to join in with my rigid posture and grumpy expression.

I sighed. Nothing was going my way today. For some reason, I hadn't prepared for reminders of college and anything from twenty-six years ago, even though I knew I'd be seeing Mea. I didn't want to talk about why I moved, so I pulled out the most generic excuse for coming to California I could think of.

"I prefer the sunshine here, and lack of real cold weather."

"Oh gosh, me too." Mea sounded like she meant it. Her smiles always reached her hazel eyes, and now was no exception. "If it weren't for needing to see my family, I'd never leave this coast. I'm sure you know that feeling?" She looked at me expectantly. I did not know the feeling and had no desire to lie about it. Luckily Mea sailed on to her next overly positive thought. "I'm loving the vibe of this town, Juliet. You really did pick the best place to start your business. Wish I lived in a house like this. Don't you? Or maybe you do? I mean, look at the view." She could carry on an entire conversation for both of us.

I didn't hate that, to be honest.

Everyone admired the view while I kept quiet. A breeze caught Mea's hair, sending it whipping across her forehead and exposing the delicate curve of her neck. Her white cheeks were flushed from the cool sea air and accented by familiar dimples, a detail I was glad to note hadn't changed along with her hair.

But Mea's good looks were one of her many drawbacks. I'd always found her distracting and yes, her attractiveness was a significant part of what pulled my attention her way. I wasn't confused about it. My love of women was a firm part of me. I'd figured out my bisexuality before ever meeting her. It was just Mea in particular I didn't understand. She grated on me, yet no amount of frustration with her personality, or hair color choices, could spare me the undeniable fact that she was lovely.

This attraction to Mea was something I'd figured would fade over time and I still held out hope, even if it was taking far too long to eventualize.

I'd tried to focus on Mea's hair because I didn't like it. Everything else—I couldn't help giving in to noticing as the group's idle chatter washed over me. Mea—full name Meadow, but mercifully nicknamed and pronounced like *Mia*—held herself with a casual confidence that felt alien to me. She was forever stylish and didn't incline toward form-fitting clothes. Her crystal rings were practical rather than flashy, as was her general attitude.

Everything about Mea was subtle and so you might think she'd blend into the background, but I always seemed to be aware of her and the way she moved. She had a distinct way of folding her arms, shifting her weight, her wrists always drew my eyes when peeking out from beneath her cuffs, and the way her shoulders shook when she laughed was more fluid than it had any right to be.

Her clothes should have seemed boring—Mea preferred to dress in black and white, and neutral tones, and maybe this was why the hair was so jarring—she had the air of someone who belonged at fashion shows and photoshoots, but not so much that her attire wasn't business-like. Today she wore wide leg black pants, a loose white blouse and an open back vest. It was chic.

Everyone else was in boring suits, me included. Well, except Aria who was in a polo, chinos and sneakers.

My gaze had lingered too long and Mea noticed me glancing at her. I avoided eye contact.

Deciding the conversational pleasantries had gone on too long, I cut across the group's chatter. "Are we going to get to the reason we're standing in someone's backyard?"

Easton and Torres shared a didn't-I-tell-you look at my expense. I knew it was rude to be so blunt and stop conversation with a brick wall, but a Witch was missing. This wasn't a social call.

"Do you know the Witch who lives here?" Torres asked me. She was somewhat shorter than Mea, with light brown skin and sharp eyes.

"No." I glanced at the house and saw no sign of the owner. "I don't know where every Witch in town lives. Who is it? Perhaps I've come across them outside their home."

"Do you know most of the Witches in town?" Easton asked rather than answer my question.

"I wouldn't say most, no. A fair few. What does this have to do with Sarah?"

Torres shrugged. "Potentially nothing."

I made a frustrated sound before I could stop myself. Keeping me out of the loop was a deliberate tactic I didn't care for.

"What we mean is," Mea cut in—the Authority preferred everyone go by their titles and last names, however I would never be able to think of her as Ms. Dubois, another annoying reminder Mea wasn't like anyone else—but I was getting distracted and she was still talking. "We're looking into possible connections between what happened here and Sarah."

Surprised, I looked around the yard again. Still nothing suspicious jumped out. "So who lives here?"

"Lana Blakely." Torres eyed me for my reaction.

"Oh. I do know her." An unwelcome sinking feeling settled within me. "We actually have an appointment for tomorrow."

Easton made a small show of surprise. "Interesting. When did you last see her?"

"Last week?" I looked at Aria as she checked the calendar and confirmed.

Easton leaned over Aria's shoulder and peered intrusively at her phone. "What were you meeting with her about?"

Everyone else was looking at me, but I thought I managed to keep my discomfort masked. "I'm sure she'd tell you. If we went inside and asked."

Easton and Torres shared another look, this one more serious.

Reyes took up the explanation at a nod from the other two. "Lana is a friend of my sister's. I stopped in this morning to pass on some charmed necklaces the two had been developing together. But she wasn't home."

It had to be more than Lana not being home. Crap. I looked through the back sliding glass door but saw nothing amiss. I couldn't feel any magic around the place either, which wasn't necessarily a good sign.

Mea followed my gaze. "Do Lana Blakely and Sarah Arroyo know each other?"

My attention was drawn back to her. "Not to my knowledge. Lana was a client of mine. She recently hired me to look into the origins of some old grimoires. I've done other, similar work for her in the past. Sarah was a regular contact, a source of information, not a client. I often consulted her, like a colleague."

"Was Sarah a friend? Do you know if there was anything out of the ordinary going on with her?" Reyes had taken out her phone, like she was expecting to write notes.

"Not that I was aware of. And I wouldn't say we were friends —our interactions weren't personal. I've known Sarah for more than two decades but only in a professional capacity."

"The people I've worked with that long, I consider friends," said Easton as if our different approaches to friendship made me somehow suspicious.

"I'm a private person. And I may conduct my social circles differently than you, that's not a crime." I liked this less and less. It didn't seem like Aria and I were here in a professional capacity. We were witnesses.

"You didn't trust Sarah enough to get close?" Easton asked, and I suspected he was pushing me deliberately.

"I never said anything about trust." *Why would he put it that way?*

There was nothing untrustworthy about Sarah. I didn't generally get close to people. Over the years I'd grown to like Sarah, but we had nothing in common on which to build a friendship. I didn't see why I needed to explain that, or any of my other interpersonal relationships. It had nothing to do with Sarah's disappearance.

My antisocial tendencies were known to the Authority Witches, and my distrust of almost everyone, officials included, was no secret in local Witch society. None of it was personal. My upbringing made me suspicious by nature, which was a good trait for an investigator. But all this, along with certain rumors about me, seemed to put Witches like Easton on edge.

Or maybe it was that I was blatantly rude to most Authority people. I wasn't so antagonistic or defensive around everyone. None of my clients seemed to find me as objectionable as people like Easton did, and the mutual weariness between the Authority and me wasn't usually an issue. My work didn't often intersect with theirs and the Authority almost always sent Edwin Bickel to deal with me, since no one liked working with either of us.

"I'm not friends with everyone I work with," Mea said, breaking the tension. "That doesn't mean I don't trust them. And you know, I'm friends with most people. It's just life, Easton. Some Witches are colleagues." She shrugged in a motion as smooth as silk.

"I'm very worried about Sarah." I hoped the truth was apparent in my tone, not wanting them to think I didn't care just because Sarah and I weren't buddies. "As I said when I reported her missing, none of her friends or neighbors have seen or heard from her. Her front door was wide open when I went by her house three days ago."

Torres nodded. "We checked Sarah's house earlier this morning. The only detectable magical traces were from the spells you cast in looking for her."

"Your spell work makes it impossible to corroborate your

claim that the house was cleansed of all magic prior to your arrival," Easton added.

I was surprised by his implication. "Do you think I'm lying?"

"This isn't about my doubts." Easton didn't sound reassuring.

I glanced from the identical frowns on Easton and Torres's faces to Aria and back. "Why are we here?"

"To help us look for connections between the two missing Witches," Mea, at least could be counted on not to antagonize me. Her genuinely friendly expression was much more calming to look at.

Mea gestured toward the house. "Lana's home was also cleansed of all magical traces. Her front door wasn't left open, but we found a half-eaten meal from last night on the table. It's like she vanished abruptly, or was made to leave with no warning or sign of struggle, just like Sarah."

My low spirits sank further. An abandoned meal might not sound overly suspicious, but coupled with the cleansed house, it was.

Witches always had protective magic cast over their dwellings. These protections weren't infallible and could be broken easily if the person after you possessed more power, but protective spells helped guard against most things. Even in the rare instance a Witch skipped protective spells entirely, no practicing Witch's house would be completely free of magical traces.

Magic was a force, and like all other forces, could be measured and observed with the right tools. It always left an echo in its wake. Cleansing a space thoroughly enough to remove all echoes was a very complicated process, requiring a great deal of power, and wasn't done lightly. Witches only ever cleansed like this when they had something to hide. It pointed to someone else being at the house, covering up their presence and any spells they cast. Unless the two Witches had faked their disappearances, and were hiding something themselves.

"We'll take over all aspects of investigating from here." Easton pulled me out of my speculative thoughts. "There isn't anything further you need to do Ms. Herrera, other than relay any relevant information you have. Anything you've come across in your previous work with these two that might help."

"Yes, of course." I didn't need the reminder they were taking over and wondered if Easton expected me to object. If so, he'd find himself disappointed.

"Maybe Terra and I can talk with you and Aria now, while the others talk to Lana's family and friends?" Mea suggested.

I agreed and Torres and Easton departed. As they exited the yard, I felt a small strain lift. This whole situation had gotten worse, but at least they were doing something now, not just standing around.

"You weren't investigating something sinister that these two women were trying to keep hushed up, were you?" Reyes gave me a hopeful look, but I suspected she was joking.

I frowned. "No. Sinister is not how I'd describe the cases I take on."

"Damn. Couldn't it just be something obvious like a secret society they'd both belonged to? Or a deadly secret they'd uncovered?"

"You can't be serious." I gave Reyes a stern look, eliciting a somewhat inappropriate laugh from her which I chose to ignore. "I have no idea what's going on, or if the two disappearances are even connected. Hopefully everything is wrapped up soon, so Sarah and Lana can get back to their lives and you all can go home."

Mea shook her head but maintained her smile. "Sick of us already, Juliet? Look, we need your help and I know Easton is a pain, but I'm not so bad, promise. I've been trying to change your mind on that since college. If you couldn't tell." Her eyes flashed like this was another joke.

"Mea, you don't have to keep mentioning how we know each other. You know it. I know it. It's irrelevant." My tone came out harsher than I intended, and Mea's casual confidence faltered.

I didn't know why Mea assumed she knew who I'd liked or hadn't like back then, and would never get used to how flippantly she referred to one of the worst periods of my life. She didn't know I considered the past that way, but I wasn't obligated to reveal that to her. I'd had so much going on back then that I'd hardly noticed Mea half the time, even as distracting as she was. I'd had bigger problems than what we thought of each other.

Now however, with my life in its current state, far removed from that time, I didn't have personal problems more significant than Mea Dubois, and I had no idea how to feel about that.

2

MEA

*J*uliet chided me, unsmiling and for all appearances unfeeling. I didn't believe it for a minute. She wasn't unfeeling, she hated me and that was a strong emotion.

Hidden somewhere beneath her precisely done up look of disapproval was a reason she despised me, but fuck if I knew what it was. I was only trying to find common ground with Juliet, be friendly, but apparently connection was irrelevant.

Maybe I should write off her dismissal as stress due to the present situation. This case was serious and I shouldn't be focusing on how much it hurt every time Juliet acted like I was the biggest pain in the ass for existing within her notice. But I was human. And Juliet used to like me, despite what I'd said. We'd been friends at first. Fleetingly.

I just didn't get anything about Juliet Herrera. I wish she'd never been nice to me, then I could have accepted her disdain without caring. Well okay, I'd still care. But her switch from friendly to indifferent made me wonder what I'd done, even all these years later. And Juliet wasn't indifferent, not really. She was just hard to read.

I couldn't help wanting to find a way to get through to her. Every time we crossed paths there would come a point where I thought I was getting closer, then she'd shut me down and make me feel like a chump for trying.

"Knowing each other isn't irrelevant," I told Juliet gently, not as a challenge but as more of a plea for reason.

Juliet clenched her jaw so hard her cheek muscle twitched. Imagine hating someone so much that acknowledging them risked tooth damage. Damn. Never mind. Trying with her was nothing more than a waste of time.

"I just don't need the constant reminder," Juliet said like it cost her with interest.

"Sorry. I won't mention it again." I smiled and shrugged. Like, no big deal, we're all good. This only seemed to piss her off more.

Terra and Aria were doing their best not to look awkward and failing. I took pity on them and got us back on track. "Would you and Aria mind going through your files on the two missing Witches to look for connections?"

Juliet arched a manicured brow. "You trust us to do that without your supervision?"

"Yes, of course." I'd work on Juliet later, waste of time or not. She wasn't rid of me. I had plans and things to accomplish here beyond finding the missing women and I'd really rather have Juliet on board than fighting against me.

Juliet studied me like she knew I had something up my sleeve. "Fine. We'll make going through the files a priority. Can Aria and I walk through the house first, before we go?"

"I thought that would be a good idea." I led the group toward the back door. "You're familiar with Lana so might see something amiss we wouldn't recognize."

Juliet treated me to a curt nod. Her long dark brown hair fell over her brow in a lovely tumble of curls.

I unlocked the door with a quick spell. The team and I had already run through diagnostic magic and preliminary revealing spells on the property, and found nothing due to the cleansing. Juliet was looking for non-magical clues now.

With nothing else to do, I watched Juliet. I had to, to make sure she didn't do anything suspicious. Not that I thought she would, but I'm just saying I *had* to look at her, not that I wanted to.

Juliet was the same as she'd ever been, put together down to the last detail. Everything from her shoes to her jewelry, to her nail color was coordinated and flattering. I always noticed Juliet's shoes. She had a habit of wearing egregiously tall heels. They hurt to look at, but I also never wanted to see her in anything else, maybe in nothing else except for the heels.

Which was an inappropriate thought I didn't need to have. Now or ever.

Juliet dressed in a way that embraced her curvy form. She liked color, but usually in small pops like a scarf or belt, paired with dark pencil skirt suit sets. It made me wonder what she wore on her days off. What was she like when she went to the beach? Long hair tied back, a cotton tank top exposing the soft brown skin of her shoulders. I bet she still wore lipstick to the beach. And why did that thought make me smile?

Juliet moved through the house observing everything with close attention to detail. She muttered to Aria occasionally, but nothing significant seemed to catch her eye.

I wondered how it would be to have her focus on me so undividedly. Knowing Juliet, she'd like me less the more of me she saw. But there was something about her sharp eyes and stiff manner that I enjoyed despite everything. I didn't get why the things that baffled and infuriated me about Juliet also intrigued me.

I met Juliet the first day of Investigator's College and we'd hit it off right away. She was outgoing, bubbly and so damn clever. The whole student group stuck together that first month, and Juliet and I were close to inseparable.

It was hard to believe that was twenty-six years ago, but the sensation of old memories feeling like yesterday was down to being a Witch. When you lived for centuries you didn't age like a Mortal, Witch-youth was actually drawn out. It wasn't only our appearances that went unchanged for decades. Sometimes I felt so much like the twenty-something I was in the nineties it was uncanny to see how different the world was now. There was no question; I was closer in mentality to that young woman, or any millennial, than to a Mortal my numerical age.

Maybe I was immature, but to some extent this couldn't be helped when you were a Witch under one-hundred years old. That was my excuse anyway. The nineties were practically yesterday, in a weird time-warpy sort of way. Back then, Juliet and I were on the way to being besties. Or girlfriends. Or both. But after that first month she'd changed her mind.

Juliet flipped some invisible switch and closed herself off. She stopped joining in when I organized drinks or study sessions. I tried to ask her about it, and she'd made some excuse about focusing on study, not distractions. She'd made it seem like building friendships was useless.

I refused to believe I'd read too much into those early days. There had been more going on, but I couldn't for the life of me see what. I'd shifted from a friend to a rival in Juliet's eyes and didn't know why. It felt like she was always trying to one-up me, keeping herself apart and treating any competition like a step that existed to push her higher. Then when she'd graduated at the top of our class, Juliet ignored all the job offers that came with her success like it had all been a game, and I realized I'd understood her even less than I thought.

If I believed Juliet now, all that history was irrelevant. Never mind my hope that whatever rift we had would heal with time.

As we moved through the house Juliet paused and spent time sifting through papers on Lana's desk.

"I really don't think any of this is useful on its own," Juliet said to Aria, and I guess Terra and myself, but she didn't look at us. "This is a pamphlet from an event on enhancing your earth magic that Sarah ran at the end of last year. So the two have at least crossed paths, but so have a lot of other Witches."

"Did you go to the event?" I wondered if that was the kind of thing Juliet did for fun.

"No." Juliet glanced at me briefly. "It was worth a look, but you'll probably get better information from Witches who know the women personally. Aria and I should go. We can start on the files I have at the office."

Terra and I walked the others back out to the yard.

"We should meet up after you've had time to go through your files," I said before Juliet could escape.

She stopped on her way to the gate. "I'll call if we find anything, and if you need copies of my files that can be arranged. Otherwise, I don't see why we need to meet again."

Terra suppressed a sigh of disapproval, her breath coming out in a huff as Juliet turned to leave again.

"You know, you might be seeing more of me soon," I called after the private investigator.

Juliet stopped, turned to face me and stared.

"You didn't hear it from me, but there could be some changes coming to the Authority. Smaller branches located outside the major cities. That kind of thing."

Juliet didn't react and I was disappointed despite myself.

"If we open an office here, you could join us," Terra added from beside me. "Best of both worlds. Living here and a career boost worthy of your special power."

"My career is exactly as I want it, thank you." Juliet turned and was out the gate before her assistant knew what to do. Aria gave us a half-wave and quickly followed.

I turned to Terra. "Nice."

She rolled her eyes. "What's wrong with offering the woman an opportunity? She's a pain, but would be good to have in support of our proposal. If I had the magical gift that runs in her family, do you know how many promotions I'd have had by now?"

"Maybe—" I stared at the closed gate. I'd never liked the Authority's focus on power and special magical ability over other skills. Terra was right, you could use these things to get promotions, but I respected Juliet for not going that way.

I wouldn't have mentioned my plans if I'd realized Terra would go straight there. Why hadn't I kept quiet? Had I hoped Juliet would stay, show interest and actually want to talk to me?

I turned away from the gate. "Variations in magical power aren't always inherited. Maybe Juliet doesn't have the same gift her mother does. She's never mentioned it."

"Like she'd tell you." Terra smirked. "God, I've never seen someone so annoyed by the sight of you. I thought you were exaggerating when you warned me."

"Yeah, no need for that. Come on, let's get back to work." I turned and walked briskly into the house.

Terra trailed behind me. "Why do you try so hard with that Witch anyway?" She was my favorite of all the partners I'd been paired with at work, but right now she was proving she knew me too well.

I began collecting supplies for a location tracking spell, borrowing items from Lana's shelves. "I don't. It's not like I was the one offering Juliet a job."

"Saying we should all meet up again—telling her you're thinking of moving to town. Seems like trying to me, Mea.

Where's I was just thinking the Authority wouldn't say no to scooping Juliet up. They love collecting people with unique gifts. If she was on board with our plan—"

"That's your aim? Using her to get what we want. Good-fuck-ing-luck. *I* was just trying to be friendly. Not scheming for ways to make our proposal more appealing."

Terra looked deep in thought, her brows scrunched together and dark brown eyes narrowed. "Okay, fine. We don't need to make things more complicated for ourselves. I know coming here is what you want."

"Mm." I made myself busy collecting candles. "Now, stop distracting me and go find a personal item."

Terra snorted and walked off toward Lana's bedroom. I went to the kitchen and opened cupboards until I came across the salad bowls. Terra was right, moving here was what I wanted. Only, it had somehow seemed simpler before today.

After coming to the West Coast, I'd found a good group of Witches to surround myself with, but my sphere had felt like it'd shrunk more recently. I hoped moving would broaden my social circle, so while I didn't need Juliet's approval to come to town, it would have been nice if she were even the tiniest bit interested in reconnecting.

How could she not want to reconcile the past? There was no reason for the two of us to clash all the time.

I didn't want to examine my reasons for selecting a town that included Juliet Herrera for my next step in life, other than to admit I didn't want to move somewhere I knew no one, or go to a completely unfamiliar place. I was running away from my life, more than running toward something new, anyway. It wasn't so much about coming here specifically but leaving LA, and if I picked somewhere too far away, Terra wouldn't want to move with me. I wasn't prepared to deal with a new work partner on top of everything else.

There were things I didn't like about the LA branch of the Authority. I was hoping to get away from some of the internal politics by moving. Terra and I shared some of the same frustrations with our colleagues and management and this expansion seemed like the perfect opportunity to get away from all that.

Was it too much to want both new and familiar? I didn't believe the two necessarily contradicted. I was determined to build the next stage of my life with balance in mind.

But work wasn't my main problem. Four years ago, my fiancée had broken off our engagement, and more recently I'd come to the conclusion that staying in the same social circles wasn't going to work long term.

Witch communities were small, even in big cities, and I didn't live a life full of Mortal involvement. Overlay the lesbian community on top of Witchiness, and everything shrunk. Even small things were complicated when all our friends were mutual. Breaking up with Michaela had devastated me. I'd moved on as much as I was able, but I couldn't keep running into her. I needed a fresh start, to build a life that was completely separate from the one I'd planned with her.

Taking part in the Authority expansion would keep me busy, hopefully reignite some of my enthusiasm for the organization, and stop me making more ill-fated relationship decisions like reviving a failing romance with a proposal. Okay, maybe no amount of work could have saved me from that flawed idea, but I could pretend.

I brought two salad bowls to the living room and set them on the floor, then arranged candles and herbs in a circle around them. By the time I was using a pitcher to fill one of the bowls with water, Terra re-joined me and placed a hairbrush in the other bowl.

Terra and I flicked our wrists in unison and the candles

ignited. We shifted seamlessly into reciting an incantation and magic hummed in the air.

We peered into the water. It reflected nothing but the room's ceiling.

"Damn it." Terra flopped onto the nearby couch and the candles went out in a puff of dark smoke. "I can feel the concealment pushing back."

We'd had the same disappointing result with our attempt at tracking Sarah.

I dissipated the smoke with a spell. "If Lana is being concealed, at least we know she's alive." A Witch's remains couldn't be masked the way living people could be, so the attempted tracking spell hadn't been entirely useless.

"True, but whoever is hiding these Witches possesses a significant amount of power. There's absolutely nothing in the reflection."

There was usually a hint of something, a sense of direction at minimum, even when a successful concealment spell was being used to counter location tracking.

A Witch's power increased the longer they were alive, so we were likely looking for a suspect close to three centuries old, going by the strength of the spell. Technically it could be someone young with very uncommon power, but either way it wasn't much of a start.

"We're not going to figure it out sitting here." I nudged Terra's leg with my toe before I started putting candles back on Lana's shelf. "Hopefully Juliet will call."

"You're lucky I'm mature and going to dump this water in the sink and not on your head." Terra turned her back on me. "You're hopeless, Mea."

"I meant call with a lead," I shouted after her.

Why else would I care about Juliet calling me?

3

JULIET

*M*ea's parting comment ate away at me all afternoon. She had to be joking. Why would the Authority want to open a branch here? Why would *she* want to *move*?

Going through my files proved a poor task for keeping my mind off the blue-haired Witch.

Aria took to the computer at the reception desk in the waiting area, while I retreated to my office to sort through the physical records. The office was tidier than it once was, with everything in filing cabinets and magical artifacts shelved in an adjoining closet. I hadn't made much effort to decorate beyond the furniture, which was selected for its classic, hardwood style and paired with vintage chairs reupholstered in bright fabrics.

My offices were located on the top floor of a nondescript, multipurpose building a few miles outside the main town center. I didn't have signage. No need for unsuspecting Mortals to try and hire me to tail allegedly cheating spouses. Herrera Investigations wasn't that sort of PI firm. I was only of any use to Mortals who Knew about magic's existence, or Witches with minor mysteries on their hands.

Aria poked her head in the doorway and eyed the papers stacked around my desk and on the floor. "Anything?"

"Not yet. Sarah is a magical historian. I have files for the work she hired Herrera Investigations to do, but most of the information she's given me over the years is mixed in with other cases. So far nothing screams disappearance worthy." I put yet another folder on the nearest pile of not-helpfuls.

Aria looked dejected. "Same for our electronic records. And there's been nothing my psychic ability can do for the case—I'm not even an investigator. I'm trying to come up with helpful ideas but feel kind of useless."

"You're not. Today went much better than it would have without you." She'd kept me organized and it was much nicer facing the others with someone by my side.

"I just wish I could do more. I know we're not technically involved in the investigation and I prefer our usual jobs, like the vanishing stock at that Mortal's boutique. But doing nothing except going through files and waiting isn't exactly easy." Aria grimaced.

I knew how she felt. Not wanting to deal with more serious crimes was in the top-two reasons I'd started my private firm rather than join the Authority.

Aria inched further into my office as if she couldn't help it. "Do you think it could be a ransom situation, or something like that?"

"Maybe. They're both well off." Many Witches were, given we had a suite of unfair advantages compared to our Mortal counterparts. "If that's the case we'd hope to hear demands soon. The longer this goes with no word, the less likely ransom is."

"I know he's busy, but maybe Mr. Bickel could help." Aria flicked through some of the papers stacked on the yellow chair visitors to my office usually occupied. "Could he break the concealment spell hiding Sarah remotely?"

Some Witches were born with rare abilities; Edwin's gift was an outlier much more so than Aria's or mine. He had a unique magical ability that allowed him to manipulate space and time, meaning he could do things like teleport and freeze time itself. This, coupled with his significant magical strength, meant Edwin could also break any spell if he combined all his powers in just the right way.

"He can't break spells remotely, no." I picked up yet another folder and wrinkled my nose at the dust. "He needs to have contact with the affected object or person to remove magical influences."

It wasn't for me to explain exactly how Edwin's trick in ultimate spell-breaking worked and I suspected Aria wouldn't ask. I'd only experienced it in action once. Such extreme measures were rarely necessary, or like now, were foiled by other complicating factors.

"Don't tell Bickel I'm disappointed to find out he has limits to his power," Aria grumbled.

She surprised a laugh out of me. "I'd never."

"Good. I guess I should get back to the computer." Aria didn't move. "Um—can I ask—what was that comment about your career Reyes made earlier? Would you be interested in working with them if they came to town? Hypothetically, like one day?"

I put my folder down and leaned my hip against the desk, giving Aria my undivided attention. "No. Not at all. Don't worry, Aria. I'm never going to close Herrera Investigations and go work for the Authority, just as you'd never quit to work for the legal system. Working privately means I don't use particular facets of my magic—which I think is what Reyes was referring to—but I'm more than okay with that, even if it's unusual and not something everyone would understand."

I couldn't bring myself to explain more directly. Aria and I hadn't discussed my possession of a magical gift. I hardly liked to think about what my ability could do, and usually managed to push it to the back of my mind. Still, Aria looked like she was putting the pieces together, realization making her expression thoughtful. She'd heard of my family, so it wasn't a far leap to fill in the blanks.

I tried not to worry confirming rumors would change anything between us. Aria had to trust I followed the law and never used my rare magic on her unknowingly. But if anyone would understand it was Aria.

On the surface she and I had little in common, but not wanting to occupy the space Witchy society designed for us was a seed of shared understanding. Aria was a psychic that didn't want to work for the courts sniffing out lies. I was another thing entirely. Both our powers had the capacity for invasive misuse, but Aria was as rigid and ethically minded about how she conducted herself as I was. It was what first intrigued me about the young Witch, and she didn't disappoint me now.

Aria smiled, a rare gesture for her, especially when not paired with sarcasm. "I'm glad I came to work for you, Juliet." With that she turned and went back to the reception desk, leaving me with a potent sense of relief.

Having a magical gift didn't mean I had to use it. I was sure Terra Reyes thought I was foolish for not furthering my career, but I had no desire to ever work for the Authority or the magical law enforcement system. Some things weren't meant to be controlled.

A‍FTER ANOTHER HOUR of searching through files my phone buzzed. I read the text message, sent a quick reply and ten seconds later Edwin Bickel was standing in my office.

"I see Aria's new filing system didn't stick." He glanced around at all the papers, no doubt remembering a not-so-distant past when my office looked much worse.

"No—this is for the case." I adjusted one of the stacks, shifting it minutely. "We're searching for connections between two women I'd never associate with one another. It's a mess."

Edwin picked up the stack of papers on the visitor chair and sat down. He arranged them on his lap, white fingers tapping out a lazy rhythm as he perused the top sheet. Edwin was dressed in his typical fashion, sporting a light gray 1920's era three-piece suit with a sea green bow tie and matching pocket square. He'd left his hat behind, meaning this was him in casual mode.

"I heard there was another disappearance." He raised a brow expectantly.

I filled Edwin in, including necessary Mea-related complaints. I wasn't more concerned about her than the case, but Mea was a bur I couldn't get unstuck. So, I tried to shake her off in Edwin's direction.

I came around the desk to tower over him where he sat. "Why didn't you tell me the Authority was opening up more offices? What's the need for infiltrating smaller towns?"

Edwin flicked a loose staple off the papers. "Expansion isn't something I'm involved with. I read the memo and forgot about it. So what?"

"Mea might be moving to town, that's what." I smacked a manilla folder on the desk and Edwin suppressed a smile, his lips practically disappearing.

Aria poked her head in. "Everything okay?"

Edwin ignored her. "Are you saying this town isn't big enough for the two of you, Juliet?" His eyes were full of laughter.

"Oh, screw you. And no, it's not. I was here first. It's bad enough she followed me to the West Coast." My cheeks felt flushed in what had to be anger. In the back of my mind, I knew I was being unreasonable, but couldn't help it.

"Have you considered Ms. Dubois' actions might have nothing to do with you?" Edwin's amusement threatening to take form in an honest-to-god smile. His serious lined mouth looked like it could barely resist, but this was Edwin so he managed.

"Mea's actions better not have anything to do with me." I was annoyed Edwin found my frustration so funny. He just didn't understand what a problem Mea was. "She keeps trying to be friends. Which makes it about me, in a way. Mea could learn to take a hint and ignore people who want to be left alone. Her persistence is infuriating. What am I supposed to think she's up to?"

"You could give in and be friends with her," Aria said with a shrug.

Edwin and I stared at her blankly.

The young Witch leaned up against the doorframe and crossed her arms. "What? Is that so unheard of? We're friends."

"No, we aren't." Edwin turned away from her.

"No shit, genius. I wasn't talking to you." Aria's frown matched Edwin's perfectly as she glared at the back of his head.

"Mea is nothing like you," I assured my assistant. "*We* get each other—she's—it's like—she's just the worst. You had to have noticed her—unlikability." Curse it, I was usually more articulate than this. I blamed Mea.

Edwin and Aria gave me matching bemused looks.

I felt cornered in my own office. What was this? It was like I was missing something when the two of them had no reason to disagree with me on Mea's annoying nature. They never agreed with each other, it was the principle of their dynamic. What the hell was going on today?

"Help, or go away," I said to them both and turned to a filing cabinet I knew contained nothing relevant. I began flipping through folders anyway.

"Should I stay late tonight?" Unlike Mea, Aria always knew when to let it go. "I'm supposed to meet Owen and Tristan for dinner, but I can cancel."

"Thank you, Aria, but there's no need." I closed the useless cabinet. "Edwin will help here. We can update you tomorrow morning before I pass anything on to the Authority."

"You just assume I don't have plans." Edwin was chiding me playfully, going by his tone. Well, if he was in that kind of mood, I knew exactly how to poke at him.

"You never have plans. Unless you were going to invite yourself along with Aria and the Mortals?" I gave him a knowing look, to which he glared in warning.

Aria was busy texting and missed our silent exchange. "Sorry Bickel, it's a friends only thing. You're not invited." She looked up and met my eyes. "If you need me, just shout."

I assured Aria I would and she departed.

"Maybe we should ask to join her sometime." The thought struck me almost out of nowhere. I'd never considered it before but liked the idea.

"Why?" Edwin made a face. "You hate group social events as much as I do."

"It's not an event, it's dinner. I like Aria and her boyfriend Owen." I took the papers Edwin was holding and set them aside. "And I thought you might like a chance to talk to Tristan."

"Juliet. Don't meddle. I have no reason to talk to him." The faint blush, not quite hidden by Edwin's freckles, said otherwise. But he was determined to stick to his stubborn resolve. I understood why and it wasn't fair of me to push too hard, so I didn't. The heat had faded from Edwin's cheeks by the time he said, "You should be concentrating on this thing between you and Mea. Not me and a man who doesn't need to notice me."

"That's not true. Why should I concentrate on Mea? What thing?" My voice was getting higher pitched against my will. "It's not the same. I don't *like* her. I can't stand her. I need to convince her not to move here. She's always acting like she knows me. It's maddening."

"Why does she get to you like this?" Edwin now seemed genuinely concerned, and maybe a little bit alarmed.

I leaned against my desk, feeling tired. I wasn't sure why. I couldn't describe the conflicting feelings. "Mea knew me before, Edwin. I don't like that she has false impressions in her head, no matter how old they are."

He took his time considering my words. Whenever he was being thoughtful, the gray in Edwin's light brown hair gave him an annoyingly wise aesthetic. "Okay, I can understand that. But what about other than Mea? Are you interested in"—he made a vague hand gesture—"it's been a while since you've dated anyone."

"And you think I want to talk about it? Now? Like that's something *we* would do?" I didn't know whether to laugh or glare.

"Of course. We talk—almost exclusively to each other. Dating just hasn't come up in a while. I'm sorry if that's my fault. Just because I don't date, doesn't mean I need to avoid the topic when it comes to you, Juliet. You can tell me anything." He smiled faintly, in a way I found reassuring. "If not me, who would you prefer to give your confidences to?"

"No one." I gave Edwin an eye roll—a childish part of me wanted to say *duh* just to frustrate him. "I'm not interested in dating right now. And I don't want to talk about my love life because of Mea. Yes, she's attractive, but liking her isn't my problem. Not anymore. If I was ever going to be anything to her, it was back then. And you know why that didn't happen."

Edwin rose from the chair and leaned against the desk next to me. "I understand."

I rested my head on his shoulder. All day my mind was stuck in the past. I let myself wallow in it for a fleeting moment. "I don't know what I'd have done without you, Edwin."

"Stop that." He jostled his shoulder, giving me a little shake but not in an attempt to dislodge me. "You don't have to think about what-ifs. We met and this timeline we live in is how things happened."

The idea of a reality where Edwin and I never crossed paths always succeeded in scaring me, no matter how many decades we'd been firmly in each other's lives. "Sometimes I think my life is too complicated to let anyone else in. The way a partner would want," I admitted.

There was so much to explain. No one knew my full story but Edwin. He was there at the time, sharing everything happened without question, for both of us.

My friendship with Aria was in its infancy and it worked even if she didn't know certain things about me. But if I ever wanted more, I didn't think I could face what opening up meant. Especially to someone like Mea, who was the antithesis of every worried and guarded bone in my body. Nothing phased her. She would never understand.

"You don't have to open up. Unless you want to." Edwin was firm in this as always. "We have each other as family, no matter what."

"Thank heavens for that." I straightened, breaking our physical contact. That was more than enough wallowing. It was time to move on, even if I could have basked in his comfort for longer.

Edwin *humphed*. "Thank something at least." With a flick of his wrist, he summoned a whiskey bottle and two glasses out of nowhere. "Let's have a drink and get through these papers."

4

JULIET

I'd planned on getting to the office early the next morning. Everything was going as usual when I stepped out of my bedroom into the living room and was momentarily distracted by the sight of a book I'd been looking for.

It caught my eye from the bottom of a stack near my two-seater couch. My living room was a large but crowded open plan space adjoining the dining room with vaulted ceilings and glass doors to the backyard. Morning light filtered in though the skylights, dappled by the oak trees outside. Shadow and light flickered back and forth on the elusive book like something otherworldly was pointing me to it.

I bent down to grab it and when I straightened Edwin and Aria were standing in front of me.

"*Oh!*" I dropped the book in shock. "*Edwin!* You didn't text."

"Sorry, Juliet. Was in a rush." Edwin balanced a tray of coffees in one hand, while holding Aria firmly upright with the other. She swayed, her face looking pale from nausea.

"Come sit." I ushered them to the couches. "What's going on?"

Aria lay down on the larger couch facing the room's stone-set feature wall and inbuilt fireplace. Teleporting took getting used to and Aria wasn't yet immune to the effects like Edwin and me. "I think I might be sick," she moaned.

Edwin conjured Aria a bucket, just in case, and took a seat next to me on the other couch.

He'd taken to frequenting the Coffee Cat Cafe since our case there six months ago. I wasn't surprised he'd gone over this morning, but he usually met me at my office afterward, rather than appearing in my home unexpectedly.

"So—?" I took my coffee from Edwin and waited for an explanation.

Aria sat up and put the unused bucket aside, her bearings hopefully recovered. "My morning hasn't been great. I went for a run—which, regrets right there—but looking back, I'm pretty sure someone was following me."

"Of course she didn't see their face, and can't recall any discerning features," Edwin complained.

"Yeah well—at the time I thought it was nothing. Just someone in the park that *happened* to be going the same way as me, before getting into a car that *happened* to drive behind me for a while. And the same car, or one like it, *happened* to be outside Coffee Cat when I got back. It still could be nothing. But when I unlocked the door to go up to the apartment, there was a letter waiting. The mail doesn't come until the afternoon and it didn't have a stamp or anything written on the envelope."

I set my coffee down without taking a sip. "Did you open the letter?"

Aria shook her head. "No, I took it into the cafe to ask Owen if he knew what it was. It wasn't until I was adding up all these odd things that the whole morning seemed strange. But that didn't quite click until Owen took the letter from me and it crumbled to ash. Then I was like—oh shit. You know?"

Edwin gave a dramatic sigh. "Fortunately, I was there ordering coffee, distracting the barista, or he might have seen. The letter's transformative magic didn't do anything beyond quietly turn it to dust, but it could have been worse in a room full of unsuspecting Mortals." Edwin extracted a plastic bag of ashes from the pocket of his dark gray vintage suit. "I'm guessing Aria was supposed to read it, but something triggered when she handed the letter to Owen."

"What a bunch of silly flare." I took the bag and examined the ash. "We can reconstruct it easily enough."

Destroying notes like this was gimmicky. Unless you also soaked the ash, the paper wasn't irreversibly ruined. A Witch who did things halfway wasn't likely accustomed to subterfuge, so my initial reaction to the note was nothing more than frustration.

Aria shot Edwin a glare. "What? We can still read it? Why didn't you say so?"

"I thought that much was obvious." He raised his espresso cup to his lips and took a small sip.

"Yeah, because I know all your investigative tricks." Aria grabbed her cold brew coffee from the tray with unnecessary aggression. "You know I'm bad at most magic."

"Excuse me for thinking you were improving," Edwin snapped.

"Oh, stop it you two." I tipped the ash onto the coffee table. "Can we focus?"

"Fine, let's see what this is all about." Edwin turned away from Aria and conjured my candles and a few large crystals.

Having him around made me lazy. Like most Witches, I couldn't summon objects out of nowhere. Transporting things through negative space was another benefit of Edwin's unique magic. He wasn't constrained by the physical world like the rest of us, who could only summon objects by sending them zooming through the air—still better than walking across the room to retrieve something, but rather conspicuous.

Edwin's trick was especially convenient when it wasn't easy to find things in my house. There was a logic to how I'd organized my many possessions, only I couldn't always remember the particular logic I'd applied to any given item when looking for it later.

With my candles lit in a triangular formation around the ash, and crystals occupying offset points, I muttered an incantation and the ash burst into flame.

An object burned in a natural fire couldn't be rebuilt like this, but putting the letter back together was nothing more than mildly complex reversal magic. The fire burned blue, and when it cleared a small card lay on the table. I opened it and set it down for everyone to read.

ARIA— Next time meet me at the third park bench. I need to tell you something about Juliet.

WE ALL LEANED FORWARD and stared for a moment.

Edwin idly adjusted his black and purple rose-print bow tie. "Wish you'd taken down that car's license plate."

"*Sorry*. How could I have anticipated this?" Aria looked across the table at me. "It's creepy."

I wanted to disagree but couldn't bring myself to lie. "I don't like that someone was sneaking around your home. We should cast more robust protection spells on you, the apartment and the cafe downstairs. Just in case." I glanced at Edwin and from his serious expression, it seemed he agreed.

Aria looked between us. "In case of what? They only want to meet me—not that I'm ever going back to that park again. Do you think this has to do with the missing Witches?" Her eyes widened in growing alarm.

"We shouldn't rule it out," Edwin said.

"But the note was left by the person following me. Not someone trying to abduct me," Aria objected.

"Why assume the person following you doesn't also want to abduct you?" Edwin cocked his head in an expression that seemed to say, *hm?*

Aria gave him a speechless look of outrage.

I picked up the note to examine it. "The message feels like a trap. But an obvious one. *Come meet me for a vague, mysterious reason.*"

"Yeah, I'd never fall for that." Aria seemed to find comfort in offense, or maybe she'd gotten over her shock enough to go back to covering her emotions as she usually did.

"No, of course you wouldn't. That makes the note an odd choice for a lure." I dismissed it as a real offer of information without hesitation. What could the writer possibly have to tell Aria about me? All my secrets were personal and unimportant to anyone else.

"Who would want to lure me in the first place?" Aria asked as if it were ridiculous. "My Witch social circle is pretty much limited to you two, and family. And if it's related to the other disappearances, why would I be targeted along with two people I've never even met?"

"All valid questions, Aria." Edwin put his coffee down on the table. "But your family isn't exactly low profile. It would pay to check your brother isn't working on anything dangerous, for a start."

Aria took out her phone and began texting her Witch-lawyer twin, Luca Belmonte. I wasn't surprised when Aria reported he was working on nothing more alarming than a contested will and ethics for a magically enhanced dating app. Still, it was worth ruling out.

Edwin stood, conjured a dark gray fedora and placed it on his head. "Before we do anything else, I'll cast protections on the cafe and Aria's apartment upstairs. No need to risk a third abduction regardless of relatability to the others. Aria—may I teleport into your living room?"

She nodded without protest or snark, and he disappeared. Aria turned to me. "Will that be enough? If this is somehow related—the other two had their homes protected."

"Having Edwin on our team is like cheating. He'll cast more than your standard spells. Everyone in the cafe will be fine, Mortals included."

"Good. But if the note and the person I saw are linked to the disappearances, the Witch should have just nabbed me when I went to shower after my run. They'd have got me as good as the others. It doesn't make sense." Aria chewed on the straw in her drink as she frowned.

"That is a fair point. We'll get to the bottom of it either way, don't worry. Once Edwin gets back we'll catch up with the Authority Witches and report it. Hopefully they've found something useful by now."

5

MEA

Terra and I were summoned to Sarah Arroyo's house early the next morning.

"We've had our first break, and it doesn't look good." Easton beckoned us into the house, his smug expression at odds with his words. Maybe he was glad for any break at all, rather than pleased he'd found something when we hadn't, but knowing him that probably wasn't true.

This sort of competitive edge and emphasis on personal success rather than good service to the people we were supposed to be helping was one of the things I hoped to get away from by leaving the large LA branch of the Authority. Easton was unfortunately typical of many Witches in his position. Hopefully at a small, bran-new outpost people wouldn't be so focused on the overall hierarchy of the organization and pushing their way up.

Yesterday, Terra and I had tracked down a few of the other Witches who'd attended the earth magic event with Sarah and Lana. None of them had anything of significance to say about either woman. We'd found no meaningful connections between the two besides the similarities in their disappearances, so at least Easton had something.

That was all that should matter.

He led us through the house to a small but pristine kitchen where Torres was leaning against the counter looking equally pleased with herself.

"You'll never guess who just called."

"Ms. Herrera?" Easton's unexplained enthusiasm only grew when Torres nodded. "Perfect. Take a look at this, you two." He indicated a small card laying open on the counter.

Terra and I leaned in to see a short note scrawled inside.

SARAH,

We need to meet as soon as possible. You know I'm displeased with our arrangement. Something needs to be worked out before we can move forward.

Regards, Juliet Herrera

"FUNNY SHE DIDN'T MENTION this before." Easton tapped the signature significantly.

I was about to say it was hardly conclusive proof of anything, but the doorbell cut me off.

"How did they get here so fast?" Torres left the kitchen, frowning.

Easton scooped up the card, which was blank on the outside, and tucked it in his jacket pocket.

Terra caught my eye and I shrugged.

Torres didn't look happy when she returned with Juliet, Aria and a familiar grumpy-faced man. I couldn't say I blamed her. I'd never talked to Mr. Bickel—a Witch so pretentious he wouldn't allow anyone of inferior standing call him by his first name—and was more than fine with that state of affairs. By all accounts Bickel was good at his job, but he was a rumored nightmare to work with. I had no idea what he was doing here.

Great. And just when I thought Easton's attitude was going to be the biggest strain on my day.

No one bothered with hellos. Juliet glanced quickly around the kitchen, eyes skittering over me without acknowledgment as she and her companions settled into the now cramped space.

Bickel was even less emotive than Juliet in her carefully neutral mask. They were a strange trio, made weirder by the fact that Aria was wearing workout gear. Okay—that wasn't as weird as looking like you were dressed for a twenties-themed party, an obnoxious quirk I'd heard Bickel put on to remind everyone of his fancy-pants time altering magic.

"Have you been reassigned to this case?" Easton asked Bickel. Some of his earlier satisfaction seemed to have faded at the sight of the other man. Apparently it was always a competition, never mind the best way to find the missing women.

"No." Bickel sounded bored and didn't elaborate. Why bother with common courtesy when he didn't have to answer to anyone but his superiors?

It was an instinct to dislike anyone wearing a fedora, but Bickel really didn't help himself. I'd heard he played up his special treatment within the organization as often as he could. Out of all the employees with unique powers, he was the Authority's most prized asset and he seemed to know it.

There was a long silence.

"I know staring at each other down is fun, but can we get to the reason we're all here?" I looked at the rest of my team expectantly. *Am I really the only one who doesn't think we have time for games and Authority politics in all this?* I'd like to have asked Juliet immediately about the note, but I wasn't leading this investigation and knew it wasn't for me to bring up unprompted.

Mr. Bickel sighed more dramatically than seemed necessary. "Aria and I came across something strange this morning. It may be related to your missing Witches. We thought we'd pass it on, in case it's relevant."

Why were Bickel and Aria doing anything together? That was more baffling than everything else we'd learned so far.

"Someone left me this note." Aria handed me a folded card just like the one in Easton's pocket.

"A note?" Easton snatched it from my hand before I could open it.

Aria and Bickel explained the origins of the message and when they got to the part about Juliet reconstructing the ash, Torres stepped forward. "Why bring this to Juliet before us?"

Bickel shrugged as if it was normal to consult private investigators over his colleagues. "Juliet, Aria and I work together sometimes. Aria is Juliet's employee, so it seemed natural to go to Juliet first. The morning's events might not even connect to your case."

"But they might," Easton pressed.

"Yes," Bickel said dryly. "That's why we brought it to your attention once we read the note and considered everything together. I'm happy to help Juliet or the local Authority as needed."

Easton crossed his arms. "But you're assigned elsewhere."

And based in a completely different district, I wanted to add, but it wasn't a helpful comment. I had to admit some of Easton's resistance might not be about one-upping but a general dislike of the other man, which I could understand. Still, more hands couldn't be a bad thing.

"Never mind him." Juliet waved dismissively at Bickel—they were standing so close together she almost hit him—then turned her focus to me. "Can you look into what happened to Aria?"

"Yes, of course," I assured her, and Juliet looked marginally more relaxed at my words.

Easton rounded on Juliet, apparently giving up on protesting Bickel's presence. "How do we know you didn't leave Aria the note?"

"Why would I write a note about myself?"

"Yeah, that's ridiculous." Aria came to her boss's defense without hesitation. "Plus, I can prove she's not lying about it. I'm a psychic."

Easton studied Aria. "We couldn't exactly take your word for it though, with no way to know if *you're* lying."

The mood in the room shifted as Aria and her companions' eyes all narrowed in unison. It was almost creepy how suddenly similar the three of them were.

The note in Easton's pocket said it was from Juliet, but that didn't mean it was. It didn't mean Juliet was lying or hiding anything. We had no evidence she would try to deceive us or harass her own assistant, and had no reason to think Aria would be complicit in covering up any of Juliet's lies. There was no reason for Easton to make such an alienating comment when we wanted them to share what they knew with us.

"We can make this interview official, with an Authority psychic, if that's what you require," Bickel offered, and Juliet nodded her agreement.

Easton frowned. "That seems like an overstep at this stage." It was like he was disagreeing with Bickel for the sake of it, and the other man didn't miss it.

They glared at one another and I suppressed the urge to groan aloud. Terra made a soft huffing sound beside me.

"The thing is, you're more and more connected to this case, Juliet." Torres crossed her arms. "Why didn't you tell us about the other note?"

"What other note?" Juliet looked from Torres to me, as if she expected something from me. What—reassurance, explanation —I wasn't sure.

It had to be a positive sign that Juliet kept turning to me out of everyone, as if she didn't totally hate me. I hoped it meant she'd talk to me. "What prompted you to meet with Sarah the day you discovered her missing?"

Juliet didn't look particularly pleased I'd skipped over her question. "Sarah called and asked me to meet the next afternoon. She had something she wanted to run by me."

"Why? Was it something you were expecting?" I pressed.

"She didn't say why. I wasn't expecting her call, but we correspond often enough that it wasn't unusual."

"Correspond?" Easton seemed to latch on to the word choice.

"Yes. You know, communicate, keep in touch." Juliet directed a distasteful gaze at my colleague.

"By letter?" the man asked as if he was on the verge of making a great discovery.

Juliet made a confused face that seemed tinged with annoyance. "No. I'm more of an email or phone call person."

Bickel narrowed his eyes. "No one modern sends letters for regular communication."

Easton took the card out of his pocket and passed it to Juliet.

She opened it and went still in surprise, her eyes widening. "I didn't write this." She looked at Aria for help.

"It's true," the psychic confirmed.

Eason took the card back. "We'll be checking that statement ourselves. The signature is spot on."

"And easy to duplicate," said Bickel.

"Be that as it may." Easton looked sternly around at everyone. "Too many links to you are surfacing, Juliet. Two notes. An association with both missing persons. Potential stalking of your assistant. Everything seems to come back to you. It makes me wonder, are you involved somehow?"

"*Involved*?" Juliet crossed her arms, looking more defensive than aggressive.

Easton had to know we didn't have enough to claim Juliet was involved, but her name was coming up an awful lot. She was more intertwined in these events than the typical person who reports someone missing, and it all being coincidence wasn't likely.

"Would you prefer I said caught up in? There's no denying that. You might even be a target of sorts. This note here"—Easton waved the card—"was found turned to ash, just as the other was. That's why it took us so long to find. If you didn't write it and it's a forgery, the person who did is trying to implicate you. Maybe they've chosen their targets because of you—we've found no other connection between them."

Juliet looked around at all of us. "But why would someone do that?"

"You tell me."

Her alarm seemed to shift to frustration as she clenched her jaw. "Well, I don't know."

Easton tucked the card back in his pocket. "If you could hand over all the relevant files you have on your work with the two missing Witches, we'll look through them ourselves. You can't assist this case in any capacity if all this has something to do with you."

"Fine." Juliet sounded like she was glad to hand everything over.

"Ms. Dubois." Eason turned to me. "I'm going to have to ask you to step aside too."

"What?" I was not cool or collected about that development.

"Sorry." He didn't look sorry. "But I think someone needs to keep an eye on Ms. Herrera."

"*Why?*" Juliet and I asked in unison. She glared at me like this was my doing.

"Did you not hear? Evidence suggests Juliet is either being targeted or is otherwise implicated in the present situation. We need to make sure she's both not abducted and not doing anything unlawful while we get a better handle on what exactly is going on here. If we think there's any chance of her disappearing like the other Witches it would be unacceptable to do nothing to prevent it."

True, all true, but I wanted to whine, *why me?*

Except I knew why. My assignment to this case was due to my acquaintance with Juliet. Terra and I were junior compared to Torres and Easton, and the Authority would have normally assigned two more experienced pairs of investigators.

I'd ignored my unease when my boss came to me, saying she'd like to make use of my acquaintance with Juliet. I didn't like when they leveraged personal connections like this because it more often than not led to biased practices. But I had nothing against Juliet. She was a challenge to work with, and I didn't mind trying to use our history—however fraught—to help my colleagues work with her more smoothly when it was on a case as serious as a missing person.

The move felt like it had been made with good intentions on the Authorities part, so I'd been willing to give them the benefit of the doubt, and Easton was right, out of everyone, assigning me to watch Juliet was probably best.

"Edwin can watch me in Mea's place," Juliet said through gritted teeth. "I object to the necessity, but if it has to be done to prove I'm not behind any of this mess, I'd much rather him than her. Edwin works for the Authority, there shouldn't be any issues."

To my surprise, Mr. Bickel nodded agreement.

"No." Easton was firm. "You two are too chummy. Bickel

might work for us, but I doubt he'd be impartial with you, Juliet."

"You don't trust me?" Bickel's blue eyes turned cold as ice in a stare I was glad wasn't directed at me.

Easton flinched but recovered quickly. "It's not good practice. That's all I meant. You can't be involved with a case involving your friend. It's not about trust, Bickel."

The dapper Witch looked somewhat mollified, and significantly less murderous. "I see your point, Easton." He sounded begrudging.

Juliet balled her hands into fists at her sides. "This is ridiculous. I can take care of myself. Just interview me if I'm a suspect and clear it up."

Easton adopted a slightly condescending tone. "A psychic interview alone can't completely exclude you from suspicion. Psychics are great when it comes to simple lies and validating intentions in court, but they are only part of a system. We need a combination of evidence and testimony in all cases. If everything were taken on psychics' word alone, justice would be left up to their discretion with no other checks. You know that imbalance isn't acceptable."

"Okay, fine. Yes. But Mea and I know each other, she should be disqualified for the same reason as Edwin." She glared at me.

"Ms. Dubois isn't your friend," Easton challenged. "So it's not the same as Bickel, is it? Or do you think Ms. Dubois will be prejudiced against you?"

"No." Juliet seemed worried for a second. "That's not—I just don't want Mea lurking around."

"Fine. Take Reyes," Easton said, losing the last of his patience.

Juliet looked frantically between Terra and me.

I was unable to resist the urge to reassure her. "It's not a big deal. Just think of it as having a houseguest."

Having someone stay with her wasn't the end of the world, but Juliet looked panicked and it was making her seem guilty. Like she had something to hide. Not that I actually suspected Juliet, but her reaction contrasted too sharply with her usually indifferent attitude. The others were noticing and likely drawing their own—and in Easton's case, less kind—conclusions.

Mr. Bickel put his hand on Juliet's shoulder. That seemed to help. She let out a long breath, closed her eyes and said, "Fine. Mea, I would rather be stuck with you than someone I don't even know."

Was it wrong that her decision felt like a tiny victory in all of this?

6

MEA

An hour later, I arrived at Juliet's house via rideshare. There was no other choice in getting here after she and her companions teleported off without me. Juliet had said she needed to get things ready, but I questioned the truth in that. She'd wanted away from the Authority and Easton's questions, and away from me. Not that I thought she was necessarily hiding anything relevant to the case, but she wasn't going to make any of this easy.

Juliet's house was no small thing, and yet managed to hide. Unlike the other homes on the street, the sprawling single story building was set back from the road, shielded by an ivy-covered stone wall and downward sloping land. Trees loomed, blocking out all sense of neighbors as I walked down the drive to the elaborately carved double doors.

I stared at the stained glass framing the entry. The grandeur fit Juliet's powerful family lineage in a way the rest of her life didn't seem to.

As I knocked, I took a moment to examine the protective spells cast on the property. They buzzed intrusively against my magic's inspection. *Stars above.* Whatever was cast on Juliet's house was orders of magnitude stronger than any protection spell I'd ever come across.

Juliet opened one of the ornate doors. "Mea." She frowned, looking gorgeous in the most corporate way possible. She didn't make any move to invite me in.

"Nice place." I gestured around me and we stared at one another for a bit too long. "Can't wait to see inside," I added in a joking tone, trying to peer past her.

Juliet's displeasure didn't crack. She stood blocking the door for another long moment before sighing and stepping aside. I joined her in an entryway cordoned off from the open plan room beyond by a decorative stone wall.

We stood in silence.

"You have some heavy-duty spells cast around here," I offered.

"I told you I can look after myself. You're going to be bored." She tapped the toe of her stiletto clad foot in annoyance.

I pretended not to notice. "Did you cast the protection yourself?"

If so, I wanted lessons. I had no idea Juliet was capable of such powerful magic.

"No, my friend cast it for me." Juliet still gave no sign of inviting me further into the house.

I set my overnight bag down. Maybe she expected me to stay here in the entryway for the duration of my intrusive visit. "Impressive friend."

"You didn't seem impressed earlier." Juliet closed the front door with a sense of resigned finality.

I was confused for a second, thinking she meant her assistant. If that young Witch could cast these spells—*oh*, she meant Bickel. Wow, it was weird they were friends, like *real* friends. When Easton mentioned it earlier I'd assumed he'd meant it in a work sense. Not that a more substantial relationship didn't fit after seeing the two of them standing stonily side by side. No wonder Juliet didn't like me, if most-powerful-and-uptight-Witch-ever was the company she kept.

"How nice of Bickel to look out for you amidst the disappearances." It was the only nice thing I could honestly say about him.

"What?" Juliet took her turn at confusion. "No. I've had the house protected like this since I moved in."

Okay, that was extreme. Everyone had some basic stuff cast on their home, but Juliet had red-alert, someone-is-out-to-get-me protection. And it'd been in place for decades?

I was going to have to ask if she had enemies. Up until now, I figured the answer would be an uncomplicated no. Damn it. Having to get personal information out of Juliet Herrera was a mountainous task I wasn't yet ready to attempt.

Waiting to be invited *all the way* inside before busting out the interrogation was probably a good idea. "How about a tour?" I did a weird let's-go jiggy motion with my arm. *Ugh*, what was that? An embarrassed blush followed, making my face hot.

Juliet cringed at my awkward—whatever the heck it was. "Fine." She walked beyond the wall and gestured before her. "This is the living room. And I'm sure you can see, over here, I have my dining area." Her tone was flat and bored.

I almost laughed at her deadpan manner, but was glad I hadn't when I ventured into the room. "Oh, how—nice."

What else could I say? The space was nothing like I'd expected. It wasn't a mess precisely, but it wasn't exactly tidy, or spacious, given it was definitely large. Chaotic was never a word I'd have put in association with Juliet before now, but there was stuff everywhere.

The dining table and chairs were vintage polished wood, and accompanied by a large China hutch, devoid of China and instead packed to bursting with random objects. An eye-catching vintage living room set might have been the room's focal point, but more noticeably, there were piles of books everywhere. Like a forest, or mountain range of pages and hard spines. There were stacks on side tables, the floor, along the backs of the couches, on the mantle, covering a significant portion of the dining table, and on several of the chairs.

To be fair, one wall housed a floor to ceiling, overflowing bookshelf. There wasn't space for more shelving due to the other walls being mostly windows, or dominated by a large stone hearth. A limitation that had apparently not stopped Juliet from acquiring all the books she'd ever wanted, and then some.

Juliet focused on me as I glanced around, her face stony and eyes unexpectedly vulnerable. It made me wonder how few people had seen inside her house. Having a houseguest might actually be a big deal for Juliet. *God*, had she expected me to be a jerk about all this, or judge her somehow? It hurt that she didn't think better of me, and I had no plans to prove her right.

"I like it. There's so much natural light in here." It was the truth. The large glass doors and skylights were lovely.

"It's good for reading," Juliet said, and I swear on my life her lips twitched in an almost smile.

"Oh, totally. Those couches look like heaven." I beamed at her.

Juliet cleared her throat. "That"—she pointed to a door off the living room—"is my bedroom. There's no need for you to see inside." She avoided my gaze as she turned on her heel and walked off in the other direction.

I followed.

"Kitchen—" Juliet led me though a spacious, fully equipped and tidy kitchen. "Outside." She pointed to another sliding glass door leading to a patio, before turning down a hallway. "Guest room, bedroom, office." We strode past three open doors and circled quickly back to the front entry.

I picked my overnight bag up off the floor where I'd left it. "You missed your calling as a tour guide, Juliet."

She smirked. It was lovely and kind of mean. "Go put your stuff in the guest room. I don't have all day to stand around with you."

I went back down the hall toward the spare rooms. "Are we going somewhere?"

"Yes, to work. I'm not twiddling my thumbs indefinitely while you Authority Witches try and figure things out. Aria is waiting at the office for me."

I entered the first room. "Oh, I love this." Another sliding glass door led to a small walled courtyard and the room's interior decoration contrasted sharply with the rest of the house. Most of Juliet's things seemed to be refurbished vintage, but in here everything was modern and minimalist.

Juliet appeared behind me. "You can't stay in here."

"What?" I laughed.

Nope, she was serious.

"You're not going to make me sleep outside are you?" The glimpse of the yard looked woodsy and inviting, but I wasn't planning on camping.

Juliet gesture impatiently to her right. "The other one is the guest room."

How was I supposed to know that? I left the room that was indistinguishable from a guest room and went to the one next door. It was smaller, much more cluttered and the bed didn't look quite as lush.

"Are you making me sleep in the small room because you don't like me?" I teased.

Juliet blushed faintly. "I don't not like you—no—it's—the other room belongs to my friend."

"Oh. Cool, no problem then. I didn't know you had roommates." I threw my bag on the bed.

"I don't have roommates." Juliet looked aghast at the idea of something so pedestrian. "It's Edwin's room, for when he wants to visit."

I knew the guy didn't live on this side of the country, but having his own room was kinda weird, right? Even for a friend. "I'm guessing he wouldn't appreciate me intruding."

"No."

Her tone didn't invite further conversation but I couldn't help myself. "What's the deal with you two?"

Juliet went instantly uncomfortable. I hadn't realized how much she'd relaxed until she snapped back into her walls-up mode. "There's no deal, Mea. It's not strange to have friends."

"I don't keep a room for anyone in my house." I wasn't sure why I was arguing. It was nice to see evidence Juliet had people she cared about in her life, even if she was being as awkward as possible about it. And who knows, maybe I'd do the same if I had a home like this.

"I have a room at his house too," Juliet said, like this made it better and not stranger. Another question was on the tip of my tongue when she cut me off. "Mea, I'm going to work. You can stay here and sit around judging my use of personal space if you want. I don't care."

Juliet turned and left in a huff. I was forced to follow.

7

JULIET

Having Mea in my house, gleaning little insights into my life, unsettled me. She'd been kind about the cluttered state of things, and I had to admit I'd been worried, but her tactfulness had thrown me off balance as much as it had relieved me.

I didn't want to care about Mea's opinions or find things to like in her. Yet, she followed me out of the house to my car like a sorry puppy and it made me wonder if Mea genuinely wanted to follow, if she cared why I was annoyed, or if she was only trailing along because she had to.

As I got in the car, I told myself not to care either way. I started the engine and Mea scampered around to the passenger side.

I hated when people made a big deal out of my friendship with Edwin. We were both deemed unlikable, and yet the fact we were friends was always so shocking. I had a bet on how long it would take Mea to ask if Edwin and I were in a relationship, because somehow that was always more logical than friendship. He and I usually found this assumption funny, but with Mea, none of my reactions were usual.

Edwin and I were close, but our history wasn't at all romantic. We were both private people and like me, he didn't have much of a social circle. It made sense most Witches didn't know anything truly personal about us, we both projected precise versions of ourselves in order to control how we were seen. Especially Edwin, and his persona at work.

What no one knew was that keeping to ourselves was a habit Edwin and I formed together, an old tool in rebuilding ourselves that had stuck around. Guarding myself wasn't something I wanted to change, other than branching out to select Witches like Aria, but being isolated created these frustrating situations that made people like Mea think I was strange. I didn't like that no one quite understood me, but I didn't want to put myself out there and do the work to change their understanding. It was the paradoxical bane of my life, and at times like this I felt I'd escaped my cage only to box myself in.

Curse Mea for bringing up my past even when she wasn't directly bringing up my past. I didn't need to think about it. Or her. I just wanted to be rid of Mea, but she was still here looking at me expectantly from the passenger seat.

I'd stared off into space, car idling, for too long after she'd buckled up. Pretending nothing had happened, I looked away and pushed the gear shift into reverse.

THERE WAS ONCE a time when I was a very different person.

The old me wasn't someone I'd chosen to be. I'd been a product of spells cast on my mind, dictating my actions and effectively forcing me to live someone else's life. For decades subconscious decisions were my only means of circumventing my restrictions.

Luckily, this all changed on a cold January day in New York, 1994, or I wouldn't be where I was today.

That day was at the end of my first month of Investigators College. My classmates and I were heading out to a bar, Mea leading the charge. She was full of ideas and lingering looks even then, and at the time I met her grin for grin. But I hadn't wanted to go to the bar with them, exhaustion had weighed me down, and I remembered the prospect of getting through the evening seemed like more than I could stand.

So I'd forgotten my day planner. Forgetting wasn't something I'd done intentionally and so the spells couldn't prevent it. However, leaving the book allowed me to make an 'acceptable' excuse to duck away from the group. I was prevented from saying I didn't want to go out—one of the sillier social restrictions placed on me to correct my standoffishness—but I could say I needed to return to the College, and then avoid meeting up afterward as long as no one asked me to join directly.

The other students had offered to wait for me, and Mea had bordered on persistent, but the evening had been cut by an icy wind which gave me an acceptable excuse to shoo my peers away. They'd left and I turned back down the block feeling I'd won a small victory. Not against them. They had no idea anything was wrong, but their understandable obliviousness only made me want to avoid them.

The cage I'd lived in was invisible and deceiving, made up of rules that governed my basic actions and reactions to others. Most of which forced me to do 'things other people did anyway,' but it was suffocating.

Even if I hadn't been magically gagged and unable to talk about what had been done to me, I'd always feared no one would believe me. It was absurd to think my personality wasn't mine, even to Witches. Why would someone alter me this way? The things the controlling spells made me do weren't bad in themselves, and might even have seemed pointless. Some people—the few that knew—even argued they were good, necessary changes. The right choices.

Being trapped in my head with emotions I couldn't express often threatened to become unbearable, but there was nothing I could do. I'd tried to manage any way I could, even when I couldn't always be sure what parts of me the spells affected. My mind wasn't my own; how could I be sure of anything? For so long everything felt wrong and every small choice that was taken from me was agonizing.

I was lonely when around others, caught in an invisible push and pull of what I wanted and what I did. But by myself I was able to be calm, and one day avoiding people led me to meet someone who changed everything.

8

JULIET

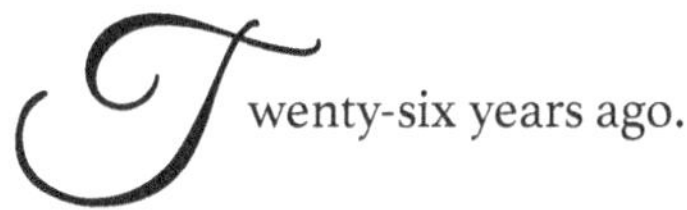

wenty-six years ago.

I WALKED AWAY from my classmates happily giving in to exhaustion. As I approached the college, an unfamiliar Witch exited the main building in a rush, and I paused.

He practically stumbled from the building's steps, plunging a hand into his pocket to extract a packet of cigarettes. He muttered to himself and seemed to be having serious trouble freeing anything from the pack, and when he finally did, he crunched the smoke accidentally in shaking hands.

He pressed the heel of his hand to his eyes.

I approached slowly and watched as the guy finally managed to get an intact cigarette between his lips. For some reason I wasn't able to look away. It was like his urgent need had trans-fixed me. I felt relief on his behalf as he clicked a lighter, but his hands were still trembling and he wasn't able keep the flame lit long enough to light the damn smoke. As the flame went out, he let out a pitiful little noise and threw the unlit cigarette and lighter into a nearby trash can. The rest of the pack followed.

I was close enough now to hear his shallow, uneven breathing and felt anguished for him, like his distress was contagious. He *needed* that cigarette. Why had he given up like the world was ending?

To my surprise, the man tore off his suit jacket and threw it to the ground. He stomped on it and stared, almost spellbound, at the heap of cloth on the dirty sidewalk.

I made a startled sound.

"*What?*" He looked up to see me stopped in front of him, staring. Without waiting for me to answer he stooped, picked up the jacket, and it followed his cigarettes and lighter into the trash.

He didn't look back at me right away, seeming as captivated by his own discarded belongings as I was with him.

Even though nothing about the situation was the least bit appealing, I found his looks intriguing. He had classically structured sort of beauty offset by a bridge of freckles across his nose, but he looked pale, even for a white guy. Maybe from stress. His hair was short and done with a styling mousse, but then ruined like he's scraped his hands through it. I'd bet he'd looked smart before he'd torn apart his outfit and thrown half of it away.

I didn't like that I was cataloging the man's appearance when he was hurting, but the combination of it all was impossible to disregard. His unbridled show of emotion bewitched me. It was beautiful in a way that had nothing to do with physical features.

Under the mind-altering spells I wasn't able to do anything so desperate or dramatic. As sick as it was, I was jealous of him.

I felt guilty about my reaction, and bad for catching him in such a vulnerable state. If only I could help, but I had no idea how. He should know I cared. That someone cared. Even in my messy mind this desire was undoubtedly real, so I latched onto it.

"Are you all right?" I asked.

His blank stare turned into a glare as he directed his attention back to me.

That was when I noticed he was powerful, much more so than me. Usually I'd only feel a hit of power in Witches who weren't actively spell casting, but with him the sense was unusually strong. Unless he was silently casting some sort of spell. His blue eyes cut through me with an indifferent sort of anger. The detachment made him terrifying and I wondered if his gaze was magically enhanced to allow him to see more than my appearance.

"Does it matter?" he lashed out.

I matched his snappy tone. "Of course it matters if you're all right."

"And why wouldn't I be?"

"You threw away what looked like a brand new jacket. There's no excuse for that."

Maybe he was as tired as I was, because his chilling glare snuffed out. He looked defeated.

"Are you from the college?" I gestured to the building beside us. "Maybe there's something I can help with?"

He shoved his hands in his pockets. "I doubt that."

"Fine, then. I'm going for a coffee. Join me." I crossed my arms, thinking he'd like a bit of challenge more than anything overly friendly.

The man now looked thoroughly confused. "Why?"

"After what you've done to your cigarettes you'll need something to take the edge off."

He laughed without smiling. "I can't argue with that."

"Okay. Good. My treat. But I have to go inside to grab something first." I turned toward the steps.

He followed me in reluctantly and lingered in the entry as I went up to the second floor.

My planner was where I left it in a lecture hall. I grabbed it and hurried back, trying and failing not to over analyze my reasons for offering coffee to the man.

Being polite was one of my mandates, but I felt my invitation came from a genuine desire to comfort him, not mere pleasantry or social obligation. I didn't have that bone deep urge to resist interaction I so often felt when my actions were taken out of my control, so I was fairly confident this was me, doing something of my own will, and for that alone I was tempted to be happy. It didn't matter if he was the worst, or if coffee was a terrible idea. Nothing mattered except choosing this myself.

When I returned, I found the man waiting by the front doors, glaring at a spot of nothing on the wall.

"I'm Juliet Herrera, by the way." I offered him my hand, pretending not to see his eyes narrow as he recognized my family name.

"I'm Edwin." We shook and turned toward the door. The cold evening had changed to a pouring rain.

I looked at him sideways. "Bet you wish you hadn't thrown out your jacket."

Edwin pursed his lips, considered me for a long moment, then flicked his wrist and a black leather jacket appeared in his hand. It was well worn and more the style of ten years ago than today, and clashed horribly with his very modern suit pants and shirt. Edwin slipped it on anyway, and with another flick of his wrist he handed me an umbrella.

Edwin noticed my startled reaction and his expression turning wary.

I knew exactly who he was now. I'd heard of him. Most anyone would have heard of his unique magical powers, but I'd heard a lot more than that from my mother and her work with the courts. I wished she'd never said anything, and feared Edwin suspected she'd gossiped from the way he was avoiding looking at me.

"Thanks." I indicated the umbrella and gave him a smile, one I actually wanted to give.

Edwin looked relieved to have my recognition of him swept away without comment. "I hope coffee is close by."

It was. We hurried around the block huddled under the umbrella. At this hour we went to a diner rather than a cafe, and sat in a booth next to the rain streaked window, cradling steaming mugs.

"I suppose you're wondering what I was doing at the college," Edwin said after a while.

I gave him a shrug. "Not really my business."

"You're a student there?"

I nodded. Now that I knew he was Edwin Bickel, I wasn't sure why he'd come to coffee with me. Then again, I couldn't let any of my second-hand knowledge of him make me think I knew him. I certainly didn't want him to think he knew me just because he recognized my name.

"That's why I was at the college," he went on. "To see the dean. I hoped to enroll. However, I've been informed I'm unsuitable."

I tried not to feel sorry for Edwin. He was so obviously hurt, and trying to act composed by keeping his features schooled into an almost-flawless mask. As if either of us could forget that hopeless sound he'd made about the cigarettes.

"If you don't have a prior degree, you can always come back once you've got one. Or apply for a life experience equivalent," I said in an attempt to be encouraging.

He was old enough to study at any Witch-run institution without meeting the entrance requirements young ones like me faced. The process for demonstrating magical competency was simple for some as powerful as he was.

Edwin's mask cracked to reveal a cold humor. "So you know about me, do you? You've heard I'm unqualified and undereducated?"

I flinched, embarrassed by my slip-up. "Sorry. No. I didn't mean—"

"I appreciate the pretense Juliet, but it's fine." It did not look fine. "You've heard things. They're probably true. So let's not pretend. You know education and competency certificates aren't my problem. My legal history has prevented me from enrolling." Edwin said the word *legal* like it tasted bad.

I didn't know how to address his blunt acceptance that I knew more than I should. We sipped our coffees in silence until I asked, "Why do you want to be an investigator?" It didn't make sense alongside the stories I'd heard about him.

Edwin averted his eyes, looking instead at his cup. "I wanted to do something right. I want a change and a new start. I want to help and be useful. To stop bad things from happening, and I know that's fucking naïve from every angle. I just—what does it even matter? People tell me I'm no good." He turned back to me with a cruel smile. "I'm sure your mother would agree. Who am I to argue?"

It was my turn to glare. "Don't assume I agree with her. You don't need character references to enroll, and you weren't given criminal charges."

"I don't need a reference, but my reputation precedes me regardless. They can still say no."

"That's not fair."

"I appreciate your unexpected support." Edwin seemed more bewildered than anything. "But I doubt you know the whole story."

"Of course I don't. I shouldn't know any of it. Unlike my

mother, I don't think talking about court cases is appropriate, even with family, but—" I ran into a mental snag here and lost my words. I pressed on, changing the subject. "Anyway. I'm sorry the college turned you away, it sounds like bullshit. But enrolling is hardly the only option if you're as passionate about studying as throwing away suit jackets would imply."

"You are rather upset about the jacket." Edwin raised a brow, almost amused.

"Don't deflect."

Scolding prompted Edwin to smile at me. The change was like a tiny bit of sunshine breaking through clouds. "You're very blunt for someone who has a good idea of who I am."

"I don't like seeing people having a worse time than me. Most powerful Witch or not, you need something other than a trash can to help you deal with—" I gestured with my hand to indicate what I presumed was his mess of personal problems. "And I get what you mean, I want to stop bad things from happening too, even if I can't stop"—I pushed through another block with vagaries—"the past."

My past, his past. One I was magically prevented from saying, and one I felt he wouldn't want to hear.

"So you feel obliged to help distraught nicotine addicts? To do good and stop innocent articles of clothing being wasted?" Edwin asked mockingly.

I huffed. "I'm not obliged. I'm trying to be friendly, and when I actually w-want—" Shit, another snag, and this one much more obvious. But I was doing better than my restrictions usually allowed.

Edwin seemed to take my stumbling as a fault on his part. "Sorry, Juliet. I'm in a bad mood, and people being nice to me often makes me want to be a jerk."

"Well that's relatable." I took a sip of coffee in an attempt to pull myself out of the conflict in my head. "You've distracted me.

I was trying to say, if you want to be an investigator, prejudiced enrollment restrictions can't stop you. Fuck them. Anyone can sit the licensing exam after paying the fee, it's run outside the schooling system for a reason. I can't promise the Authority would hire you, if that's what you were wanting, but you could work privately."

Edwin looked out the rain spattered window. "And how would I learn the material to pass the test without attending lectures or training?"

"I'd teach you."

He turned and peered at me. "I can't ask you to do that."

"You didn't. Besides, it will be a great way for me to master the material. So really, it's in my interest."

"I can't accept that kind of favor. It's a two-year commitment. You don't know me." He shook his head as if I were being ridiculous.

"Maybe I'll get to know you." I was going off on a whim here, but I'd bet we had a lot in common, and I wanted to get to know him as genuinely as I'd wanted to buy him coffee.

Edwin pulled his jacket tight around himself. "Why would you want to?"

"Why does anyone want to know another person? Why stop in the street to reach out to someone? Maybe I'm some selfless do-gooder, or maybe I'm—maybe—" Fucking, fuck. My words tripped, caught in a snare, taking me down and slowly killing me with silence.

"Feeling sorry for me?" Edwin said, trying to finish my thought.

"No. *God*, it's like you've never heard of the concepts of friends."

"It's like you've never successfully made a friend."

He wasn't far off the mark. I had plenty of friends, a rich

social life, but it wasn't real. "Seems like we'll get along great then."

Edwin smiled and dropped his head back against the red vinyl booth. "You're actually offering to spend all your free time teaching me the principles of magical investigation?"

"It's not a big deal. I hate free time."

"Okay. As long as you don't have an ulterior motive." Edwin looked more bitter than I'd have thought possible. "Don't think that doing me a favor will get you one in return. I don't do magic for others."

I felt a flash of guilt, but I didn't really have an ulterior motive. I wanted to help and be his friend, but I also hoped he could help me, against all odds. Even if he couldn't, I'd still do what I could for him. If we were anything alike, he needed it.

My heart raced as I tried to figure out how to communicate this next bit through my restrictions. "I don't want favors," I said slowly, feeling the words like they were physical things. "Not that. But I hoped—"

I ran into the topic I was prevented from even dancing around. These particular spells were so well incorporated into my mind that the thoughts themselves were hard to form, but I saw an opportunity here. I couldn't waste it.

Edwin said he wanted to do good. Stop bad things happening. This wasn't a favor, it was a plea.

I stuttered, trying to get out impossible words, and Edwin looked confused as my strange attempt to talk failed. I took a breath and tried again. My voice came out small and tentative. "Maybe I hoped someone would stop in the street and reach back."

Edwin considered the roundabout callback to my earlier statement. His gaze turned as intense as earlier but without the unfriendly edge. It was like he was waking up, like I'd pulled him out of his own muddled mind. "Is something wrong, Juliet?"

I felt the smile stretch across my face and wanted to scream. "No." My voice turned light and girlish, but I reached for his arm and gripped him hard.

He looked closer. I felt trapped, as caged as ever. Everything in my mind was so unbearably jumbled. And for once someone saw the realness of all this inside me. Edwin's face shifted in recognition. I didn't know how he saw when no one else ever had. If there was magic in his stare that allowed him to see beyond, if it was our physical contact, or if we were the same. However it happened, he knew something wasn't right and I wanted to weep with relief.

Of course I couldn't. My smile tasted like acid lies. But this was the closest I'd ever come to breaking free, and he'd given me an idea.

9

JULIET

*D*riving across town only took so long, so I kept my memories focused on that day as best I could. So much of what followed was messy and complicated. The important thing was to remember that my idea had worked in the end. The spells on my mind were long gone.

I managed to extricate myself from memory by the time Mea and I reached the Herrera Investigation offices. We ascended the stairs to my office and I held the frosted door open for Mea. Her smiley thanks came across almost flirty. But that couldn't be right. She wouldn't act like that now, would she?

It was like the woman ran on sunshine and rainbows. I'd been completely rude to her, then ignored her in the car, and yet she wasn't deterred in the slightest. If it weren't for the blue hair, we could have been back in college, the way she was acting.

Mercifully the illusion was broken by Aria's presence at the reception desk, and the lack of New York skyline out the window. Aria waved before turning her attention back to the computer and her second love—cold brew.

Mea took her time looking around the office. It used to be organized in a similar fashion to my house. I had Aria to thank for the new filing system and more organized space. Mea seemed to approve. *Not that I care what she thinks.*

"Where's our teleporting friend?" Mea asked.

"He's in some other state, working on some other case," Aria replied, unconcerned.

It was best Edwin wasn't here. I was overcome with the urge to talk about our past. I wondered how often he thought about that day.

Mea turned to look at me. "So. What are we doing? You don't need to go through the files relating to the disappearances anymore."

Could she not deduce the logical answer, or did she just like the sound of her own voice? I had other work, obviously. This was a business after all.

Instead of explaining, I walked around Mea and entered my office.

She trailed after me. "Juliet—"

I sat behind my desk and smoothed my blouse. "Is part of your assignment to inventory everything I do?"

Mea sat in the guest chair opposite me. She ran her hands over the upholstery. "I mean—kind of. Not everything, but I need some information from you, Juliet."

I looked at her expectantly. We could both play the game of waiting for everything to be stated plainly.

Often there was nothing more fun than being difficult. There was a time when I wasn't able to act like this, and it never ceased to give me joy now. Besides, Mea was no chore to look at. I could easily be difficult, staring at her all day.

Mea's hazel eyes threatened to soften my resolve, so I refocused on her lips.

She didn't rise to my childish mood, was instead annoyingly professional. "Can I get a list of everyone you work with regularly?"

I turned my attention to my computer, not sure why I was disappointed.

What was my problem? People were missing and I was over here playing games. "I'll print out a list, including contact details. And I'll make a separate list of all my recent clients. I might as well print out my calendar. Prepare to be bored by everything I've been doing over the last few months."

"Okay. That'd be great." Mea unlocked her phone and tapped out some message or note. Her brows knitted together as she concentrated on the device. I didn't like seeing her worried, though if I had to guess it wasn't anything major.

Wait, when did the intricacies of Mea's facial cues become part of my knowledge base?

She bit her lip in concentration.

Why did she have to be so cute? I didn't need to notice how her blue hair fell over her face like a silken waterfall that I wanted to run my hands through. Having her stay with me was going to be a disaster.

The printer sprang to life and Mea got up to retrieve the paper. "I have to ask, Juliet, considering someone could be targeting you, has anyone been dissatisfied with your services? Is there anyone you worked for who rubbed you the wrong way or didn't feel they got their money's worth?"

"No. I haven't ripped anyone off or screwed up any cases. Like I've said, I haven't worked on anything Witch-snatch-worthy. And I don't charge, I work on a barter system. There is no money's worth."

"What do you barter for?" Mea came back to the desk and sat at attention.

"Depends on the person. Sarah and I traded information. Never anything personal or sensitive, but she would help me find obscure facts as needed, and I'd share anything of interest I came across in return. Witches can hire me for the price of a favor, if a direct exchange doesn't suit. Mortals usually barter with physical goods, and some insist on cash payment. It's not an exact system, I work however people need me to."

Mea looked baffled.

"It's not a hard concept to understand," I said more firmly. Sometimes I wondered if people were determined to find me weird, no matter what.

"No, it's just—why? Owing favors sounds like trouble."

"No, it doesn't. I'm not trying to trick anyone, or cash in for blood and first-borns. It's like, if I help you figure out who cursed an old family chest, I might ask to study the chest as a favor. Or I might come to you one day and ask if you know more about eighteenth century woodwork. People can always refuse."

"But then they might never pay."

I shrugged. "So what. You saw my house. I'm doing all right." Initially my money came from family, which I was uncomfortable talking about for several reasons.

"So you're only in this to help people out?" Mea's inquisitive gaze sent an odd tingle through me.

I didn't usually like scrutiny, but she wasn't judging. Mea was looking at me with understanding, like she'd clicked something into place. And it was something she liked. As if *I* was someone to like.

I almost smiled. Shit, I hadn't felt like this in so long. Temptation to lean into whatever this moment was almost got me.

"Can I ask one more thing?" Mea waited for me to nod. "What about enemies? Are you aware of anyone who might want to target you? If not for reasons relating to your work, then anything else?"

"No." A chill went down my spine, my brief moment of happiness gone.

I wasn't lying, but I wasn't going to go into all the caveats. There was no need to detail my irrelevant trauma. All of my conflicts were resolved. If I thought anything from my past was connected to the current events, I wouldn't hold back.

Mea watched me closely. I feared she'd push, but she let it go. "I want you to feel like you can talk to me, Juliet."

I turned my attention to the computer. "That's nice, but my feelings are my own. I'll keep you posted on anything relevant."

Mea bit back a sigh. "I was hoping we'd be able to relax, get to know each other. Since we're stuck together."

"No, you're hoping *I'd* relax. This is how I am, Mea. We aren't going to share confidences and bond. Deal with it."

I stole a glance to find Mea looked personally affronted, which wasn't fair. The two of us had different personalities. I didn't have to bend myself into whatever she wanted me to be, and I wasn't apologizing for it.

It wasn't my fault if the assumptions she held about me were wrong. If Mea thought I'd somehow turn back into the girl I was when we first met, she was dead wrong. That me wasn't real and I hated that Mea preferred her.

"I'm the only one the Authority thought could deal with it," she muttered.

"What does that mean?" I leveled a piercing stare at her. I'd been taking lessons from Edwin and had a very cutting gaze of my own these days.

Mea was disappointingly unaffected. "It means I was assigned to this case specifically to work with you. To help things run smoother."

Her words brought me up short. Out of everything she could have said, I found this humiliating. Like I wasn't just some regular person but something to be managed. The Authority usually sent Edwin for similar reasons, but this felt different. I'd been unaware and never would have agreed to this, whereas the arrangement with Edwin was mutual. This felt like the Authority trying to manipulate me.

"It's okay." Mea was either oblivious to my reaction or trying to gloss right over it. "I like working with people I know. This isn't a big deal. I bet we could work well together, if we give it a chance."

"Yeah? But only if I loosen up and act how you want? Don't count on it. I don't need special handling. It hardly matters if it was you or someone else I was stuck with."

And to think I'd felt momentarily guilty for not giving Mea a full, honest answer to her question. She wouldn't understand what held me back any more than she would understand how right I was not to trust her with that part of myself.

10

MEA

As soon as we returned to Juliet's house she disappeared into her bedroom without a word. I stood in the living room feeling the silence.

Time stretched and Juliet didn't reappear. Should I wait, or retreat to the guest room? I wasn't sure if she'd like me wandering off without permission so I browsed the books. Maybe they would lend some useful insight into my hostess.

There was no discernable order to the haphazard stacks. The shelves were loosely grouped by genre, but finding anything would be a nightmare. I supposed you could summon the book you were looking for, but if it was at the bottom and a four-foot pile you were risking a cascade. Not to mention, sending books flying through the air was a gamble when anything might topple over at the slightest nudge.

I abandoned the books and went to look out the glass doors. The wooded yard stretched beyond my line of sight. It was gorgeous but had an underutilized quality. I'd say neglected, but didn't mean the appearance or landscaping. Nothing was overgrown. I was just hard to imagine Juliet going out there often. It was the kind of yard I'd kill for—not literally—but something like this was perfect. Shielded from neighbors and ideal for small enchantments.

I heard Juliet's bedroom door open behind me and turned.

She walked through the room, focused ahead, wearing a slouchy beige knit sweater and black leggings that hugged the curve of her hips. Her feet were bare. Seeing her dressed down shouldn't have startled me, but it felt unexpectedly intimate. I wanted to think this was her relaxed, except her posture was stiff as ever.

Juliet turned to face me. She'd taken her makeup off, except her lipstick. Something about me standing around caught her off guard. She blushed, her eyes going ever so slightly wide.

I couldn't help but smile.

"What are you doing?" Juliet took up a defensive stance, shutting down her subtle display of emotion. Even the flush disappeared from her cheeks.

I fought with disappointment. "Nice yard." I gestured unnecessarily out the window. "You should get a dog or something. It's perfect for animals to run around in."

Juliet gave me the most flabbergasted look I'd ever seen. "Why didn't you change?"

"Was I supposed to?" I was still in my loose leg pants and sleeveless blouse. It wasn't like we'd discussed plans for the night, let alone what we wanted to wear.

"Are you going to spend the whole evening in your work clothes?" Juliet's cheeks turned an even deeper pink than before as she crossed her arms in front of her chest. "Should I not have —I can go get dressed properly again." She looked back toward her bedroom.

The secondhand awkwardness was painful and impossible not to find endearing.

"No, it's fine. I got distracted by all the cool stuff in here. I'll go change." I moved away from the window and headed toward the hall. "You don't have to entertain me. Just do whatever you usually do. I can stay out of the way."

Juliet looked displeased by my accommodating words. "True. You're not a guest." She walked off to the kitchen. Hips swaying.

I disappeared into the guest room and checked my phone. No messages.

The rest of my team hadn't contacted me since I'd left this morning. Had it really been less than a day since I'd been tasked with Juliet-watch? It felt longer, and I had no idea how long I was expected to stay with her.

Spending the afternoon at the Herrera Investigation offices had been painful. I couldn't talk to Juliet for more than a few minutes without pissing her off. I was usually much better with people, not that I was a social butterfly, but I was generally able to move through my days without inspiring loathing.

Except with her.

It was maddening, but Juliet's unreasonable responses only drew me in further. Every time she perplexed me with her actions, she threw off what I thought I knew about her. She looked so perfect and predictable when she was anything but.

I needed to figure out how to talk to Juliet without her shutting me down. I had no idea why the thought of opening up or getting to know each other sent her into defensive mode. Not that I'd helped myself by revealing I was assigned to the case because of her, but she also made a way bigger deal out of it than I understood, and now I had to repair the damage that oversharing cost me. Juliet needed to trust me.

For reasons relating to the case. Obviously.

So what if I also wanted to show her it was safe to be comfortable around me. I found the mystery of Juliet endlessly intriguing, and couldn't help wanting to understand her better, both to ease my frustration and satisfy my curiosity.

But as personal as my desire to get to know Juliet was, she needed to tell me what she actually thought about the Witch disappearances and how they related to her. I didn't believe her clipped responses to my brief questioning earlier. More was going on with Juliet than she wanted to admit. She was hiding something, or given the protection on this house, hiding from someone. I needed to know who, and why.

Another glance at my phone and there was still nothing from the rest of my team. I shucked off my work clothes trying not to worry silence meant they were getting nowhere, and dressed in shorts and a T-shirt advertising my family's apothecary shop back home.

I exited the guest room only to stand in the hallway, uncertain. Juliet was making noise in the kitchen. It was almost seven and I couldn't deny food sounded like a good next step. Would Juliet be annoyed if I joined her? Who was I kidding, of course she would. Juliet wouldn't be happy unless I hid in the guest room until the Witches were found.

Cautiously, I made my way into the kitchen and hovered by a small dining table near the back door.

Juliet was cooking, like actually cooking. Without magical assistance. She had an apron on and a pan on the stove. Something was in the oven. I didn't know any Witches who bothered cooking manually when eating out and spells were much more appealing options.

Juliet measured something and put it in a bowl. "I can feel you staring, Mea."

"Sorry." I came closer and leaned against one of the cabinets. "What are you making?"

Juliet looked at me. It seemed like it was supposed to be a darting glance, but her eyes caught. Juliet blinked, her gaze running quickly up and down my body like she was searching for something before turning away.

"Baked tofu tacos."

"Yum. But—why?" I looked at all the ingredients she had laid out.

Juliet's shoulders tensed and she went completely still. I could never anticipate what triggered these reactions in her, other than anything I ever did or said.

Her utter stillness only lasted a moment. Juliet resumed mixing the contents of the bowl with her hands, her posture unrelaxed. "Why does anyone do anything, Mea?"

"Um—depends?"

She still wasn't looking at me. "I cook because I enjoy it. Even I have hobbies."

"Of course you have hobbies. Reading for one."

She let out an involuntary laugh.

I took it as encouragement to go on. "Cooking is kind of cool, actually. Though, seeing you do all this makes me feel lazy. I've never bothered learning a complicated skill magic can do for me instead. Food prep always seemed like a chore. Not that I don't know how to do chores—just—why learn to cook a lasagna when magic guarantees I won't mess it up?"

For some reason my arguably annoying tendency to ramble didn't appear to bother Juliet. She considered my words carefully. "Cooking can be a chore if you have to do it all the time, or if you're busy. But I find it relaxing."

Juliet placed a ball of masa in a tortilla press and flattened it.

"So you can relax?" I teased.

Juliet gave me a withering look, but the tension was gone from her shoulders. She slapped the tortilla onto a hot griddle and made another.

"I'd offer to help—"

"Please don't. You're doing more than enough by being here."

I chuckled at the sarcasm in Juliet's tone and she treated me to another sideways glance. The gold and amber in her eyes seemed to spark with mischief. Then she was back to focusing on her task.

Juliet made a stack of tortillas as I watched. Her ease of movement told me she'd done this countless times. She met my eyes again. I smiled and she turned away, her movements going clumsy. I decided to give her some space and went to look out at the dark backyard. I could almost feel Juliet's ease return, now she was free of my attention.

"You can go outside if you want," Juliet said after a few minutes.

I smiled, not that she could see with me facing away from her. "Maybe later. It smells good in here."

"Thanks," she huffed. It was almost a laugh.

Juliet took a tray of tofu out of the oven and tossed the baked cubes in a bowl, coating them in sauce. "What's the deal with the Authority opening more branches?"

"Oh." I shifted my weight trying to decide what to reveal. "We're expanding now there are more people in the Authority workforce. Population growth—they're finally catching up. The more Witches around, the more problems. Or something."

Juliet did a spectacular eye roll as she arranged tortillas on a plate. "And you think they need to come here?"

"There's an open submission for new branch locations. Terra and I are putting one forward. I suggested here."

"That didn't answer my question." Juliet dished out the tofu and topped it with slaw and cilantro.

"Right." I inched into the kitchen looking for a distraction. "It's the beginning of the programs so there's no wrong suggestions."

"So in other words, everywhere is in need of Authority presence?"

"It's not an invasion." I didn't like the way she made us sound.

Juliet made a *humph* noise, picked up her plate and went to sit at the little table. "You don't think the Authority expanding is unnecessarily invasive?"

"Protecting the secret of magic and the power imbalance between Witches and Mortals happens everywhere, not just in key cities." I filled two glasses with water and set them down next to her.

"But has there really been a large enough increase in magical problems to justify what they're doing, or is this just the Authority's preoccupation with surveillance getting the better of them?" Juliet looked at me in open challenge.

I turned away to grab my plate. Juliet had hit a nerve, her words capturing my initial gut reaction to the expansion announcement. But after some thought I'd decided change could be a good thing. Spreading out was a chance to do things differently, do things better, move away from the rigid structure that was in place now and the problems that came with that.

Facing my host, I took the positive angle. "It's an opportunity and it will change how the Authority works. Lots of Witches live in this area, so the choice of location isn't random, but it's not about watching what people are doing. It's about being more accessible to people when they need us."

"And what about the people who don't need you? The ones the Authority doesn't like, do you think this will be better for them?" Juliet eyed me as I joined her at the table.

Setting my plate down with care, I avoided her graze. "I don't know. But that's why I volunteered. Opening new branches is a chance to address these things. And I need a change of scene in general—just not too much of a change."

"I see." Juliet folded her napkin and put it on her lap.

I shouldn't have been disappointed that she didn't press me for more details about that last bit, but I'd much rather focus on my personal reasons for wanting to move than my murkier professional ones, even if Juliet wasn't the right person to confide in. Juliet had probably only asked because she didn't like the Authority and clearly hated the idea of them coming to town. It hadn't been a personal question, I only wanted it to be.

I might like some form of friendship with Juliet, but I couldn't make up for the mismatch between us if she didn't meet me halfway. If she didn't care to be friends, we never would be.

"You're not going to the dining room?" I asked in a desperate attempt to change the subject and spare us the pained silence we were descending into.

Juliet shrugged like nothing mattered. Not the conversation, and not where we sat to eat. "I don't usually."

We sat in silence. I examined my plate instead of eating, too busy being annoyed with myself for caring what Juliet thought of my potential plan to move.

I looked up to find her considering me.

Juliet tapped her fork on her plate. "You're right about one thing."

"Um, which thing?"

"There is a high Witch residency here. Higher than the national average. You can put that in your proposal. And placing yourselves here would make access to other, smaller central-state locations easier."

"That's a good way to put it." I didn't mention that these were things I'd already considered. What—was she supporting the idea now? She knew that meant she might actually see me around town. Right? Or was this the same as resigning herself to having me as her unwanted house guest? She'd rather it was me than other Authority people she liked even less?

I picked up a taco, resigned to never understanding this woman.

"Wait—I forgot to ask if you had any food allergies." Juliet looked stricken at her lack of consideration.

I let out a surprised laugh at the contrast between her care and previous antagonism. "Relax. It's fine. I eat anything."

Juliet pursed her lips in response.

I put my taco down, an idea taking hold. "Want to eat outside?"

Juliet's reaction was worth speaking the whim out loud. She looked how I'd imagine someone would respond to being told we could eat on the moon. "It's dark out, Mea."

"So?" I stood up.

Juliet could probably do with some fun in her life. Like no offense, but if her BFF was Bickel, she needed a lighthearted influence to balance out all the seriousness. And I didn't want to get stuck on the Authority and our differences, I wanted to give her the opportunity to see positive things about me. She'd never open up otherwise.

"I have a good feeling about tonight. It's not that cold, and I love your yard. Come on?"

"I guess we could." Juliet looked resigned. No one had so plainly humored me in all my life, but she was agreeing and I had no doubt that if she didn't want to play along, she'd let me know.

Juliet opened the back door and grabbed our plates. I took the water glasses and followed her outside. A small stone patio with an adorable wooden table and chair set sat beyond the edge of the lawn, almost hidden in the dark. We made our way over and I found myself surrounded by a low-lying garden, overlooking a small, albeit dry, creek.

I sat down. "This is great."

Juliet crossed her legs, brushing my knee with her slipper clad toe. "Sorry."

"No worries." I nudged her back playfully.

The table was small and placed us much closer together.

The potential for a romantic date in this spot was strong. But Juliet was right, it was too dark.

I muttered a quick spell and my rings flashed, setting twinkling lights glowing in the surrounding plants. A perfect addition to the space. Magic should be fun, and I loved using it to make the world more glittery.

I mean, how could you sit in a twinkling night garden under the stars and not smile?

"Cute, Mea. This is very you." Juliet seemed pleasantly surprised, and maybe like she was continuing to humor me.

I picked up a taco and dug in. It was delicious. "Thanks for cooking for me."

"It's fine." Juliet took a bite before adding, "It's nice to cook for people."

Sharing a meal was nothing revolutionary. I knew it could be an act of friendship or caring, or not a big deal, but something about it being the two of us had me disoriented. Possibly the garden was *too* romantic, but that wasn't a thought worth dwelling on.

I wiped my hands on my napkin. "Do you cook for many people?"

Juliet made a noncommittal sound. "Edwin mostly."

"I can't imagine him cooking."

"Oh, god. He doesn't. Brooding is the only thing I've ever seen him do in a kitchen."

I couldn't help snorting at that. "But he's good company?"

"Yes." Juliet looked at me like she was trying to decide if I was hassling her, which I wasn't. I genuinely wanted to know—anything—about her. Juliet must have decided my motives were acceptable because she added, "Edwin is good for conversation and testing out new recipes. Like you, he'll eat anything."

It was hard to imagine good conversation between them, but it wasn't something I was going to dispute. "Cool. Sounds like you two are a good match. A cook and a tester—" This time I could see Juliet's mood about to turn in the way her features seemed to still. I rushed on. "A good match as in friends, I mean. Like Terra and me, but not."

There was an awkward pause in which Juliet didn't bite my head off, so I must have gotten something close to right. Instead she settled into assessing me, as if she didn't quite trust me.

I slumped in my seat. "I'm sorry if I keep making this difficult." What the hell, might as well get things out in the open.

Juliet still wore a weary expression. "What do you mean?"

"I keep stepping in it. Like I'm oblivious to something. I don't know why I always upset you, or saying the wrong thing—"

The rest of my words were swallowed by a thundering boom.

11

JULIET

*M*ea and I froze.

A piece of tofu tumbled out of the taco in Mea's hand and splatted on her plate. "What the—"

Another clap of thunder sounded. It wasn't really thunder, there was no lightning, not a cloud in the sky, but it sounded just like it, echoing as the air buzzed with magic.

I stood up, almost knocking my chair over. My heart raced as I looked around.

Even with the twinkling plants you couldn't see much. Mea's lights actually made it harder to see beyond the garden. Abandoning sight, I searched the area with magic.

Mea jumped up as another boom shook the ground beneath our feet.

My magic revealed there was no one else in the yard. Not that there could be with the spells Edwin cast on my property. But someone was trying to get in. The protective magic hummed as the intruder sent shockwaves through the complicated spell work, but it held.

Of course it held. It was impossible for anyone to break the protections but Edwin himself.

I was safe in my home. Unreachable. These facts should have been comforting but I found myself shaking.

Was the Witch lurking out of sight? On the street? In a neighbor's yard? Were they nearby, or powerful enough to try to break my defenses remotely? And if they knew about my defenses, had they been scoping me out? Or had they assumed I'd be an easy target and been caught off guard?

There was a howling sound, like a gale force wind, but none of the fallen leaves rustled.

"Look at the trees next door." Mea's voice was alert but calm, even over the noise of the wind swaying the neighbor's trees. "Definitely not a regular wind."

"We shouldn't have eaten out here." My own words came out pitchy and harsh with fear.

"From a magical point of view, it makes no difference if we're inside or not. Your whole property is protected. We should see if we can figure out where the attack is coming from." Mea went to walk off into the yard.

I made a small sound.

She stopped and looked back. "You can go inside. Grab my phone from the guest room and call Terra or Easton."

I looked toward the house. It seemed impossibly far across the small stretch of grass. All I could think was: *I don't want to know who is doing this.*

I tried to keep my mind in the realm of rational thought and facts—someone was targeting me, but we had no proof this was any different than what happened to the other two Witches. It didn't mean this was personal. It didn't mean the attacker was a Witch I knew—but I couldn't ignore my deepest fear. It didn't matter that what I was most afraid of was impossible.

"Juliet." Mea had come up to my side without me noticing. She touched my elbow lightly. "Let's go inside."

I let the woman guide me across the yard and into the house.

She closed and locked the back door even though the gesture was unnecessary from a security point of view.

"Sorry," I mumbled, arms wrapped around myself and shaking whether I wanted to or not.

"Don't be. Are you okay?" Mea peered at me, concern evident in everything from her posture to the intensity of her eyes. If only I could drown in those green and gold flecks, I might be all right.

I ignored her question. "We need to figure out who's doing this."

The sound of the wind was muffled now we were inside but the thunder was just as loud. The house shook as the mess of magic raged around us.

"We can do that just as well from here. Come on." Mea gripped my arm gently and led me into the formal dining room. She scanned the contents of my China hutch. "Candles?"

I shook myself and went to help, retrieving several candles from one of the lower cupboards as Mea took a few bunches of the plainly displayed herbs over to the dining table.

"We don't need to look around in the dark. If the person is physically nearby or not, we can see them just as well this way." Mea disappeared into the kitchen.

There was no need to explain, but I appreciated it. It kept me focused and stopped me freaking out more than I already was.

Mea returned with a bowl of water. She set it on the table with a sloshy *thunk*, lit the candles with a silent flick of her wrist, and began to murmur under her breath.

I was being utterly useless and couldn't for the life of me get my heart to slow down. It was like my mind was stuck on the desire to not know who was behind this, even though I knew we *needed* to figure it out.

Mea distracted me. I could focus on her and the way her hands were braced palms down on the table, her head bowed forward, blue hair hiding her downcast face from view. The candleflames danced and the water rippled. Mea's crystal rings sparked. The magic assaulting the house shook and shuddered, air electric.

I didn't need to look in the bowl to know Mea's spell was getting nowhere. The opacity of the attacker's spellcasting was almost tangible now Mea was trying to force the Witch to reveal themselves. They might be no match for Edwin's robust protection, but they weren't weak-willed. Even frozen in fear, I wasn't so distracted that I couldn't pay attention to what all the electricity in the air was telling me.

The Witch failing to break past my property's enchantments was working just as hard, if not harder, to conceal themselves. Almost like anonymity was more important than breaking in.

Fear coursed through me. Like a shot of coffee, it woke me up.

"Damn it." I turned and ran toward my bedroom in search of my phone. I should have called Edwin right away.

I looked frantically around my room. There were books everywhere, naturally. But my phone was only likely to be in one of a few places. Yes—it was on my vanity by the window.

I cued up Edwin's contact and pressed call.

It wasn't guaranteed he could do anything. If the Witch was concealing themselves from afar, in the same manner Sarah and Lana were concealed, then Edwin wouldn't be able to see their identity any better than Mea. But if they were lurking in a neighboring property, he'd be able to find them.

Edwin answered on the second ring.

"Someone's trying to get in," I told him in a rush.

Edwin didn't respond but half a breath later he materialized at my side. "*Hell*," he muttered as another thunderous boom sounded.

Then, everything went unnaturally still. The activity in the air vanished.

For a moment I thought it was Edwin's doing. His quizzically raised brow told me otherwise. The attacker must have given up—the ceasefire happening as Edwin arrived, coincidental—but he still had time to act.

Edwin gave me a nod, and did one of his more impressive tricks. He stopped time. Not that I was able to tell until after it was done because he didn't take me with him. I only felt a faint disruption in the air and noticed Edwin's instantaneous shift in position from next to me, to directly in front of me. His chiseled features went from concerned to disappointed.

"Nothing?" I asked.

"No Witches lurking anywhere within a mile radius. Other than the ones who live in the neighborhood, but they were all frozen doing boring, law-abiding things." Edwin ran a hand through his gray flecked hair, betraying his worry.

"Knowing that is good," I said, mostly to reassure myself.

I shouldn't have been relieved by the culprit's physical absence. It would have been easier to catch them if they were nearby, but distance gave me the illusion of safety.

"Um—hello?" Mea called from the living room.

"Shit." I grabbed Edwin's arm and dragged him after me. "I don't want her coming in here."

We found Mea heading this way, having abandoned her spell work at the table. "Oh, you're here. Missed the action, Bickel."

"Hardly." He made himself at home in an armchair, all outward signs of concern gone from his demeanor.

For once this didn't comfort me. I didn't know if I could act like everything was fine, and didn't want to feel alone even though I knew Edwin's impassive face was nothing but a mask.

I collapsed on the two-seater couch, exhausted, hands trembling slightly. My heart hadn't gotten the memo to calm down and pounded on. I reached for my usual composure but found it impossible to grasp.

Mea paced back and forth in front of us. "Whoever's doing this can't keep lurking out of sight. We should still search the street. Look for clues or disturbances. Just in case they were here."

"Already done." Edwin waved a dismissive hand.

Mea stopped and looked at him. "What?"

"I just spent hours combing the surrounding area." Edwin conjured a glass of whiskey he'd likely been drinking back home before I'd called. "If someone was here, they'd have been caught in my time-stop. No one was concealed, or practicing deceptive magic anywhere near here."

"What, you just froze everyone and everything to go snooping all over the place? How do you know it wasn't one of Juliet's neighbors? Did you search their homes? Without a warrant?" Mea gave my friend a look of distaste.

"Of course I didn't go into people's homes. Save your moral outrage, Ms. Dubois. Just because I have the power to violate most rules, doesn't mean I do. Perfectly legal investigative magic can tell me what spells are being used without trespassing. I only looked for anyone practicing concealment, or trying to break defenses. I'll file a full report on my search with my superiors. No need to worry about overreach." Edwin narrowed his eyes at Mea briefly, before turning his focus to his drink.

"Oh." She deflated and plopped down next to me on the couch. "So we're still no closer to figuring out who's doing this."

Neither Edwin nor I responded.

I was occupied with avoiding my own thoughts. At least my heart had slowed down. I closed my eyes, tempted to ignore everything and sleep this off. When I opened them I found Mea peering at me.

"I need to call the others. Tell them what happened." She looked at me expectantly. "They'll want to come investigate."

"Why?" I sat bolt upright. "Edwin's just searched everything more thoroughly than they possibly could. I don't need people poking around my house."

"We can't do nothing," Mea argued. "With the letters, it was only implied you might be a target. Now we know for sure someone is trying to get to you."

I wanted to deny it with every bone in my body.

"I'm sorry, Juliet." Mea put her hand on my shoulder, her touch warm and inviting.

I shivered, the urge to fall into her almost getting the better of me.

Mea gave me a pat and took her hand away. "Juliet, I need to know if you have any idea who could be behind this. With your name in the notes, you could even be the primary target here. Casting suspicion, then coming for you. Is there anyone who has it out for you?"

Edwin and I made eye contact.

"I already told you I don't have enemies, Mea."

She looked between my friend and me. "What aren't you telling me? What was that look?"

Mea had been a comforting presence through this whole ordeal. I couldn't deny that. But now I wished she'd go away. There was never any real danger, not with the property protected. I'd been afraid and Mea helped me effortlessly, despite my irrationality. I was grateful, and glad she hadn't made a point out of my failure to handle the unexpected. But none of that meant I trusted her.

My fearful reaction gave away more than I wanted Mea to know.

The thing I was most scared of didn't even fit the current events. I didn't want to have to explain myself, only to admit I was afraid of my past and projecting old trauma onto the present situation unnecessarily.

Besides, Edwin knew every detail I'd never share with anyone else. I wasn't keeping vital information from the Authority by not opening up to Mea. I just didn't want everyone to know, to talk, to draw conclusions and look at me with extra scrutiny, when what happened back then had nothing to do with anything now.

Mea turned to Edwin. "What are you two hiding?"

"This isn't a conspiracy," I said, drawing Mea's attention back to me.

"So there's nothing you haven't told me? You haven't the slightest suspicion what this could be relating to?"

I tried to think of something rational that fit the facts. If I stopped being distracted by my past and irrelevant things, what did I think was happening? Why would someone target me?

With my mind slightly clearer, a possible motive for present events came to me on an old memory. "It's possible all this has connections to my family. That's the only thing I can think of."

"Your family?" Mea looked between me and Edwin again, but she wasn't getting any hints from his stony face.

"I'm sure you've heard," I said dryly. "My mother sits on the Judicial Committee in New York City. Her mind-altering power always attracted complicated company. Growing up I was often around Witches who shared our rare magical gift. Everyone knows it's only legal to use mind-altering magic within the court system, but Witches who possess the power themselves often attract trouble, whether they use it or not."

"You think someone is targeting you because you possess mind-altering abilities?" Mea looked like she was expending effort to keep her features neutral.

I tried to ignore that. "It's possible."

There, I wasn't holding everything back. I'd confirmed for

Mea I had the power myself. And what I said was true. Witches who had this power were sometimes targeted by people who wanted to gain control of the ability for themselves.

This happened to one of my mother's colleagues—a Witch tried to curse him into submission, to turn him into a tool to wield mind control outside the law. But it's quite hard to get one over on a mind control Witch and the attempt was unsuccessful.

The ability to magically alter minds was the most heavily regulated of all magic. Any use of my power to alter someone's mind had to be court approved and be explicitly consented to by the affected party, otherwise it was illegal.

The only practical use for this power was within the court system. Witches like me were used to erase the memories of Mortals who wanted their knowledge of magic undone. There were very few other approved uses. Not all Witches who used their mind control for the courts were judges like my mother, but it was a power you could use to work your way up, like she had. We were considered powerful assets, even if we were hardly allowed to use our power.

I wanted nothing to do with any of it. I wished this ability didn't exist and so didn't use it myself.

The spells that had been cast on my mind growing up were completely illegal. I was taught as a child that no one with our powers acted outside the law. And I was sure most Witches like me never would, for moral reasons or because the punishments were harsh, but nothing was failsafe. Rules always got broken.

Some mind-altering magic was irreversible, like the erasure of memories. Other, more subtle spells were only reversible by the person who cast them. Or Edwin.

I didn't need to tell Mea that someone had once trapped me in my own mind. That problem had been dealt with more than two decades ago. The fact I was still scared of it happening again wasn't rational. It wasn't possible for that Witch to get to me now. I was haunted by my past, but it couldn't touch me.

It was much more likely someone had heard I possessed this rare power but didn't use it, and wanted to steal it for themselves. How Sarah and Lana, or Aria, fit into that scenario, I couldn't tell you.

It was possible for your average Witch, one without any unique gifts, to approximate mind control through curses, but cursing someone's mind to alter their behavior or memories was unreliable. The magic didn't always last and had unpredictable outcomes, meaning it was dangerous in a way my kind of mind control wasn't. It was also much more detectable. The spells placed on me had been seamlessly integrated into my thought patterns, it was how the power functioned, which was why no one noticed. A curse couldn't interact with the victims' mind in the same way, but it could still, in theory, force someone into submission as was attempted on my mother's colleague.

Mea appeared deep in thought. "Do you have any idea who would target you for your power? Anyone overly interested in your abilities?"

"No. It's only a guess as to why someone might target me. I don't have any evidence to back it up as a motive. I rarely tell people I have an extra ability, but people assume that because my mother is high profile and has the trait, that I do as well. Edwin's always known, and I told Aria yesterday. But that's it. Mind magic was never a subject of any of my work at Herrera Investigations, and I've never had anyone try to hire me to use my power, legally or otherwise."

"It's a long shot lead." Mea ran her hands through her hair, frowning.

"I don't deny that." It was still a more likely scenario than anything else I could think of.

Mea looked at me like she was giving me room to say more. She needn't have bothered.

The other reason I was hesitant to share my full history with Mea, was the sheer unlikelihood of what happened to me. Believability was always a fear of mine. *Why* was a question I was never getting a satisfactory answer to. How could I expect anyone else to understand, when I didn't?

I couldn't bring myself to share the most vulnerable part of me only to have it met with skepticism. I didn't want this old violation to keep hurting me. Denial of the reality I'd lived through was a pain I couldn't cope with.

I didn't want to be faced with proving myself, even if Aria's psychic sense could attest to my truth, and Edwin could corroborate everything as a first-hand witness.

He'd broken the spells the only way it was possible to, using unprecedented risky magic. Which he'd done without hesitation.

Then we'd dealt with the spellcaster ourselves. That chapter of my life was closed.

My paranoid fear of falling victim to mind magic had nothing to do with the attempt to break the protections on my property. Someone after my mind wouldn't bother with protections cast on my house.

"I should fill the others in on what happened," Mea said when it was clear no one was offering more information.

I acknowledged her with a tired nod, and she left the room.

Edwin vanished his empty whiskey glass, giving me his full attention. "I can stay."

"You don't have to. Really. The house will be too crowded with three."

He tapped the chair's arm rest. "I think we can manage."

I shook my head. "It's not necessary. If anything happens, I'll call. Without delay next time."

"If you're sure?" Edwin stood and offered me a hand up from the couch.

I didn't want Mea wondering why I was so frazzled I needed powerful Witches to hang around. What I needed was to get back to my usual self before anyone noticed. But from the look Edwin gave me, he knew where my mind had been tonight.

"I'm sure. You can go, it's fine. I'm just being paranoid," I whispered.

Edwin gripped my shoulders in a grounding gesture full of reassurance. "As anyone would be, Juliet. Worry isn't unreasonable after everything that happened." He looked down at me, his blue eyes soft with loving concern. "I'll look into it."

I sagged in relief at being so understood I didn't even need to speak my concerns out loud. Edwin knew how my mind worked, how I worried, and how I held it all together. We supported each other in dealing with our respective traumas. Not having the world know our business was not inconsequential; he knew that more than anyone. Only Edwin could comfort me without me having to spell it all out.

I trusted him completely.

And this way, with him looking into it, I wasn't hiding anything. Not keeping secrets or denying potential leads to solve this case. If against all odds my past had anything to do with what was happening now, no one was better placed to figure it out than Edwin. And if the past had nothing to do with current events, Edwin knew I needed my mind put at ease discreetly.

I needed my wall of privacy. It kept me upright.

12

MEA

The next morning it was like nothing happened.

I woke up to find Juliet in the kitchen slicing fruit. She looked impeccable in a form-fitted black dress, matching blazer, gold belt and pale pink scarf as she popped a slice of apple in her mouth, the juice clinging to her red lips.

"What do you want, Mea?"

I blinked. "Um—nothing. You're up early."

"No, I'm up at my usual time. If you aren't dressed in ten minutes, I'm leaving for work without you." She turned back to her fruit.

Juliet had been so shaken last night. It was like whiplash seeing her acting calm and unaffected. I'd always suspected Juliet's perfectly presented unreadability was a mask, but I never expected it to be so all encompassing.

I made it to the entryway dressed and ready just as Juliet opened the front door. "Are you sure about going to work today?"

She held the door open and ushered me forward. "Is that not self-evident?"

"Well—"

The door slammed. Juliet was already walking away.

I trailed after. "I mean, if you need to take a day off after everything."

"I'm not hiding at home just because someone made an intimidating but useless magical display in my direction."

A few days ago I might have taken this comment at face value. Believed her unaffected. Now it looked like a bullheaded attempt to avoid acknowledging what had happened, and how she felt about it.

Should I ask Juliet how she was really feeling? I wanted her to know she didn't have to pretend everything was fine in front of me. Damn it. Last night would have been the time to speak up, but with Bickel there I got distracted and missed my chance.

I held my tongue and got in the passenger seat of Juliet's sleek black car.

One uncomfortably silent drive later, we found Bickel alone in the Herrera Investigations reception area holding a tray of coffees. Juliet grabbed one and marched into her office without a word to anyone.

Bickel set the tray down and followed. "The cold brew is for Aria," he called over his shoulder before shutting Juliet's office door.

Well, shit. Close me out, why don't you.

Was the snub more than their usual rudeness? Juliet had to be hiding more than her emotions. Acting 'normal' wouldn't convince me otherwise. But I knew Juliet well enough to be confident she'd never impede our investigation. She just didn't make it easy to trust her.

This secrecy was doing her a disservice, even if it was in line with both her and Bickel's personalities and not necessarily suspicious behavior. I could imagine them having a closed-door conversation about the weather, or coffee. But standing out here I couldn't be sure. I'd liked to have weaseled my way in, but popping in uninvited wouldn't prompt either of them to include me in their discussion.

I took the fourth coffee and sat in one of the chairs opposite Aria's reception desk. Removing the lid, I found a drip coffee with cream and—a sip revealed—the perfect amount of sugar. Exactly how I took it, light roast and all.

How the hell had Bickel known my order?

Maybe he had a creepy coffee-related sixth-sense, or maybe Juliet had told him.

I'd stuck to the same simple order since college. Juliet likely had that information stowed away in her busy mind—ready to pull out as needed—the same way I was sure she still remembered the textbook curse-breaking principles off by heart. But I smiled like Juliet remembering and asking her friend to get it for me meant something.

Maybe getting her to open up to me wasn't a completely lost cause, if I could be patient enough.

The door to the office banged open and I jumped, almost spilling the hot drink everywhere.

Aria entered, suppressing a smile that told me the almost disaster hadn't gone unnoticed. She tossed her keys on her desk and slid into her chair.

"You've got to be kidding." Aria picked up the cold brew and shook her head like the coffee was bad news.

"Not what you wanted?"

"No, no. It's my go-to." Aria turned on her computer and logged in. "It's just—the reason this Witch has a vested interest in Coffee Cat is something I'm not sure what to do about."

"Right. Can't help you there, sorry." I didn't bother asking why Bickel's choice in coffee shops was a concern. There was enough on my mind.

Aria sucked on the drink's straw, reaping the benefits regardless.

"How've you been since yesterday? Any more trouble?" I asked once Aria seemed settled in.

The cold brew ice clinked as she set it down. "No, all good. I skipped the run today, to avoid potential stalkers, and haven't had any more letters."

"That's good. Are you worried?"

"Only a bit. I'm on the lookout, and will probably lay low, but hanging out at home is my preference. The Witch-snatcher can't get in the building now there's Bickel-level protections in place."

Interesting. Juliet didn't mention Bickel was doling out more protective spells.

I drank my coffee and exchanged texts with Terra and Easton as Aria tapped away on her computer. My three colleagues had almost no luck interviewing Witches in the community. No one knew about the note to Sarah. Both Witches seemed to live quiet, average lives with not so much as a bitter ex or family squabble to point toward possible motives or suspects.

The only thing of note was another destructed letter signed by Juliet, this time found in Lana's trash. Easton sent me a picture of the reconstructed note. It simply detailed a date and time to meet, without the allusion to trouble Sarah's note had possessed.

The supposed meeting was set for the night before Lana was discovered missing, but didn't correspond with anything on Juliet's calendar. Easton was of the mind that Juliet wouldn't write such a thing down if she had done it—no one put criminal activity in their calendar—and okay, *maybe*. But looking at her calendar, Juliet wrote everything down. The missing meeting could also mean the note was a fake planted by someone trying to point us toward Juliet.

We had email evidence of Lana and Juliet arranging their appointment for the day after the disappearance, just as Juliet had told us. Why would she arrange things twice? And why do anything by hand?

When I texted Easton back with my objections and a potential alibi for Juliet, written in her calendar for the night in question—*'dinner with Edwin - sushi - new place'*—Easton tried to find reasons to dismiss it. I ground my teeth. He really seemed to have something against Juliet, and even if it was just a general dislike due to Juliet's unfriendly attitude toward the Authority, Easton shouldn't let it into the investigation.

I only replied that I would ask her and Bickel to confirm the alibi with a psychic. Easton didn't reply.

I put my phone away and waited for Aria to finish whatever she was typing. "Can you think of any clients who've rubbed you the wrong way?"

Aria poked her head out from behind the computer monitor. "Not really."

"No one's made any odd requests? There's nothing that seemed normal at the time, but looking back now, feels off? Like with your run."

"I've only worked here six months, nothing stands out in that time." She paused to consider. "The jobs we do are low-key. Oh —but I do fend off social calls. That's not ordinary, but also nothing to raise the alarm over. It's a Juliet quirk. There's nothing wrong with the requests themselves."

I tried to catch Aria's eye, but the computer was still mostly in the way. "I'm sorry, what?"

"I'm Juliet's buffer. Not that I mind at all. Fielding emails and stuff is my job. Besides, I get wanting distance from Witchery at large." She rolled her chair out from behind the desk. "No offense."

"None taken. But what do you mean, fending off social calls?"

Aria paused, now seeming to select her words more carefully. "Every once in a while Juliet will be contacted by Witches she used to know, wanting to catch up or reconnect. I respond to those enquiries along with the business ones. I usually just let whoever it is know Juliet's busy and can't meet, or come to their event, or whatever."

"Usually?" I pressed.

"Well that's usually it. I say 'no' on Juliet's behalf, and they leave us alone until the next time they're in town. Some people even take the hint that Juliet doesn't want to see them and stop contacting us. But there was this one time, a Witch insisted I rearrange Juliet's calendar to make room for a lunch date. We went back and forth for days, but I didn't cave. Eventually he took no for an answer."

"Uh-huh." I marveled at Aria's ability to roll with odd work requests. "Who was this Witch?"

Aria couldn't remember and so went trawling through her emails before saying, "Jasper Suarez. Want his email address too?"

I pulled out my phone. "That'd be great, thanks. What did Juliet have to say about Jasper's persistence?"

"Nothing really. Juliet just said if he kept asking to tell him she didn't eat lunch, so the whole scheduling conflict was irrelevant."

I stared at the psychic assistant. "But Juliet does eat lunch."

Aria laughed at me. "It's called a lie, Mea." She disappeared behind her computer again.

Juliet's management of social callers wasn't exactly a surprise, but Witches trying to push their presence on someone who so obviously didn't want it didn't sit right.

I logged into the Authority database—yes, we had an app— and did a search on Jasper. He had no criminal history, but was in our system due to his position as a court clerk in New York. He was otherwise unnoteworthy.

Being persistently rejected for a lunch date with Juliet wasn't much, but I texted the potential lead to Terra anyway. If someone was targeting Juliet for her mind-altering power, it wouldn't be outrageous to think they'd tried to contact her in person first. An ulterior motive could explain Jasper's unusual persistence, even if it was more likely he was just a pushy type of person.

"Are you planning on sitting here with me all day?" Aria asked after a while.

I gestured toward Juliet's office. "I'm waiting for Bickel to leave before I go in."

"You think he's going to use the door on his way out?" Aria gave me a *come on* look.

Right. The man would teleport off when it suited him and Juliet would happily leave me sitting out here, waiting for her until five.

I got up and knocked on the office door. Juliet called for me to come in, and sure enough the dapper Witch was gone.

"Who's Jasper Suarez?" I asked as I sat in the guest chair.

Juliet raised a flawless brow. "I don't know, why?"

"He sent Aria an egregious number of emails trying to meet with you. Are you sure you don't know him?"

Juliet turned her attention back to her computer, but it didn't hide her as completely as Aria's did. "If Jasper's request was work related, I'd have reviewed the emails and met with him. But his name isn't familiar, so you'll have to ask Aria."

"I did. Jasper was very interested in lunch with you."

Juliet tapped her manicured fingers against the hardwood desk. "You think he was trying to meet with me to scope me out?" She glanced at me, but I couldn't tell if she seemed worried or annoyed.

I put up a hand. "I have no proof of that."

"Hm. If he was up to anything dodgy—and was smart, or

knew me at all—he'd have posed as a client to meet me. Sounds like he wasn't that clever. That doesn't fit our culprit's airtight abductions and flawless ability to cover their tracks." Juliet turned away. Conversation over.

I shifted in my seat. "It's possible Jasper only wanted lunch. Doesn't it get boring turning everyone away? What if you missed out on some good friends?"

"What if I saved myself from this Jasper's evil plot?"

"But you just said he wasn't—"

"I'm only going off what you said, Mea. Now stop trying to influence my social life. I'm not about to start hosting dinner parties or going out with people. I might be stuck with you for now, but don't assume it's going to leave a lasting effect on me."

Ouch, that stung more than it ought to.

Juliet must have realized. She flinched. "Sorry, Mea—it's just —I only mean there's no use encouraging me. I'll be busy reading for the next decade at least. My calendar is booked." She offered me a soft smile.

This had to be the first time Juliet apologized for one of her snappy replies, and seeing her make fun of herself had a warming effect, like we were getting somewhere after all.

I returned her smile. "I hadn't thought of it that way, but you make a good point. I neglected to consider the books."

Juliet suppressed a laugh, her lips twitching as she resisted smiling.

"Aww, look. We're all friends now," said someone from the doorway.

Juliet and I turned to find Terra. I wanted to be glad to see her, but she had the worst timing.

Juliet shifted smoothly back to her all-business attitude. "Any news?"

"Nothing worth repeating." Terra pulled up another chair and joined me in front of the desk.

Juliet made no effort to disguise her annoyance. "Then why are you here?"

"I have an idea." Terra gave me a wink.

"You couldn't have emailed?" Juliet turned away from us and began typing with practiced speed.

I'd like to think she was annoyed at the interruption for the same reason I was, but this felt more like her general annoyance at all things Authority.

Terra didn't seem bothered by the unwelcoming reception. "I could have, but I wanted a moment away from the other two."

"Oh—" Juliet considered this thoughtfully. "I suppose that's fair."

Terra was checking her phone and didn't acknowledge Juliet's comment. "So nothing suspicious to report since last night's drama?"

Juliet shook her head and I said, "No," because Terra's attention was still diverted and she wasn't looking at either of us.

My co-worker barreled on. "Good. And I'm glad you're here, Juliet. Not hiding at home." She looked up from her phone and mercifully put it away.

"Oh? You don't think I should take it easy?" Juliet's sharp attention landed on me, as if to say, *see*.

"Nah—this is better," Terra insisted. "The attacker now knows they can't get to you at home. So if they're going to make another move, it'll be while you're out."

"Isn't that an argument for staying in? Oh—" It looked as if something had just dawned on Juliet. "Is that what you were getting at this morning, Mea?"

"Doesn't matter." Terra cut in before I could speak. "We can play into this. Give the culprit ample opportunity to come for you, Juliet."

I made an incredulous noise. "What, like bait?"

"Exactly." Terra nodded a little too enthusiastically. "But I don't think it will look like bait, not to our attacker anyway. Juliet has carried on, business as usual, without missing a step. It looks like she's not bothered. If this Witch is targeting you more so than the others—as putting your name in notes implies—I'd say they'll take the next opportunity to get you, while you're away from your fortress."

"It's a perfectly normal house," Juliet muttered.

"I don't know about this." I couldn't be the only one feeling uneasy. This wasn't exactly putting wellbeing first.

Terra turned in her seat to face me fully, looking confident in her plan. "It's our best bet at catching them. With all the concealing magic, and almost random-seeming selection of our other victims, other than their loose association to Juliet, this might be our only real break."

"I'm going to go about my life as usual anyway, Mea. There's no point worrying. If they show up while I'm away from home, you can nab them."

I ran a hand through my hair. "While I appreciate your faith in me, I can't say I'm keen on the idea. What if they overpower me?"

"I'm not defenseless. It'll be two against one." Juliet sounded as confident as Terra, making her fear last night feel almost like a dream.

"Make that three," Terra added. "I've got another layer to the plan. You won't exactly be going about your usual schedule, Juliet."

13

JULIET

So much for Terra's grand idea.

Her suggestion boiled down to going out to dinner. The rationale being the less time I spent at home, the more likely someone would make a move. But I wasn't so sure.

I had spells cast on myself as well as my home, so I couldn't be surveilled magically. For the culprit to know I was out tonight, they'd have to be watching me as any Mortal stalker would, and that felt unlikely. Tailing me in person didn't fit with prioritizing secrecy and concealment.

However, being out and about as potential bait was still worth a shot and better than doing nothing.

Dinner was uneventful and, in an effort not to retreat too soon, Terra dragged me and Mea out to a cocktail lounge. The excursion felt less like a necessary part of a plan, and more like an excuse to be out on a Friday night.

"You didn't want to change?" Terra had shed her work suit in favor of a black romper and had already asked about what I was wearing once before.

"Mea didn't change," I pointed out.

But Mea looked stunning in loose slacks and a lightweight

top, not at all out of place. Her style morphed from professional elegance to chic woman on the town with nothing more than a change in locale.

I had an unusual urge to explain my stiff appearance. "I don't really own anything between boardroom suits and loungewear. It's either or."

To my relief Terra gave up on me, her attention turning toward securing drinks at the crowded bar. She was right about tonight being a disruption to my routine. I couldn't remember the last time I'd been anywhere other than my house or Edwin's after nine thirty.

"What about when you go to the beach?" Apparently Mea wasn't ready to let go of the clothing topic.

I gave her a baffled look. The single glass of wine she'd drunk with dinner must have gone to her head. "Why would I wear beach attire to a bar?"

"Never mind. Let's just have fun." She gave me a quick, devastating grin. The low light made it hard to see clearly but the details of Mea's lips were somehow imprinted on my memory.

I looked away scanning the growing number of people in the lounge. "Is now really the time to be having fun?" I knew this was a stodgy thing to say, but there were two missing Witches. My worry for them hadn't gone anywhere.

"Stressing won't help the situation." Mea seemed to read my mind. "But I understand if you're nervous about running into anyone dangerous. The whole situation isn't conducive to a good time."

Mea put a gentle hand on my elbow. Luckily, Terra was occupied ordering drinks and missed the gesture.

However, Mea was wrong. I wasn't nervous or worried about something happening to me, and yet her touch was warm and comforting, tempting me to respond with a touch of my own.

Maybe the glass of wine *I'd* had over dinner had gone to *my* head.

I shifted away. "It's fine."

Mea looked like she was about to apologize for touching me, so I cut her off sputtering inelegantly about finding us a table and walked away before she could comment.

Too many little moments with Mea were adding up. She was probably tallying up everything I did, and I wasn't doing enough to keep her at a distance.

For a moment I had trouble remembering why I should. What if I leaned into her touch, gave in to her incessant need to talk and bond? The idea made my stomach flip with anxious fear, and maybe something else.

I didn't want Mea to notice me more than she already had, or get to know me in any real sense. I'd much rather Mea dislike the performance I put on than find out what she thought of the rest of me.

Ever since my mind was returned to me, I'd analyzed my interactions and almost always selected my reactions based on what I wanted to portray rather than how I felt, erring on the side of purposely unlikable. In contrast, the me under mind control had been very likable. It was no wonder Mea had been drawn to me then.

Mea rejecting the public version of me now was fine. Anything else was a risk not worth taking. She probably thought the girl she'd met back in the beginning of college was the real me, and that me opening up would turn back the clock to reignite what we'd been. She was bound to be sorely disappointed.

And if I wanted to show Mea something 'real,' it didn't matter. I didn't know how. Not after wearing my public face for so long. There might not be anything underneath.

I found a high table in the semi-crowded courtyard and

perched on a barstool. Fairy lights and lanterns crisscrossed overhead, slung from the building to the fence. The atmosphere wasn't as nice as my garden last night, but it would do.

It was too bad Edwin hadn't come along tonight. Somehow I wasn't preoccupied with real versus fake me around him, everything felt natural. We'd have darkened the sidelines of this establishment together, but he was busy with a Judicial Committee dinner in New York and looking into things for me. He had the worse evening by far.

So far Edwin had found no indication my current trouble was connected to my past. But neither of us were lying back in relief just yet.

Maybe I should have invited Aria out with us. She would have been a welcome presence, not as stoic as Edwin, but far from the bubbly Mea—who was currently flitting through the crowd in my direction.

"Hope you like fruity cocktails." Mea plunked two garish drinks down on the table. Whiskey neat was more my speed, but the offered drinks were oddly appealing.

"Oh—perfect. Yes—um—that's—thanks." *Has my tongue been tied? What was that fumbling mess?* "Where's Terra?" I asked in an effort to cover my inexplicably flustered state.

"She got sucked into chatting with someone." Mea didn't sound like she expected the woman to come back any time soon.

"She's working hard," I teased.

"Terra will be ready if anything happens," Mea assured me, more serious than my comment warranted. She seemed to be taking looking after my nerves as her main objective. Which was all my fault for how I'd acted last night.

"I'm not worried, Mea." And I told myself that her attention wasn't comforting.

The red cocktails loomed like a dare to enjoy the night. I picked mine up. It was an effort to take a sip without being hit in the face by the garnish. I managed to maneuver the thing, but Mea embraced fruit hitting her in the cheek as part of the experience. The cocktail tasted like spiced strawberries with a kick.

We sipped in awkward silence.

A band was setting up, so I focused on them. One of the musicians struggled with a tangled cord for so long I almost marched over to help him, but his bandmate came to the rescue, saving me the trouble.

My attention slid back to Mea. What was I supposed to talk to her about? We'd exhausted work chat over dinner.

From her posture, Mea didn't look uncomfortable with our silence. She slowly sipped her drink and looked around. The lighting was better out here, actually brighter than inside the bar. Mea's blue hair looked mesmerizing, deep and mysterious with undertones of purple. It contrasted with her pale skin and made her eyes pop, dark green, all the hints of gold and brown overshadowed by the night.

"Is there garnish on my face?" Mea wiped her cheek.

I blushed and hoped it wasn't noticeable between my brown skin and the night. "No. Sorry—your hair—" I looked away.

Mea shook her head, sending blue strands flying around her. They settled in a wild tangle. "Yeah—I bet you hate it. Right?"

"No. I—um—like it." This wasn't embarrassing to admit, so why was my face feeling hotter?

"You should try dyeing your hair," Mea said, like my compliment didn't matter to her.

"I don't think so."

"Why not?"

I didn't know. I wasn't sure if it was something I'd like. Obviously the stiff boring Juliet everyone knew would never do such a thing. But the real me—who knows—whimsical hair felt like something other people liked. How would I know if it was genuinely me or not? Not knowing made the whole idea sour.

Oh honestly, who cared. It was all stupid anyway.

Unable to come up with an answer, I made no response to Mea's question.

Mea didn't react to my silence, as if she'd assumed I'd ignore her. It made me realize how rude I was all the time. Not that I didn't know. I was often purposely rude. It was just, suddenly I felt guilty about it. Mea shouldn't accept such disrespectful treatment. She deserved better than someone who ignored her.

When the band started to play, I caught a glimpse of Terra and a few people dancing across the courtyard. She caught my eye and waved us over.

"Go on if you want," Mea said. "I'll watch the drinks."

I snorted. "I don't think so. You go."

Mea picked up her drink. "No, I'm good. I'll stay here."

"You don't have to pretend you don't want to dance just to sit here with me. I'm fine. I know you like getting out there." I had vivid memories of Mea dancing in college. Someone as graceful as her in everyday life was beautiful on a dancefloor.

Mea only shrugged in that fluid, effortless way of hers, and stayed at the table.

I didn't take her decision personally. There were plenty of reasons not to dance with Terra that had nothing to do with Mea wanting to spend time with me. All we were doing was sitting in silence, she couldn't be enjoying this.

"I know I said I wouldn't bring it up again, but remember—" Mea looked at me expectantly, waiting for my permission before finishing her thought.

Figuring her mind had gone back to old memories as mine had, I waved her on. I was thinking it already, she might as well talk.

Mea looked like I'd indulged her in some sort of treat. "Remember that time at the dive bar?"

"Vaguely." I sipped my drink, making it clear I wasn't going to offer more. She could recount the story if she wished. I'd listen but that was it.

Many of my memories from before were hazy due to the mess of spells tangling my thoughts, especially when the magic was making me do things differently than I would have chosen to, but I was certain Mea was referring to the first night we went out with the other students. There was a dive bar a block away from the college and that night, Mea had danced on a table with one of the bartenders.

Even through my haze, the sight of her had given me an uninhibited feeling of attraction. Remembering the moment my feelings for her hit, made me smile despite everything.

"Whatever happened to us?" Mea wasn't looking at me now. She turned her drink in circles, focusing on the mess of perspiration it was leaving on the table. Like she was nervous about my answer.

I should have blown the question off. I'd done it enough times before. I was practically an expert at shutting this kind-hearted woman down, but Mea's face was so open. Real curiosity and confusion made me hesitate. She looked close to vulnerable.

Not knowing why I cut her out bothered Mea. I'd always known that, but I didn't like hurting her, and couldn't keep pretending I wasn't.

Maybe I gave an honest answer to put the matter to rest. To get Mea off my back. But that wasn't the whole reason. I didn't know if this particular secret was actually saving me any pain, and even if it was, that wasn't worth seeing Mea like this.

I looked away, down at my own drink. "I don't see it as anything happening to us, Mea. The things going on with me back then had nothing to do with you. I—wasn't okay in college. I was going through one of the hardest times of my life. I couldn't deal with anything else. I didn't ignore you because I didn't like you, or changed my mind about you, I ignored you because I had to focus on myself. I was too busy making it through day-to-day life for anything more."

"Juliet, I—I'm so sorry." Mea looked like she wanted to rush around the table and hug me.

"There's nothing to be sorry for," I insisted, but it still seemed like she was holding back her hugging instincts. "Really. I'm only telling you because you keep asking." I felt kind of frozen. I didn't want her to hug me. She didn't need to feel obligated.

Mea shifted in her seat like she suddenly couldn't get comfortable. "God, I've been pestering you about this for years. But I didn't know—did something happen? After that first month? Sorry. What an intrusive thing to ask. If you don't want to say, you don't have to."

I was avoiding looking at her again. The melted ice had created a watery gradient in my drink. "Yes, something happened. I don't want to try to explain."

"That's okay. Thank you for telling me. I—I'm sorry I've been badgering you about it all this time."

When I met Mea's eyes, I felt lighter. "You weren't badgering me—well maybe. But how could you have known? That was the whole point. You didn't."

"Still. I get it now and I'm sorry if I made anything worse. I hope you had someone, back then—to help get you through?" Mea was getting that overly worried look again, but I hadn't told her this to make her feel guilty.

"Really, it's fine. I had Edwin."

Mea's shoulders sagged almost like she was relieved.

Watching these new bits of information about me filter through Mea's thoughts was anxiety inducing. I tried to push away fears she'd see more than I'd revealed, or that this would somehow change everything.

"He's an interesting guy—Bickel. I hope to get to know him better." Mea's shifting opinion of the man written all over her face, like she was begrudgingly admitting to herself he wasn't terrible.

I hoped Edwin wouldn't be miffed that I'd shattered the illusion he was nothing more than a selfish prick. Authority employees were the last Witches Edwin wanted to gain insights about him, but Mea wasn't going to tell people what she'd learned about either of us.

It was almost like I trusted her. Except for the fact I'd still told her as close to nothing as possible.

"So what about now?" Mea asked.

"Now?" Had I missed something? Was she asking if I was okay now? And did I want to answer that?

"I get why we didn't end up as friends back then. And why you don't like me bringing it up—again, I'm sorry. But—what about now?" Mea raised her glass as if to say *come on, let's give it a try*.

Ah. I should have seen this coming.

Keeping everyone at a distance was how I operated, and part of me didn't want to change that. But pure stubbornness wasn't enough of a reason anymore.

If only I could avoid Mea comparing me with who she used to know me as. I didn't want her thinking that was me, and that something broke me and turned me into this, when it was the other way around. That was reason enough not to be her friend —since I was clearly looking for one—but maybe I didn't have to open up any more than I already had. Tonight wasn't so bad. Why couldn't we just keep doing like this?

"You are nothing if not persistent, Mea," I said with none of my usual bite. I liked her persistence. If she didn't care about me on some level, she wouldn't bother with me.

It wasn't like the world was going to end if I acknowledged tentative friendship.

Before I could commit out loud a man—a Witch—approached our table. His half full beer sloshed in its glass as he leaned against the stool next to me, invading my personal space.

"Juliet Herrera?" he asked loudly, ignoring Mea and giving me an inebriated grin.

"Who's asking?" My hard, business-like tone snapped back into place. I felt my face shift automatically into a blank slate, not even realizing how relaxed my expressions had become in the previous conversation.

The man stuck out his hand. "Jasper Suarez."

Mea made a choking sound and put down her drink.

I eyed the Witch. He was young, handsome and well dressed in an uninspired way. His dark hair hung in loose curls and his brown skin mirrored my own. Jasper let his hand fall when I made no move to shake it. Not deterred, he sat down and leaned an elbow on the table.

"Did I invite you to join us?" I asked.

He had the grace to blush. "Can I? Sorry. I've tried to meet with you but you're a very busy woman."

I turned away from Jasper in favor of looking at Mea.

Was Terra right? Were Witches lurking in the shadows, waiting for me to become easily accessible, poised to pounce the moment I didn't spend my evenings at home or teleporting off to remote dinner locations with Edwin?

"How do you know Juliet?" Mea asked the intrusive Witch. She was alert but her tone friendly and unassuming, as if we hadn't been talking about this guy hours ago.

Jasper put his drink down. "I don't know her. That's the reason I was trying to reach out."

"You've tried to get a hold of Juliet recently?" Mea prompted.

Jasper looked between us. "No—a few months back. I was in town. My friend said I should look you up."

"Why?" I scrutinized him. "Unless you were trying to hire me. In which case I'd have seen you."

"No, not for a job. I'm friends with Ben Shaw—you know him. He said to get in touch when he heard I was heading out West to visit my cousin. He thought we'd hit it off." Jasper smiled at me.

"You don't say." I didn't hold back my look of skepticism.

Ben was an old acquaintance of mine and Mea's from college. We weren't friends. Ben had tried to ask me out a few times, eons ago, and I'd refused. He'd been in touch once or twice in the intervening years, but I'd never met with him. Even before Aria, I was a firm no to social calls.

I didn't see why Ben would send someone else my way. It could be a lie, but why would Jasper bother? Someone this sloppy couldn't be involved in the disappearances. Why approach me half drunk? What was he trying to achieve here?

Terra thought someone watching me would make a move, but this didn't feel like the move of the Witch behind such well-planned abductions, or the work of someone scheming to curse me into giving over control of my power.

"What brings you to town this time?" Mea asked Jasper.

"Oh, same deal. Seeing my cousin, Juan." He gestured across the courtyard where another Witch waved in acknowledgment. "I um, didn't bother about asking you to lunch this time, Juliet. But running into each other is rather serendipitous, no?"

"No."

His smile fell. "Okay, I can take a hint," Jasper said, despite ample evidence he couldn't. "Maybe I'm interrupting something with your—um—girlfriend?"

Mea looked like she was about to object but I got there first. "Maybe it's none of your business, Jasper. Excuse us."

I got up, rounded the table and tugged on Mea's arm to drag her away with me. She complied, linking our arms together and we left Jasper behind.

Mea leaned close. "What are you thinking?"

"I don't know. Keep an eye on him." I led us into the flow of people dancing closer to the band.

"Do you think he was telling the truth?" Mea's breath tickled my ear.

Our arms were still linked and I didn't want to let go. It was nice to be this near to her. Mea's skin brushed against mine, our mingling body heat feeling like a force all its own. But I couldn't be distracted. I spun Mea away from me and for half a second it was like we were dancing. Then I turned my attention away and scanned the rest of the crowd. Besides the three of us, Jasper and his cousin Juan were the only other Witches here.

My ability to magically alter minds came with a few useful, and less problematic, advantages. I never used my ability to control, but the power had a side effect that allowed me to assess other Witches' magical activity with greater accuracy than typical Witch-senses allowed.

Witches like me could tune in to others' thought patterns in a way that was similar to psychics, but rather than detecting someone's emotions we could sense magical activity. The general ability to harness magical forces came from the mind, so I could sense a Witch tapping into their magic even if the Witch wasn't actively using it to cast spells. In other words, I could detect otherwise undetectable magical activity.

This sense allowed me to see the difference between a Witch minding their own business, and one subtly readying for action.

I turned my attention to Jasper. He wasn't harnessing any of his magical abilities. I'd have expected him to be reaching out with his magic to subtly inspect me and our surroundings if he was planning anything untoward.

I explained to Mea what I'd observed, keeping my voice low. "Jasper might be telling the truth about why he wanted to meet with me, but we should check his story. It feels suspicious, even if he doesn't seem to be preparing to make a magical move tonight."

Mea was back at my side, but not as close as before. "Agreed. It's an easy story to fact check. I'm not in touch with Ben anymore, but I can reach out. Unless you think we should be more discreet?"

"It would be better if our questions didn't get back to Jasper, in case he's up to anything more sinister than networking. It would be good to keep the element of surprise on our side."

Mea nodded. "Maybe ask Bickel to poke around? He and Ben are both investigators at the same branch, right?"

Something about Mea suggesting I ask Edwin made me smile. Like the three of us were all on one team. "Yes, good idea. I'll let you know what he says."

I turned my attention back to Jasper, who was across the courtyard laughing with his cousin and a few others. My snub didn't seem to have left a lasting impression. If Jasper wasn't completely ignoring me, he was an excellent actor, and he still hadn't done so much as access his magic.

"Hey. You're dancing." Mea pushed my shoulder playfully.

It would be more accurate to say I was swaying in an effort to blend into the dancing crowd. "Wow Mea, your observation skills astound me. Just—don't make a big deal out of it. Okay?"

With Mea smiling at me I almost enjoyed pretending to dance, even if it was awkward and felt like I was trying too hard. Everyone could probably tell I was hopeless, but Mea didn't seem to think so.

She took my hand and spun me.

I blushed and hid my face with a turn of my head. "I still prefer finding a comfortable corner," I mumbled.

"Fair enough." Mea let go of my hand, even though that's not what I'd meant. "I'm having fun with you tonight."

"Really. Fun?" There was no need to exaggerate. Our conversation hadn't been light or enjoyable. It wasn't exactly a night to remember. "I'm sure we can do better."

"I'll hold you to that, Juliet." With a devious grin Mea grabbed my hand and spun me into her arms.

I felt delicate in her embrace. My curves seemed to fit perfectly against her frame. I wanted to do something silly, like run my hands through her blue hair.

She was looking at me like she'd seen something extraordinary. She had no reason to look at me like she'd never seen me before. I wasn't acting so different tonight. Was I?

Who was I kidding, I'd never have let her hold me like this before, and I didn't know why she'd decided to do it now.

"Oh good god, Mea Dubois. Behave." I shimmied free but didn't back too far away.

14

MEA

*S*ounds in the kitchen roused me from sleep. A look at my phone told me Easton was stopping by this morning, so I got up and dressed. Even though I wasn't looking forward to seeing him, I found myself smiling.

Was waking up in anticipation of good things silly? I hoped Juliet and I would build on last night's comradery, unless she decided to act like nothing had changed between us. I could picture that all too well.

The smell of coffee wafted down the hall as I exited the guest room.

"Meadow—" Juliet's voice followed the coffee aromas in a sing-song tone. "Is that you?"

I froze. She'd never sounded so light and airy. And hearing my name, my full name, said so happily lead my thoughts down a pleasurable path.

"Good morning." I entered the kitchen to find Juliet looking adorable, standing at the counter wearing house slippers, leggings and another cozy sweater.

"Coffee?" She handed me a mug.

I took a grateful sip of the brew prepared exactly as I liked it. "Thanks."

"No problem." Juliet picked up her own cup, her eyes darting from it to me and back again. "I'm—um—going to sit in the living room." Instead of turning to go she paused expectantly, like she was waiting for me to do something.

I smiled, hiding it with another sip. It was as if Juliet couldn't quite bring herself to ask me to sit with her, but she wanted me to, if her hopeful expression was anything to go by.

"Lead the way." I gestured ahead of me.

Juliet made a pleased sound and hurried off.

"So what are you reading these days?" I asked as we entered the book filled room.

Juliet sat on her two-seater couch and I took the other. "The books on the end tables are the ones I'm currently reading, or planning to read next."

This hardly answered my question. There were dozens of books on the various tables, but it seemed like an honest answer, not a diversion. We chatted about our favorite recent reads. Juliet had a lot more to say than me, but I was fine with that. Preferred it, actually.

"I hate to kill the mood," I said when our coffee cups were empty. "But Easton is stopping by soon."

"There's no mood to kill. It's good he's coming over. Maybe there's an update on the missing Witches." Juliet's spirits seemed dampened, despite her insistence otherwise. She looked guiltily down at her mug, as if she felt bad for living her life while the case went on without us.

I tried to think of a good response, but her thoughts had apparently moved on.

"Maybe I should get dressed." Juliet frowned at her slippers.

I was in shorts, a tank-top and bare feet and felt no need to dress up for my coworker's arrival. "You don't like people seeing you in anything casual, do you?"

Juliet looked up at me, her face falling to that familiar snappish beauty as if she were about to challenge my observation, but she didn't go for her usual defensiveness. "No, I don't."

"Go on and change then, before Easton gets here."

Juliet nodded, looking almost confused. Had my response surprised her? What had she expected me to say?

As Juliet left the room I tried to think what I'd have said a few days ago. Probably that what she wore wasn't a big deal, and that she shouldn't worry about it. I certainly didn't. But this sort of thing really mattered to Juliet.

She made it back not a moment too soon. The doorbell rang and Juliet went to answer, high heels clicking on the tile floor. She returned, followed by a sour-faced Easton. I wished the others had come with him to balance out his not-so-glowing personality.

"You're looking casual, Ms. Dubois." Easton sat down in an armchair, pointedly adjusting his tie.

"It's Saturday morning."

He let out an exasperated sigh. "I'm aware, and can see you're taking the opportunity to lounge around. At least one of us has an easy assignment."

Like it hadn't been his idea to remove me from the investigation and plant me here. Easton's comment stung, but I refused to be put off balance.

"Why are you here, Easton?" Juliet asked at her most harsh and unforgiving. It was strangely soothing to see her directing that tone at someone else on my behalf.

"I have news." The Witch shifted his attention in Juliet's direction. "A third disappearance. We've been making our way around, personally warning all of your regular contacts that someone has it out for people known to work with you. Unfortunately, showing up to one Witch's house proved too late. She was gone, house cleansed, no friends or neighbors with a clue what happened."

Juliet went pale. "Who?"

"I think we'll keep that confidential for now." Easton leaned back in his chair, maybe expecting an objection. He didn't get one. "Perhaps it's best if you pause your work completely, Ms. Herrera."

Juliet blinked in momentary shock. "Really? I don't see why anything I do would be causing people to disappear."

"Neither do I." Easton frowned. "Your cases are almost uninteresting. Tracing the lineage of a local family. Breaking petty curses. None of it warrants anywhere near this kind of attack. But someone is picking off your associates. There's no other link between the victims."

"Was it one of my current clients who disappeared?" Juliet gripped the edge of her seat, rigid with tension.

Easton considered before answering. "No, but I'd suggest contacting anyone with an open case to say you won't be working with them any longer. At least until we get a better hold on this."

So much for Terra's idea of subtly tempting the attacker into their next move by acting unaffected. Instead of trying for Juliet again, they went for someone else. Perhaps targeting Juliet wasn't their only aim. In that case, would shutting Herrera Investigations have any effect?

I leaned forward in my seat, resting my elbows on my knees. "What are Juliet and I supposed to do now?"

"Nothing." Easton seemed annoyed I'd asked. "You two will just have to wait and see. Try to do a better job identifying the culprit if they strike against the house again."

"That's not within our power." I bristled at his implication that we'd let them escape. There was no way to break the concealing spells without knowing either who we were dealing with or where they were.

Easton didn't acknowledge my protest. "At least try not to make anything worse."

Juliet cut me off before I could object. "Fine. I'll close Herrera Investigation, Easton. But you better be doing more than talking to Witches door to door. If current clients aren't the targets, shutting my business may have no effect. Your request feels like a desperate attempt, grasping at nothing." She got up without another word and disappeared into her bedroom.

"Walk me out, Ms. Dubois?" Easton stood and turned to go without waiting for a reply.

I followed him out of the house. Easton hadn't pulled his car into the driveway, forcing me to walk with him out onto the street, past the boundary of the house's protection.

"Right. Now we're away, how's it really going?" Easton leaned against his car.

"What, are you worried Juliet's listening in on conversations on her property?" I glanced back toward the house.

Easton shrugged. "Better to be careful. Please tell me you've gotten some information out of her. What's Ms. Herrera up to? Other than drawing trouble to the community."

"She's not up to anything. None of this is her fault. She was happy to help Terra and me yesterday."

The blame he was placing on Juliet made my blood boil. It wasn't the first time I'd come across this attitude in Easton and resented how nothing had changed since then, even though I'd made my complaints known.

Easton made a *harrumphing* sound. "Ms. Reyes's little plan was a waste of time, but I could have told her that if she'd talk to me about it first."

"We might need to have given it more time—"

"Reyes said you and Herrera were getting chummy. So what did you find out?"

His phrasing made me want to keep everything to myself. I didn't trust Easton. Working with people like him made everything feel impossible and created unnecessary problems, yet the Authority seemed to have no issue with keeping people like him around.

I told Easton the bare minimum of what he needed to know about Jasper's odd attempts to get an audience with Juliet and how we ran into him last night, while avoiding clueing him in to the fact that Juliet and I were on better terms.

He looked disappointed. "You're looking into this Suarez Witch?"

"Yes, I'll fact check Jasper's story, but I'd be surprised if he had anything to do with the case. The guy was more annoying than anything else."

"Keep me updated." Easton checked his watch. "A few higher-ups have contacted me about this mess. It's not looking good. The rest of the Authority is checking up, so you can expect to be contacted. We're pulling more people in. Make sure you're on board with any requests, and get Herrera to cooperate as well."

I glared, hoping he could tell I resented his implication that Juliet or I were the ones being difficult. "Of course I'll work with whoever is on the case, and so will Juliet."

"Good. Judges from all over are watching. Expect a call from New York soon." With that ominous comment, Easton got in his car and left.

I slowly made my way back to the house.

Judges getting involved wasn't necessarily bad. It was out of the scope of their role, but any extra help was better than none.

Easton was probably worried he hadn't made enough headway and was panicking that a third disappearance made his handling of the situation look inadequate, but that was no reason to act like this was all Juliet's fault. It seemed like he'd rather take out his frustration on others and cast blame about without cause than try and actually figure out what was going on. I didn't really care how this debacle made us look to Authority superiors as long as we were able to find the missing persons. And if Easton or the rest of us weren't doing a good job, maybe they should do something about it rather than keep assigning us to cases like none of this stuff mattered.

Terra had been casting location spells several times a day, to test for any change to the magic cloaking our victims. So far they were all still concealed, and thus alive. We could still resolve this without the worst happening.

When I returned to the house, I wasn't surprised to find Bickel sitting in the living room. Juliet was out of sight, talking on the phone in her room from the sound of it.

"She called you?" I sat down across from dapper Witch, trying not to stare at his blindingly yellow bow tie.

Bickel inclined his head in subtle acknowledgment. "Yes. Juliet said you had a troublesome clerk for me to look into."

I recounted the Jasper tale yet again. The more I thought about it, the more of a waste of time it seemed to be.

"You aren't officially part of the investigation, are you?" I asked Bickel after he agreed to check up on Jasper's connection to Ben.

"No." Bickel examined his fingernails and didn't look inclined to offer any further details.

So he wasn't one of the higher-ups being brought in, or the call from New York I could be expecting. I wondered why not him, if New York was getting involved. It wasn't clear what their branch had to do with anything, but wasn't Bickel supposed to be their best guy? He was helping anyway, maybe they knew that and were sending even more support. Bickel seemed to be in a different tier than the rest of us as far as rules and reporting, maybe that had something to do with it.

Juliet reentered the room. "I'm officially closed for business. Not that I think it will do much good."

"You don't think closing you down was the culprit's aim?" Bickel was still focused on his nails. "Perhaps a new PI will open up shop on Monday."

"You can't be serious." I stared at the Witch until he gave me his attention.

Bickel's eyes flashed with amusement. "Fine—you got me, Mea. I'm not serious. But that's what Easton seems to be thinking along the lines of."

"Your joke telling skills need practice," I muttered.

Bickel snorted but didn't smile so I wasn't sure if he was amused or annoyed. He stood and buttoned his suit jacket. "I'll let you know if I find anything on Jasper."

"Wait Edwin, before you disappear, why don't you come back for dinner?" Juliet asked in a rush.

He glanced at me briefly, as if Juliet's invitation had something to do with my presence, and agreed. Then he was gone.

15

MEA

The rest of the day passed in a somber haze. Juliet seemed restless, like she wasn't used to having nothing to do. Eventually she settled on the couch with a pile of recipe books, looking for something to make for dinner.

I was in a similarly unsettled mood. With no way to help the case I decided to work on the stack of forms to be filled out for my branch proposal, but I found thinking about it harder than I had previously. My mind kept wandering, almost like I was deliberately avoiding the task.

After a long, comfortable silence where we were each occupied with our own thoughts, I felt Juliet's attention shift to me. "Why do you want to move?"

I glanced up from my form. "Like I said before, I need a change." This was still true, I needed to get out of LA, but I was less enthusiastic about my exit strategy than I had been.

"Oh." Juliet looked disappointed, maybe at my short response, and turned her attention back to the cookbook in her lap. It didn't look like she was actually reading. After a minute she glanced up again. "A change in your work?"

"In part." This morning made me want a different working

environment even more than before, so I didn't know why I was hesitating. The expansion was the only chance to change things, I had to take it if I didn't like how things were now.

"I don't think working for the Authority here will be very different from what you're doing in LA." Juliet sounded almost scolding.

Was she still trying to talk me out of coming here? I'd hoped we were past that, but this felt more like the kind of comment Juliet used to make. She always made me feel wrong-footed.

I folded my form in half, looking away. "I didn't say I wanted a career switch. But things could be different away from main organization and its rigid same old way of doing things. It could be a change if I make it one."

"Why not work privately? If you want away from all that?" Juliet closed her cookbook with a snap.

"I don't know—" I trailed off, trying to examine Juliet through the bangs that had shifted to hide her face.

She tapped her manicured nails on the book's hard cover. "You might like it better. I do, obviously. Not that I've ever worked for the Authority." She made a face.

"Maybe." I bent the edge of my form. "But it feels worth giving this a chance. I know you don't like the Authority, and it's not as if I like everything about it either. So what if this opportunity could be a good shift?"

"Hm." Juliet sounded unconvinced.

"You think I'm being too hopeful?"

"I didn't say that."

"Well, I need to be optimistic. Things can only get better if we try, right? Besides, I need to get out of LA. I want a change of scene more than any change in my work. But if I can get them both in one hit, even better."

"Oh." Juliet paused like she wasn't sure how to respond. "Is there a reason why you want to leave? Or are you just sick of the place?"

She'd given me an easy out. I could hide behind general complaints without making this weird if I wanted. But I didn't. If I wanted to get to know Juliet better, I had to let her in as well. And I couldn't pretend that sharing more with her wasn't what I'd always wanted.

"Did you know I was engaged a few years ago?" I gave her a sheepish smile.

Juliet stiffened. "No."

I put my crumpled form aside. "You're not really in on the gossip, are you?"

"Of course not." Juliet seemed truly outraged by the idea.

Why is disapproval so hot on her? I snorted a half-laugh, both at her reaction and mine, and Juliet gave me a sly look. Her dark brown eyes were sharp and expectant. Making me want—

I cleared my throat. "Anyway. You know Nora Lin, right?"

Juliet's cheeks darkened with a blush. "I dated her about a thousand years ago."

"Damn, you look good for your age."

Juliet threw her head back and cackled at my joke. "Mea, you're a little devil. What about Nora? She and I didn't keep in touch."

"You know her best friend Michaela—well I asked her to marry me. I mean, we'd been together for years so it wasn't weird. Asking was a perfectly normal thing to do." I felt hot all over and lost my conviction to keep talking.

Why was I making this so awkward for myself? It wasn't even a recent break-up.

Juliet set her cookbook aside. "I didn't think it was weird, Mea."

"Right, good. Um. Anyway, the whole thing was a disaster. She said yes but we were doomed before the proposal. Michaela called things off eventually. I don't think she ever wanted to commit, but said yes to be nice, not hurt my feelings. I guess."

"That isn't nice. She should have been upfront with you." Juliet looked at me seriously but not unkindly.

I let out a sigh full of Michaela-related exhaustion. "It's complicated—After circling each other for years I've decided I need more space. I don't want her to always be hovering on the edge of my life."

Looking back, a lot of my relationship with Michaela had been one sided, and our post-breakup interactions were the same. I felt like the only one bothered by our continued proximity. I'd been the driver of the relationship, more committed—and yes, overcommitted—and when Michaela left it seemed like she wasn't that affected by our time together. Not like I was.

Maybe Michaela was holding back and pretending she had no complicated feelings, only acting like seeing each other wasn't hard. She'd held back in our relationship and kept everything to herself, so maybe it was the same. But after we split, I just felt like she didn't care, and had never really cared.

She wasn't concerned when the two of us were supposed to attend the same event, while I always worried about needing space, giving her space, and stepping back. I was always the one to bow out. It made sense if she was never that invested in our relationship, the aftermath wouldn't be as fraught for her. But maybe I was taking a self-centered view, even if there was no doubt my ex had always prioritized herself.

I didn't know about explaining all this to Juliet. Michaela and Juliet weren't completely dissimilar. They were both closed off. Mystique was always a draw for me, but I didn't know if that was a good thing. I didn't want to be the one left with most of the emotional work, trying to conform myself to a mysterious unreachable partner.

But an uncaring, unaffected interpretation of Juliet's character was starting to feel outdated. She might be all the things I didn't need in my life if I only considered her at surface level, but I suspected an open Juliet was another story.

The only problem was, I didn't know if I had any power to affect which Juliet I would be presented with. I didn't understand why she acted the way she did. I didn't understand what I could do to allow her to feel she could be whatever she wanted around me, and not just someone focused on pushing everything away. Getting too close to someone who might change like flipping a switch, without communicating why, wasn't what I wanted.

What I wanted was to understand who Juliet really was. I didn't think any of her snappishness was rooted in cruelty or mean spiritedness. I liked her uptight and mean when she was deploying these characteristics reasonably. Like with Easton. Juliet wasn't a push-over and I admired that. I liked it when she was stiff and unsure and trying to navigate situations in earnest. And I liked her when she showed me her delicate side.

I wanted to hold all these different versions of her at once and figure out what made it all come together. I didn't want to peel back the prickliness she used to push people away and discard it. It was part of her. That was where I'd been wrong before.

The more Juliet showed me, the more I wanted, and I hoped she'd want me too.

Juliet was regarding me silently like she was making up her mind. "It feels like you've already made your decision, Mea. You should move, if that's what you need."

"But what if it doesn't work out? I might not get chosen to transfer here." I let myself acknowledge this possibility for the first time. I'd pinned a lot to this semi-thought-out plan and didn't know what I'd do about work if I didn't get the opportunity to try and impact at least some of how the Authority operated.

"I doubt this is your only option if the Authority is spreading its web." Juliet made a face that made it seem like she disagreed about Authority's initiative being an opportunity to do better. Then added, more kindly, "You'll find something, Mea."

"That's true, there should be lots of opportunities. But this is the one I want. I don't want to uproot my life completely. I still have friends I want to see and be close to. I want something more, not to start over from scratch."

Juliet nodded. "I see. It's a specific balance you're after. Moving here sounds perfect for you. I'll help."

"How?"

"However I can. You couldn't wait to tell me you had your eye on my town when you arrived. You must have thought I could offer something in the way of assistance."

I made a face in mock-offense. "Your town now, is it?"

Juliet gave me a haughty look. "No, but I know who among the Witches would be happy to see you suits set up shop."

"Witches unlike you?" I couldn't help laughing.

"Yes, yes, I'm no fan of the Authority. But I'd rather have you than someone like Easton moving in. For more than a few reasons. I'll let the right people know you come recommended. Now let me see that." She held out an authoritative hand for my form.

I handed it over.

16

JULIET

*E*dwin arrived with a bottle of Bordeaux.

After a long day being trapped inside doing nothing I needed to unwind. We all did. Mea was, as ever, determined to look on the bright side, and in this situation I really had to commend her sunny nature.

After dinner she brought out a pack of cards and demanded we play while enjoying the rest of the wine. Edwin requested poker and poor Mea had no clue what a bad idea it was to agree.

"We're playing outside." Mea threw open the back doors with a flourish.

"Last time we made use of my yard the night went to shit." I didn't know why I said it. There was no need to dampen her spirits, but the effect of the attack lurked in the back of my mind.

"So you're never going out there again? Come on. I found this animal rescue online that I want to show you. I've got some ideas on how to utilize your space better."

"I thought you were working on your proposal." I followed Mea into the yard, Edwin closing the back door and trailing behind.

Mea plopped down in one of the seats at the garden table and pulled out her phone. "I was. But these ducks are so cute."

Mea told me all about the benefits of caring for animals while Edwin trounced us at cards and the evening slipped away. We laughed more than I'd have thought possible under the circumstances, Edwin included. Neither he nor I seemed to be able to help ourselves tonight.

After several games, Mea's phone rang and she excused herself. I watched her walk off into the dim periphery of the yard. She'd lit the garden again, expanding her twinkle lights out to the trees.

"This isn't terrible." Edwin puled my attention away from Mea's ethereal form.

"High praise." I rolled my eyes.

He shuffled the cards with deft fingers. "I know. I just didn't expect such a pleasant evening after your rant the other day."

I almost choked on a sip of wine. "There was no ranting."

Edwin's responding look told me he wasn't fooled. "Either way, Ms. Dubois seems to have become suddenly tolerable in your eyes."

"Minds can change." I didn't know if my mind really had changed or if I'd only admitted what I'd been trying to hide from myself. Resisting Mea along with the rest of my past had been a misplaced effort.

"Yes. It seems a few things are changing." Edwin looked wistfully off into the yard. Something in him did seem different, but I couldn't put my finger on what exactly.

Maybe he was thinking about the barista. If I could change my mind, so could he. Perhaps we'd both been too rigid in pushing everyone else away. We had our reasons, and I could only speak to re-evaluating my own, but didn't Edwin and I both deserve more? I wasn't sure if he'd ever want a partner, but the more I thought about it, the more I wanted one.

My attention slid back to Mea, who was wandering among the twinkling trees, still on the phone. Wanting her terrified me. I didn't know if it was enough. The idea of a relationship was one thing, actually opening up to one was another.

"Change might be good for us." I sounded as unsure as I felt.

Edwin's dreamy look disappeared. "Maybe. I don't know." He turned his attention to Mea. "Something about the two of you together is contagious. I'm not opposed to doing this again."

"That's a change, right there. See it is good." I slapped him playfully on the arm and he tried not to smile. "I don't know if you'll be invited next time. Part of me wants to keep her to myself. But honestly, I like that idea of all of us spending time together. Maybe Aria can come too."

"Hmm—don't push it." Edwin narrowed his eyes, like he was wary of what I might suggest. Was I wrong about that wistful look? Even if he was thinking about Tristan, that didn't mean he wanted anything about that particular situation to change.

"I meant only Aria. It's probably best not to invite the Mortals given how Mea keeps enchanting my yard," I said, giving Edwin an out.

He looked almost disappointed. "That's for the best."

Mea returned, thoughtfully tapping her phone against her chin.

"Any news on the case?" I looked at her hopefully.

She reclaimed her seat. "No progress, just Witches getting organized."

"Took them long enough." I couldn't seem to help criticizing the Authority, even if I worried Mea might take offense on behalf of her colleagues.

"Hm." Mea put her phone away, not looking bothered. "We'll see if it comes to anything."

I waited for her to say more, but Mea avoided my gaze as

well as Edwin's. I glanced at him, wondering if he'd expected more too. He half shrugged.

"I think I'll leave you two, if that's all right?" Edwin got up and put on his hat. "I don't need to stay for the case critique."

"I wasn't critiquing." I gave him a betrayed glare. "Only commenting on the pace at which *your* colleagues have gotten their shit together, Edwin."

"My point still stands. If the conversation yields anything worthwhile, do text me." Edwin tipped his hat and was gone.

"Do you really think the Authority is screwing up on this?" Mea asked as she gathered up the poker chips.

"I didn't mean to be harsh. It's easy to judge from the outside. I just can't shake my anxiety about all this. And I can't do anything to help. I'm frustrated, that's all." I collected our glasses and led the way back into the house.

"I get that."

I tried not to be disappointed that was all Mea said. She probably wasn't at liberty to divulge whatever she'd learned on the phone, which was fair enough. I'd just have to wait and see.

I shut the back door behind us, cutting off the subtle night sounds. The room was jarringly silent, making me extra aware of Mea. She placed the empty bottle in the recycling and turned to take the wine glasses from me, her fingers brushing mine.

"Can you believe us right now?" Mea saluted me with the glasses.

"Believe what?"

"Us. Getting along. Having a pleasant evening."

"It shouldn't be hard to believe. I thought the whole evening felt natural, but I know what you mean." I'd never have seen this night as a possibility a few days ago.

Mea cleaned the glasses with a poof of smoke. "I've imagined having a lot of great times with you, actually."

I laughed. "Oh, please." I needed to deny it because the

possibility was disorienting. Mea had always been friendly, but over the years I never imagined she noticed me the way I noticed her. Not like when we first met.

And maybe she hadn't thought of me that way for a while, but now—could I accept that she'd spent time thinking about me?

"Like you haven't?" Mea put the glasses to the side and faced me, eyebrows raised, her hip leaning on the counter.

I wasn't quite sure what to do or how to respond to that playful look. I had imagined. Maybe it hadn't felt real or achievable given everything, but that was the thing about imagination. You could entertain impossibilities. Like trailing my hands through Mea's hair and running my fingers down her neck. Kissing her like nothing else mattered.

I'd always told myself whether she wanted these things too didn't matter. I wasn't going to try even if she did. She didn't know me, and if she liked anything about me it was only an old unreal version of me. But that wasn't true. She seemed to like me well enough right now.

It was disorienting to think a few nights of half-friendship could open us up to so much.

"So am I wrong?" Mea asked as I stared at her.

A lie would have been easy. Snapping at her now would close this door permanently. It would be smart, but I was sick of being guarded.

"No." I took a confident step forward. We weren't quite touching, but it was close.

Mea looked at me like I suspected I was looking at her. With a longing that seemed to want to focus on lips and eyes.

I'd never wanted to be friends with Mea. I'd always wanted more, but knowing we were now on the same page didn't make me ready to let her in. I still wasn't sure. Everything felt risky after coveting isolation for so long. But so what? I was tired of thinking and calculating. With a beautiful woman standing in front of me I didn't see why I had to.

I longed to feel Mea against me. To satisfy my lust but also to feel cared for and precious in the way only a lover could provide. To make up for lost time. I wanted to steal some of her sunshine, and if Mea was right, it was easy to open up, to relax and do as you wanted.

"I don't want to pretend I don't like you anymore, Mea." I moved a stray strand of blue hair out of her face.

Mea's lips parted. I resisted brushing my thumb over her bottom lip.

"Is that all you want?" she asked, breathless.

I swallowed my nervousness. "I also want to kiss you."

"Oh, good. I was thinking the same." She sounded fluttery, excited. It was all the encouragement I needed.

I leaned in, pressing us together and placed my hand at the back of Mea's neck. Her smile was bright before it disappeared against my own. My hand shifted to tangle in her hair. Hazel eyes consumed my view, and I let go.

Mea didn't hold back once my lips touched hers. I sucked in a startled breath that turned into a moan on the way back out. We tasted like wine and the fresh dark night as our tongues found each other.

I'd always found the first go at physical intimacy with someone clumsy and tinged with self-consciousness and this was no perfect kiss, not some magical moment where we tele-pathically knew what the other liked. There was eager clashing of teeth and giggled *sorries*. But these things didn't pull me out as they might have normally, they only took me under.

I'd never been so free of my consuming, circling thoughts. Everything was Mea. How soft her hair was, how strong the muscles of her back felt under my palm, how her body leaned against mine, the two of us fitting together even better than when we'd danced.

Mea put her hand at the back of my neck, sending shivers up and down my spine. "My imagination didn't do you justice, Juliet." She rested her forehead against mine, panting slightly.

I was making her pant. Me. And I wasn't interested in talking about it.

I kissed Mea down her neck and felt her arch, giving me access. My hand at her back slipped under the loose fabric of her top, resting on bare skin. My lips traveled along her collarbone and she made the most desperate little sounds. Heat shot straight to my core in an aching need.

"Where else are you going to let me kiss you?" I asked.

Mea's hands were roving, pulling me tight against her. "Anywhere you want, just don't stop."

I took my lips from Mea's skin, making her whimper in protest. I smiled wickedly. "Oh, come on. You should have seen that coming."

Mea's desperate look seemed to intensify. Her eyes were wide, a rainbow of light browns and dark greens shining like her twinkly lights in the yard, tempting me to enjoy everything in front of me. "Please, Juliet."

I kissed Mea quickly before taking her hand and leading her to the living room, not feeling so carefree that I'd strip us down and screw her in the kitchen. I had my limits.

Mea collapsed on the couch in a graceful heap, her gaze fixed intently on me. I stood before her, not quite hesitating. I wanted to savor this.

I blushed, feeling all the places my suit clung to my body as Mea drank me in. My clothes had never felt more like a disguise and for a moment I didn't know how she could be looking at me that way when I was so buttoned up.

That problem had an easy fix. Less clothes. I shed my jacket and stepped out of my shoes.

"No, leave them on." Mea bit her bottom lip in a way that seemed involuntary as a blush bloomed on her cheeks.

Her reaction was glorious, but appreciation didn't stop me from being thrown off kilter by Mea's request. My face must have shown my surprise because she backpedaled. "You don't have to if—never mind."

"You like my shoes?"

"Yes." Mea swallowed. "I like everything about you."

Her look of genuine desire ignited a burning need in me. I slipped the shoes back on and removed my silk scarf instead, my movements slow. *Everything?* She liked everything?

The scarf fell to the floor.

I straddled Mea's lap, hiking up my skirt mainly out of necessity, but the extra exposed skin gave me a small thrill. "Is this all right?" I asked in her ear.

Mea's hands ran up my bare thighs. "Yes, but only if you kiss me."

Our lips met less frantically than before. Mea touched me reverently as I kissed her. I let myself explore the rest of her, tracing the elegant lines of her body, making her squirm, and soon she was letting out a whole array of needy sounds.

I leaned back, feeling only a little bit smug. "You couldn't believe we were having fun playing cards, now what do you have to say about us?"

Mea looked debauched. Her breath was coming short and fast. "This is so much better." She pulled her tank top over her head and tossed it away, revealing an unlined lace bra.

I traced the black lace with my thumb before dipping my fingers beneath it to graze her bare nipple. I pulled back the fabric and bent forward to kiss her. When I caught her nipple gently between my teeth, Mea gasped.

I let my hand wander down her stomach, hesitating at the waistband of her shorts. I paused my kissing to look at Mea.

"Yes." She pulled my mouth to meet hers.

My hand slid between us, undoing the button and zipper. Instead of teasing her, I slid my fingers under the lace of her panties, finding Mea wet and sensitive to my touch. She jerked her hips, pressing against my hand. I massaged her clit with an urgency meant to undo her. Mea moaned, moving under me, rocking herself against my hand. I couldn't quite get enough friction of my own but didn't really care. I wanted her to come apart and loved how achy that made me.

Mea held onto the back of my neck and let her head fall back against the couch. She shuddered, moaning as she came against my fingers.

I felt a devious smile twist my lips.

Mea hadn't even caught her breath when she went for the buttons on my blouse. Soon it was on the floor. She ran her hands over me almost rhythmically, before cupping my breasts. Her touch was hot as if my skin was cool, but in reality I felt like I was burning up.

I shifted my position so I was half kneeling, sitting astride one of Mea's legs, notching one knee between her thighs. Mea pulled my skirt up further so she could touch the fabric of my panties stretched over my ass. She pulled me harder against her and I let my hips roll.

"I can feel you against me," Mea breathed into my ear. "So wet."

I whimpered. She could feel me against her leg and I hadn't even taken my underwear off. It somehow felt more exposing than if I was naked. I couldn't remember the last time I'd felt this desperate. I didn't have the capacity to think about anything but the way this felt. I kissed Mea hard on the mouth, moving against her as she rocked into me, and my orgasm crashed over me.

Mea's shuddering movements and rapid breathing told me she was almost there with me. We didn't stop until she cried out and went boneless.

I brushed Mea's wild hair back and she lolled her head against the back of the couch. My knees were a little stiff from holding my position so I shifted away and stood. "Come to bed with me tonight?"

Mea jumped up and took my hand. "I'm allowed in your room?"

"Don't give me those big awestruck eyes. There's nothing special about my room," I teased. But she was right. I'd deliberately kept her out.

I led us into the bedroom and perched on the end of the bed.

Mea stood before me. She didn't look around, her focus making it seem like she saw nothing but me as she slid off her shorts and underwear and unhooked her bra. Perhaps I should have been doing the same, but she had me captivated. She was nothing but elegant subtle curves, covered in gooseflesh.

"You're so beautiful," I whispered.

Mea's lusty expression softened into a sweet smile. "So are you, Juliet."

Then she was pressed up against me, undoing my bra and tossing it away. She kissed me, her breasts brushing mine in a silken touch. The sound that escaped me was even more desperate than a whimper.

We lay back on the bed and kissed for what felt like forever. Mea rid me of the rest of my clothes, leaving me as naked as her. I tore my mouth away from hers and trailed kisses down her neck to her chest where I teased her—almost maddeningly, going by the pleading coming out of her mouth—until I moved lower, kissing her stomach and hips, her thighs, before settling between her legs.

"You're going to kill me," Mea gasped with half a laugh.

"Do you want me to stop?"

"What. No—" She propped herself up on her elbows. "I just meant—this is so—"

"I know." This, between us, was something. More than getting off or giving in to physical need. I'd always seen Mea as something more, it was a large part of why I'd kept her away.

"I want you, Mea," I whispered, not looking at her. I kissed a freckle on her hip.

Mea ran a hand through my hair. "I want you too."

I let myself get lost in us together, my mouth on her most sensitive place until she came with her hands tangled in my hair.

We twined together in the rumpled sheets kissing and touching lazily.

"That was more than worth how long it took us to get here." Mea smiled against my neck.

"Yes." I held her tighter.

Being together like this was worth everything, but to me this didn't feel like the culmination of our shared past. It wasn't the destination we'd reached at the end of a road that lay behind us. It was the beginning of something else and I wanted it more than anything.

17

JULIET

 woke up snug under the covers and less worried than I'd been in a long time. Even before the stress of the disappearances I hadn't been at ease like I was now.

Sun streamed onto the bed. I hadn't gotten around to closing the curtains last night, but I'd been worn out enough that I'd slept past sunrise anyway. Mea lay beside me sleeping on her stomach, blue hair fanned out on the pillow. My pillow.

I leaned over to kiss her bare shoulder.

She stirred. "Good morning."

"I'd say so." Hell, I sounded smug.

Mea rolled to her back, happily laying shirtless and uncovered by the blankets. I felt myself blush as I swept my gaze over her body.

"You going to do more than look, Juliet?"

I looked long enough that Mea begged me to touch her, and I didn't have it in me to deny her.

LATER, Mea met me in the ensuite.

She switched on the shower and waited for the water to heat. "I have to meet someone about the case today, will you come with me?"

"I thought we were supposed to be laying low?"

"Yes." Mea slipped into the shower, her form becoming obscured by the steam and frosted glass. "Easton also asked us to cooperate with any requests. The Authority is calling in some bigger players. They want to talk to you, hear from you directly."

I followed her into the shower. "Okay. As long as no one accuses me of endangering the community because I left my house."

Mea paused in lathering herself with soap. "No one will do that."

That's pretty much exactly what Easton had implied yesterday. I didn't mind pausing my work on the off chance it affected the culprit's behavior and prompted them to stop abducting Witches, but I didn't appreciate the guilt Easton had tried to saddle me with.

Mea reached out to touch my cheek and my scowl softened.

"We can't get too distracted," she murmured as she caressed my face.

"That's not what your touch is saying." I captured Mea's mouth before she could try and contradict me.

Our bodies were soft and slick with warm water. I pressed Mea against the tile wall, eliciting a gasp from the cold.

"Don't worry, I'll make it worth it," I whispered in her ear before making good on the promise.

We were in a rush after that, but I couldn't quite find the energy to care. My whole body was loose and relaxed. I was smiling almost uncontrollably.

"Where are we heading?" I asked as we got in the car.

Mea clicked her seatbelt. "They're meeting us at Coffee Cat, where our first meeting was supposed to be."

"It's closed on Sundays."

"Really?" Mea looked momentarily panicked.

"Don't worry. We can have the meeting at my office if that helps." I started the car and took us in that direction.

Mea pulled out her phone, looking strained. I wasn't sure why. She wasn't usually one to sweat details like this, that was much more me. She quickly made a call, her side of the conversation clipped. From the sound of it our Authority visitor had shown up at the closed cafe and wasn't happy.

Luckily we arrived at the office before our guest. I let us in and Mea went to peer out the window and down into the parking lot.

I flipped on the lights and checked my desk was presentable. "So who are we meeting?"

Mea whirled around to face me. "Your mother, actually."

I blinked at her, my relaxed attitude freezing over. I'd misheard her. There was no way, no *reason* for the woman to get involved. "I'm sorry, what?"

Mea scanned my face and tried to give me a smile, but her manner had changed. She stayed hovering by the window as if she didn't want to get closer to me. It was almost like she wished she could get away, like she knew her announcement of my mother's arrival wasn't inconsequential. Like she was hiding something.

Mea swallowed. "Your mother called last night."

"And you didn't think to tell me?" My tone was as razor sharp, causing Mea to flinch. I stood in the doorway to my office gripping the frame, my nails digging into the wood, waiting for her to explain.

"She said there was no need to tell you. She'd talk to you at the meeting."

Panic broke through the frost encasing me. "She told you she was coming to—to see me? Last night?"

Mea shrugged without her usual grace. "Well, yeah. You're so tied up in this case. From the notes to the attack—"

"Why didn't you tell me? I asked about the call." The strain it took not to shout made my head ache.

"It—it—didn't seem important." Mea avoided eye contact with me and looked back toward the window.

My control broke. "Didn't it? Then why the hell are you acting so guilty now?"

"Because you're yelling at me, Juliet." Mea looked more worried than I'd seen her during the entire case, with lines creasing her forehead and a deep frown keeping her dimples away. "With everything else going on last night I honestly didn't think about it."

"Is that why you—is that why we—to distract me while you were plotting behind my back? To break me down—before—before—" What had begun as a snarl petered out. My anger failing to protect me from the horrible truth.

What had Mea done?

"Juliet—" The traitorous woman looked baffled. "What are you talking about? I'm not plotting. Of course that's not why we slept together. How can you even say that? Easton told me New York was getting involved—"

"You never told me that! You deliberately kept this from me." I frantically tried to retrace my memories of the last few days. Everything I felt for Mea, everything she did to tempt me to open up. "Has anything you've said this whole time been true?"

"What? Yes, everything I've said is true. Juliet, I'm not deliberately keeping anything from you. I'm telling you now." She took a step toward me. "Why does it matter? Just take a breath, let's talk. We're all on the same side. It's only your mom."

I almost broke down and cried. I couldn't deal with any of this right now.

My mother wasn't coming because of the case. What the fuck did a judge have to do with anything at this stage of the investigation, other than to throw her weight around? Abuse her power. My knees were weak and the uneasiness in my gut turned painful.

She couldn't come here. Not after so long.

I would not see her.

No one could make me.

"I'm not doing this." I stomped over to my purse where it was abandoned on Aria's desk. With shaking hands I searched its depths for my phone. All I had to do was text Edwin. I could manage that. Then I'd be gone in a flash. Teleported off to someplace no one could reach me.

I might not come back.

"Juliet, why are you freaking out? Just tell me what's going on." Mea came up and grabbed my arm, maybe to still my shaking, but I suspected she was trying to stop me from using the phone I'd just wrapped my fingers around. Like her job was to deliver me to my mother. Stop me escaping.

Mea had to know I was going to call Edwin. She was trying to manipulate me just like she'd done all this time. Getting under my skin, into my bed, stealing my trust and lying to me. Telling me *I* was freaking out, like what she'd done was nothing. Like I was being unreasonable.

I yanked my arm out of Mea's grasp, her touch burning. The frantic gesture sent my phone flying across the room.

"*Just tell you.*" I growled at Mea. "There is no *just*. I have told you things—I have—and you—you've fucked me over—" I took a heaving breath. "Even if you didn't do all this to get my guard down then—you're so clueless. Not everything is simple sparkly perfect rainbows, *Meadow*. Did you even stop to ask yourself why a judge was calling? *To think*. Or do you just take everything at face value? Do as you're told without question? Assume everything is exactly as it seems? Like you honestly believe everyone is who they pretend to be."

Mea was rigid with shock, her eyes wide as I laced my words with anger. Deep down I knew it wasn't fair. Mea didn't know what she'd done.

But what if she did, a nasty voice inside me hissed. The thought stopped me short on the way to retrieve my phone. What if Mea knew more than she implied? She'd been talking to my mother after all.

Was Mea betraying me deliberately? Was I only hoping she'd done this in ignorance? And did it matter when the outcome was the same either way? Maybe I was the clueless one for trusting Mea just because she smiled at me and acted like I was worth knowing.

I reached for my phone, but it slid across the floor away from me. Summoned by magic.

"Mea—" I spun around to see, not Mea, but my mother standing in the doorway. My phone in her hand.

"Juliet." She sounded blandly pleasant, her face neutral. "Your personal calls can wait until after we talk."

Like everyone else, my mother would have heard about my friendship with Edwin. He worked under her court's jurisdiction, and even if our friendship wasn't well known in the Authority, I was sure mother would have deduced it by now. No one else could have broken her spells.

Taking my phone meant she knew I was trying to run away. She knew I was scared. I tried to pull my armor on, my mask of indifference, but I was scattered into a million pieces.

"Mother." By some miracle my voice didn't waver.

My tone was ice, but it didn't seem to cut her at all. She looked exactly as she had the last time I'd seen her. Pristine, slim, expensively dressed and classically beautiful with hard unrelenting eyes.

"Judge Herrera," Mea said in a composed, business-like tone. "Thank you for coming."

I glared at Mea. She'd trapped me. Whether she was colluding or blindly following my mother's orders, it didn't matter. I hated that she had any part in this.

The last time I'd seen my mother was several years after graduating from the Investigator's College. I'd gone to a function hosted by a retired lecturer, then living in LA. I hadn't realized the guest list would include his old colleagues from before he taught at the college. I hadn't expected to see my mother there, and by then I was sure she'd suspected what I'd done.

I'd managed to avoid being alone with her but I hadn't been to a Witch-society party since, just in case the next time I wasn't so lucky.

My mother had tried to contact me since the event, but I'd ignored her. At first I'd worried she would come see me in person and try to force a conversation like she was doing now—I'd never gone into hiding completely, only gotten away and protected myself—but she'd never showed up. I'd always feared my mother was watching me instead, piecing together how I'd slipped free, biding her time and waiting for something I couldn't identify.

When Edwin had broken her mind compulsions after he and I first met, I'd decided the best way forward was secrecy. At first, I'd acted as unaltered as possible in public. I'd continued my studies, went through the motions around anyone that might pass on information about me, and continued to see my mother as I would have otherwise been forced to.

Initially, I didn't want my mother to know the spells had been broken. I'd needed a refuge and time to find myself again. Pretending was frighteningly easy after a lifetime of being someone else. Far easier than being me, and without the fog in my brain it almost felt safe. It became my lie, my secret, my defense. It was the best of both worlds. I could use who I'd been to make people see one thing while being another, and take comfort in knowing I was using the mask by choice.

Yes, Mea, and maybe the other students, had noticed a change in me but they didn't matter. They wouldn't give me away and being able to choose my actions more authentically around them motivated me to uphold the rest. And I had Edwin, who was there for me however I wanted to be.

That game was supposed to be temporary. A reprieve until I was ready to confront my mother, but when I finally got there, that conversation hadn't gone as I'd imagined. My expectations of her had been naïve. She'd only tried to twist the new situation to hurt me. She couldn't get at my mind through magic any longer, so she fell back on other manipulations. Or tried to, at least.

Not that she was aware of that now, standing in my doorway. I'd stolen the memory of that failed confrontation from her, erased like it had never happened, and went back to pretending. To an extent. There was no fooling her into thinking the spells were still in place forever. What was the point of being free and still living the life she'd dictated?

It turned out, what I wanted wasn't completely unrelated to the Authority path she'd tried to set me on. I still wanted to keep my investigatory career, just not in the way she wanted, with the people she deemed appropriate. In my eyes choosing my career wasn't the most important part of being rid of the spells, it was all the small choices that I valued. The rest was secondary. So it might have looked like very little changed, but to me, life felt vastly different.

The subtle shift in my career to a private investigator had a convenient side effect. I was sure it filled my mother with doubt: Had I broken her spells? Then why hadn't I thrown it in her face? The hole in her memory combined with my seemingly minor life changes must have made her hesitate and wonder what exactly she knew and didn't know, and it worked well as a layer of protection.

And my mother had stayed away. Until now.

I walked away from the two women and into my office. My computer had a version of my texting app installed. I'd message Edwin that way. I would not be trapped. Walking away from this conversation was as much about exercising my will and refusing to bend to others' demands as it was about not wanting to confront my past.

My mother followed me. "I've heard about the awful disappearances plaguing the area."

I glared at her and slipped behind my desk. She met my stare, unflinching.

Was she behind everything, as my most paranoid fear wanted me to believe? Edwin had found no proof, not a single hint she was involved. Neither of us could see the logic in it. My mother didn't act irrationally. What was the point of snatching people tangentially related to me? It wouldn't help my mother get what she wanted from me.

"We appreciate you coming out to help," Mea said into the strained silence.

The two of them sat down in the guest chairs in front of my desk as if we were actually having a meeting.

"How will your presence here help, *Judge* Herrera?" I asked, since Mea gave no sign she was going to ask critical questions.

"I was worried about you, Juliet." Mother gave me a concerned smile that I was no longer foolish enough to believe. "I wanted to make sure you were all right. If someone is targeting my daughter, I can't sit by the wayside. I came here for you."

I turned on my computer with a humorless laugh. "*Supporting* me isn't a part of the investigation. Why tell everyone you're getting involved officially, to assist the Authority's efforts, if you're only checking on me? That's personal and requires no communication with the rest of your organization. What are you doing here?"

"You're being rude, Juliet." My mother gave Mea an apologetic look. "I thought I raised you better than that."

I gripped my desk so hard my knuckles cracked.

The comment was meant to sound innocuous, but my mother had to know how I'd take it. She hadn't raised me better. She'd punished any deviation from her arbitrary definition of 'the right way of being' with spell after spell. Corrections upon corrections that sometimes contradicted each other, taking my ability to choose my own actions away from me and molding me into a person that wasn't real. A pleasant and acceptable ghost. That wasn't parenting.

The spells had started out small. I was only a child, and when I didn't respond to traditional punishment, my mother gave up and used her power on me. It was like I was a bother, annoying and not worth the effort of trying to understand. It was like she didn't want me unless I was one particular way.

At first I'd tried to get it right, to be 'good.' But that was the reaction of a kid who hadn't yet realized that in a system of nonsensical rules I would always lose. It wasn't about right and wrong, good or bad, it was about control.

But somehow, after everything, my mother's admonishment for my rudeness had the same effect, today in my office, that it would have when I was small. The anxiety it triggered was unbearable, fear from another time rendering me helpless, even though I knew she couldn't touch my mind now.

I tried to breathe through it without gasping and giving myself away.

As my computer loaded, I spared a glance at Mea. I didn't want her to see this. Whether she'd betrayed me deliberately or not, I cared what she thought of me. I wanted to be real around her, but not exposed like this. I felt as powerless as I'd ever been, stripped of choices and trapped. Mea was seeing a truth in me she was never meant to. I hadn't given permission to share any of this with her.

All I wanted was control over my own life, to be in charge of how people saw me and what they knew about me.

Mea was looking at me with a strained expression I couldn't interpret. Maybe she was holding back now we weren't alone, but something about her reaction hurt and confused me. I looked away, focusing on my computer screen.

"So you're here to check on me, mother," I rambled, blocking Mea out as I typed in my password. "I still don't see how that benefits the case, or why you were ringing around the Authority pulling rank, instead of contacting me directly."

"So you would have seen me if I'd called you?" The judge sounded amused.

I refused to look at her. "No, I wouldn't have." The messenger app loaded at a pace set to kill me slowly.

My mother made a *tutting* sound. "Then you left me no choice but to contact you through more reliable means."

"Checking on Juliet wasn't what you mentioned on the phone," Mea said tentatively.

Mother ignored her. "I'm here to offer you my help, Juliet. Someone has it out for you. That much is clear. Why don't you take a break, come home. We can discuss your options."

I stared at her. *Options?* Was that a euphemism? A threat? Under no circumstances would I discuss anything. I felt my soul harden under the pressure of all that remained unsaid and unacknowledged between us. When I spoke, it was venomous. "Is it you?"

Judge Herrera didn't even blink. "Me? What could you possibly mean?" She sounded innocent and almost sweet, as if she were trying to act like a kindly grandmother, but her gray hair and simpering fooled no one. "All I'm saying Juliet, is you should take some time away. Until the situation is under control. If people are disappearing because of you, you can't keep going on as if nothing is happening. The fate of your friends is at your feet, my dear."

And if I don't, then what? Was she implying she had control over the fate of my friends because she was behind it after all? Or was I being paranoid? Her smooth, concerned expression gave nothing away.

I stole my eyes away from the judge and dashed out a message to Edwin.

"The Authority has already asked Herrera Investigations to pause temporarily," Mea said and my mother looked at her like she'd forgotten anyone was sitting beside her. Mea faltered but pressed on. "It isn't Juliet's fault. She's another victim. We haven't proven a connection to Juliet is *why* people are going missing. Only that it's a way the victims are related."

"Hasn't it been proven?" My mother arched a thin brow. "Clients and associates gone, threats and failed attempts aren't enough proof? None of the victims have any standing or power on their own to be worth all this trouble."

Footsteps sounded in the waiting room, signaling Edwin's arrival.

I wished I had the ability to read minds as I stared at the judge. Even Aria's truth detecting would have been invaluable here. "You seem certain it's all about me."

"It's not a hard message to interpret, Juliet." My mother spoke as if she were addressing a confused child.

But is it her message we're interpreting? Had she lost all reason? Was she honestly doing all this to intimidate me? Perhaps she was only taking advantage of the unexpected opportunity the disappearances provided to—what exactly?

How could she use this situation to force me to do anything if she wasn't behind it?

Sitting here glaring at one another wasn't going to get me answers. I stood from my desk. "I'll walk you out, mother."

She crossed her ankles primly. "No. We aren't done. We have things to discuss."

"Then discuss them." I felt bolder knowing my escape lurked in the other room. I had someone in my corner.

My mother's nostrils flared, her only sign of anger. "We can't discuss personal matters in front of your companions. I believe someone is waiting for you in the entry, though I don't remember allowing anyone else into this meeting."

I didn't care if she knew exactly who was waiting for me. The judge wasn't in charge of this 'meeting.' There were the things she wouldn't say in front of Mea and Edwin, but why even try to bring our history up now, after so long? What did she think we'd discuss? I'd hoped we were done years ago. I'd wanted to believe that the impasse I'd created had forced the final word between us.

I tapped my shoe in an obnoxious, impatient gesture. "Either say what you mean or leave."

My mother didn't rise from her chair. "You're such a disappointment, Juliet. Not content with wasting your career, you have to ruin your family's reputation with bad behavior as well."

"You think Mea cares how I'm acting? That she'll tell all her colleagues how rude I am? So what. I don't give a shit." I marched out of the room and found Edwin waiting, frown lines creasing his forehead.

He took my hand.

"She has my phone," I whispered before he could take us away.

Edwin's lips disappeared into a thin line as if he were thinking hard. Then, with an almost undetectable surge of power, he stopped time around us and the air stuttered to an unnatural stillness. "What the hell is going on, Juliet?"

I couldn't bring myself to let go of him. "Mea screwed me—" My voice broke on the words and to my dismay, I started crying.

My friend pulled me close and I sobbed into his suit. Part of me wanted to stay trapped in this bubble forever, let the rest of the world be frozen and forgotten. I didn't want to deal with it. But being suspended in a moment of self-pity and fear would be hell. And besides, Edwin and I might actually get sick of each other with nothing else to occupy us.

"Right." I said after I mopped my face with tissues and dried Edwin's jacket with a spell. "I need my phone and to get that Witch out of my office."

Edwin glanced toward my open office door. "Can't we just leave her, or do you think she'll snoop through your files if we disappear?"

My thoughts raced. "Why wouldn't she? Either she's behind everything and will take the opportunity to look for more targets, or she's trying to manipulate the situation to her advantage, in which case she'll look for anything she can hold over me."

Edwin and I walked back into my office where the others were frozen. Mea was turned toward the door like she'd followed my progress out of the office, a look of confusion on her face. My mother was facing forward, expression set in unreadable stone.

"Why don't we leave Mea to keep an eye on mother dearest?" Edwin circled my desk examining the frozen scene. "Mea wouldn't let her raid your office."

"I don't know if I can trust Mea." My stomach fluttered and I wished what I said wasn't true, but trusting her too much, too quickly had gotten me into this mess.

Edwin gave me a pointed look like he wanted to disagree. "That's nothing new, you didn't know if you could trust her the other day. Besides, you don't have to trust Mea. All you have to trust is that your mother will preserve her standing and image above all else. If she's behind this, she's being excruciatingly careful. She won't give herself away by doing anything as blatant as searching your office."

I crossed my arms. Edwin had a point, but I was uneasy leaving anything to chance. "Coming to see me already gave her away. If she hadn't come here, I'd still be telling myself it was paranoid to wonder if she was involved. Yesterday I'd have said a meeting like this was too bold to fit how she operated. We can't know what she'll do next."

"Her presence only has significance in your eyes. This meeting doesn't give anything away from Mea's, or the rest of the Authority's, point of view," Edwin reminded me gently.

He had another good point. My mother's visit was cloaked in official business, and it would make me appear ridiculous if I tried to use it as proof of anything more sinister. All her comments only held meaning to me, in the context of our history. There was too much no one knew. She wouldn't give that protection up just to search through my things.

Edwin stopped his circling to stand behind Mea. "So, we'll leave Ms. Dubois behind then?"

I opened my mouth and closed it. I should leave her behind after today, but no matter how convinced I was that everything between us was a mistake, I couldn't let go.

"Things have changed, Edwin. Mea needs to come with us. I need to know—" My throat threatened to close again. "I don't want Mea alone with my mother. The judge can still do plenty of damage without giving herself away."

"Okay." Edwin perched on the corner of my desk. "So what exactly are we doing from here? Explaining this time-stop is going to be complicated enough as it is."

Edwin's time altering magic was monitored by the Authority.

He was required to account for his actions in an effort to manage his unprecedented power, but we couldn't explain the reason I'd called him when everything in the past was veiled in secrecy.

Edwin frowned, thinking aloud. "I can't exactly report to my keepers in New York—of which your mother is one, let's not forget—that I didn't trust her alone here."

Guilt joined the anxiety coursing through my veins. "I know. I'm sorry Edwin, I didn't mean to make a mess for you."

He shrugged. "You're not."

"For what it's worth, I don't know if my mother will mention the exact details of this visit to her colleagues. I doubt she'll admit we used your time freezing power to take back a phone she all but stole from me, and left her here, clueless as to where we went. It won't make her look good and would be awkward to explain."

Edwin stroked his chin. "I can work with that. Reporting in a minor issue. But we'll need to leave your mother unsupervised if we're taking Mea with us. The judge would love to catch me out for doing something wrong, like transporting her somewhere against her will."

I agreed as I retrieved my phone from my mother's purse. Maybe I was being overly cautious. I wasn't positive she'd find anything useful on the device or in my files, but there was too much information about me stored on my phone and in this room, and I'd have no idea how she'd use it.

There was one tedious solution that left nothing to chance.

"Shall we vanish all the papers and things from the office? She can snoop through empty file cabinets all day." I looked around, glad Aria had helped me tidy the palace.

Edwin tapped his chin in thought. "That's not a bad plan. I'll leave it out of my report, of course. She can't mention missing files without admitting to searching your office illegally, so we should be fine." Edwin sighed and got up from the desk. "At times it's like I'm your personal mover, Juliet."

I caught his eye and he gave me a joking smile, cutting off my apology.

Turning to open the nearest drawer, I teased, "And you once told me you don't do magic for others."

"There's a difference between doing others' bidding and working together." He was serious once again.

"I know." I reached out and pulled Edwin into a tight hug.

He started in surprise, going stiff before patting my shoulder awkwardly. Edwin was always better at comforting me than receiving any in return, not that he needed it any less.

We cleared the room of anything remotely noteworthy. Edwin sent the files and laptops magically through space into my already overcrowded living room.

"Now we just have to deal with Mea." I glared at her and my mother.

"There's a hell of a lot more to do then that, but I suppose we have to start somewhere." Edwin offered me his hand and placed his other on Mea's shoulder.

The three of us disappeared.

18

MEA

One second I was in the office watching Juliet walk away, then I blinked and I was in an entirely different room, overcome with the worst nausea I'd ever had.

I groaned. "What's happening?"

Luckily I was sitting, and put my head between my legs. The white carpet under my feet definitely wasn't there a moment ago.

"Is she going to need a bucket?" Bickel's unfeeling voice came from somewhere behind me.

Juliet's manicured hand appeared between my face and the floor, thrusting said bucket at me.

I took it and made an embarrassing—thankfully dry—retching sound, took two deep breaths, and sat up. "What the hell?" I looked around frantically. "Where am I?"

"We're in New York City," Juliet snapped, as if I should know.

She stood in front of me, arms crossed and sure enough, behind her was a wall of windows displaying Central Park and the New York Skyline. The clouds were an ominous gray.

The look of disdain on Juliet's face took the discomfort in my gut to a new level. It was as if everything that had happened between us over the past week had evaporated. Or maybe had never happened at all.

"We're at my apartment." Bickel sat himself in an armchair that looked like the descendant of a piece of modern art. The couch I was on was of the same fashion.

"You can't just bring me here without asking." I tried to sound outraged but was too disoriented. "Where's the judge?"

"Sitting alone and disappointed in my office, I suspect." Juliet hadn't stopped glaring at me.

"Why? What are we doing here? What the hell is going on?" I got a handle on my outrage and tossed the bucket aside. "Juliet, I'm working on a case. Even if I'm not an active member in the investigation, I need to be in California. How's it going to look having you two kidnap me? I can't abandon senior members of the Authority mid-meeting."

Bickel leaned forward in his seat, looking alarmed. "We aren't kidnapping you, Mea. I'll take you back right now if you want."

"But I won't be joining you," Juliet added.

I looked between them, Bickel as impassive as ever despite his momentary concern, Juliet concealed by a mask of rage. They were hiding something. Scratch that, they were hiding everything. "I'm not going anywhere until you explain what happened back there."

"So just to be clear—" Bickel held up a hand. "You aren't going to accuse me of abducting you, right? Because—"

"Fine, whatever. No, I don't actually think you'd kidnap me. I'm glad you didn't leave me behind." I stared the man down the best I could.

Bickel nodded and set his hat on a side table, leaning back, legs crossed as if everything was now settled.

Juliet did not look satisfied. "What happened was, you were

easily manipulated, and had no idea what you were doing. Or did you purposely sell me out to my mother?"

"What? No, I didn't sell you out." I jumped off the couch. "And I do know what I'm doing. Stop talking to me like I'm an incompetent child. Why did your mother want to meet with us if not to help the case? Why are you acting like I betrayed you?"

Juliet took a step back, toward the window. Her rage slipped to reveal something more vulnerable. "Because you did."

I moved around the coffee table, closer to, but not crowding Juliet. "How am I supposed to commit treachery without context? I only did what made sense with the information I had. Not being clairvoyant doesn't equate to cluelessness. I can't help you or betray you if I don't know what the fuck is going on. Meeting with a judge was perfectly reasonable."

Juliet's stony expression resolidified but she didn't speak. A glance at Bickel revealed him to be as unreadable as ever, though I suspected he knew all the answers I was looking for.

Uneasiness joined the frustration and anger coursing through me. I couldn't even imagine what was going through Juliet's mind. How did I know so little about her? Was I wrong to think anything we'd shared in the last week mattered? I didn't know how she could be standing there looking at me like that.

But Juliet might have been right about one thing—I hadn't thought to question the judge's request—though I still resented how Juliet was treating me because of it.

Judge Herrera had asked me not to mention the nature of the meeting to Juliet, but only in a casual way. I doubted anyone would have seen her offhand remark as a red flag. I'd genuinely had the meeting out of my mind the rest of the night. Once Juliet and I had gone inside, I hadn't thought about the phone call until the next morning.

She should know me well enough to believe that.

Taking a breath, I tried to even out my tone but didn't temper my words. "Trusting no one got you here, Juliet. Maybe if I'd known whatever it is you're not saying, I'd have acted differently. But you have to see what I'm getting at. This secrecy is making the situation worse. For yourself. For everyone around you. Keeping information to yourself is affecting how we're running the case. It's selfish and irresponsible. So stop blaming everyone else for—"

"Don't call me selfish for looking out for myself." Juliet's anger ebbed out of her tone with a sense of finality. She looked defiant but fragile, like someone who had been struck out of nowhere.

Had I been too harsh? I had the urge to apologize, but why should I when Juliet refused to do the same? She'd let her anger fly and hadn't cared about my feelings when she called me clueless. And she still wasn't explaining anything.

But stubbornness and wanting to get even with Juliet wasn't going to help this situation.

"I didn't know that's what you were trying to do, Juliet. How is disappearing from a meeting with your mother looking out for yourself?"

Juliet didn't make any indication she was going to answer.

I took a breath and told myself I hadn't expected any different. "I can't help you if I'm walking around in the dark. You brought me here instead of leaving me behind, so tell me why. I just want to understand."

I tried to convey how layered and deep that desire to understand was with more than words. Could she see it in my eyes? Maybe I could will Juliet to feel how much I meant it.

She avoided my desperate gaze and pushed past me. I expected Juliet to storm out of the tastefully decorated living room, but instead she collapsed on the couch, kicked off her shoes so aggressively one hit the coffee table, and curled her feet up underneath herself.

Bickel watched her with sharp focus. I wondered if he was concerned.

Juleit ran a hand through her curls, almost tugging on them and sending them every which way. "I suppose you leave me no choice—"

"Nope, don't do that." I settled myself at the opposite end of the couch. "I'm not forcing you to talk to me. I only hope you can see why you should."

I wanted Juliet to trust me. Hadn't we been headed that way all week?

"I—" A war of emotions rippled over Juliet features like she'd much rather believe I was cold-heartedly forcing her to open up. "I wasn't going to tell you any of this."

"Why?"

"Because I never tell anybody." Juliet looked assured, like she was reminding herself as well as me. Her words sounded like a stock response.

I frowned. "Am I just anybody? Is that how you want this to be?"

"I don't know." Juliet looked like she couldn't believe I'd gone there—pointing out that there was more between us—but the outrage didn't stick. She wilted, probably feeling exhausted. I couldn't imagine what it was like putting so much energy into closing yourself off.

"Don't you think you brought me here because, on some level, you had something to say to me? Or am I totally wrong? Is it something else?" Of course, I wanted Juliet to tell me I was here with her because she cared about me.

"I—well— This might be the end anyway." Juliet gave me a strange look.

End of what, the *us* she didn't like me alluding to? Was she hoping I'd contradict her? Give her reassurance? If Juliet didn't like the idea of me being just anyone to her, it was in her power to change that outcome, not mine.

There was a long silence. Juliet looked at Bickel but he didn't give any indication of his thoughts. I didn't know what else to do but wait. The only way forward was through this conversation. I tried not to feel remorse—worried Juliet was right and that this was the end of anything between us.

But Juliet didn't shut me out. She told me the most unexpected story starting with college, meeting Bickel, and so many other things I couldn't imagine, spanning her whole life. She talked in an emotionless, almost bored tone that put me on edge the longer the story went on. My anger faded and my guilt intensified.

Juliet was right, I had been manipulated and I couldn't deny I'd been too trusting. Even though there was no way I could have known what lay between her and her mother, I could have prevented this meeting from hurting her.

Maybe I was always too trusting, giving every situation the benefit of the doubt. And yes, sometimes this was a good thing, but I'd already had my doubts about the Authority. They'd been growing for a while, and I already knew the case wasn't being handled well. Easton was letting personal grudges and judgments color his decisions. Why had I expected anything better from the rest of our organization when I also knew they let this sort of shit go unchecked and didn't deal with problematic people?

But I was making this about me, and while I probably should reflect on a few things, now wasn't the time.

Juliet was looking at her hands and I didn't know what to say. I was finding it hard not to cry. Expressions of sympathy felt inadequate. I wanted to hug her, wrap her up and not let go, but I didn't think Juliet would welcome that, so I went with trying to convey that I understood, not what she'd been through, but where she was coming from in her reaction today.

My hands were balled in my lap. "I'm so sorry you went through any of this, Juliet."

Juliet nodded and shrugged, her reaction disorientingly calm.

I squirmed, rambling on. "I understand why you didn't confide in me. We've barely started getting along. And I'm sorry for calling you selfish. I get it now, and I won't ever repeat any of this, you know that right?"

"I believe you Mea. I probably wouldn't have told you otherwise." Juliet sounded matter-of-fact but seemed almost surprised by her own words. Otherwise, she had almost no reaction to what I'd said.

This explained so much about Juliet's closed off nature. I wondered if she was shutting me out right now, almost seeming to ignore my sympathy, because anything else was too painful. Of course she'd guard herself and push everyone away after the one person that was supposed to protect her had done something so horrible. And she hadn't just been betrayed by a parent, but someone who sat at the top of Witch society's power network. It was a marvel Juliet trusted anyone and that she'd let me in at all.

"How did you get away?" I asked when trying to express what I was feeling became too much.

Juliet ran a finger along the arm of the couch, seeming relieved that I'd stopped trying to convey my sympathy. "That was the thing I was going through when I stopped talking to you. Edwin broke the spells. He didn't know exactly what was wrong with me and I couldn't tell him, but he figured out something wasn't right." She looked over at her friend, who I'd almost forgotten was here.

As if he'd received some silent permission, Bickel took over the explanation. "I can break any spell without exception, and without needing to know its nature. Not by way of counter-magic, but by detaching the subject from all facets of our reality."

"That's possible?" The knowledge made me uneasy and even more wary of Bickel despite everything else I'd found out about him. He had a perfect storm of powers.

The Witch gave me one of his unimpressed looks, like I should have known exactly what he was capable of. "You're aware I can teleport and stop time. If I combine these powers in a precise way, I can go to a place that doesn't exist in this physical universe. A place disconnected from our timeline and all physical being. Like an in-between plane of existence."

"And you asked him to take you there?" I turned to Juliet, in awe of her past boldness, especially given everything else that was happening in her life at the time.

"I only asked Edwin if it was theoretically possible." Juliet waved her hand as if it weren't a big deal to essentially leave reality. "Meeting him gave me the idea. I hoped my theory about his power would be a work around to breaking the damn spells."

"I'd never attempted anything like it before helping Juliet. I probably never would have on my own. I don't like messing with that scale of magic." Bickel looked momentarily thrown by this small admission, like he hadn't meant to let it slip, but pressed on. "Leaving our universe was an out of body experience—as you might imagine—and I think, easy to get lost in. It's not natural to remove yourself from earthly ties and then come back. But it does remove *all* earthly ties, any spells or influences, without exception. So I took Juliet to this other plane, so to speak, and back again."

"What did you do then?" I looked between the two of them. "I'm surprised you didn't disappear, get as far away from your mother as possible."

"I didn't want anyone to know." Juliet looked at me like this should be obvious. "Running would call attention to something changing in my life. I needed to figure out what to do before she knew I'd broken the spells."

It must have felt impossible. What could Juliet have done against someone in such a powerful position? There was no good way to complain about the Authority. Judges were supposed to oversee the wellbeing of our world while also protecting the Mortal world from magic. But there was no good way to deal with them when they were a problem.

I'd known this in theory but never considered the brutal reality. It made me angry at everything the Authority did poorly and all the ways we didn't work well. Juliet was left with no one to turn to but the exact system where her mother held a position of unchallenged power, and what, she was supposed to trust that it would take her side?

Maybe with all my optimism I should have expected justice to be done regardless, but I knew better than to think that the Authority worked without prejudice. And obviously, sitting here with Judge Herrera still in her position all these years later, Juliet had come to the same conclusion back then.

I ran a hand through my hair, feeling at a loss. "You shouldn't have had to figure out what to do on your own."

"I didn't. I had Edwin." She gestured to him and I was glad she'd had someone. "But I think I know what you actually mean, Mea. My mother had proven she didn't think it was wrong to use her power against me, what was to stop her from doing it to everyone else in order to cover it up? So you're right, I had to figure out what to do on my own. I didn't trust trying to go to the Authority. Even with psychic corroboration I worried I wouldn't be able to prove what had happened, not against someone as respected as her and not when she could alter minds to force anyone who wasn't already on her side to join her.

"So I confronted her myself, with Edwin, but she refused to understand." Juliet's demeanor turned hard. She scowled at the past like she might still show it how much she hated how it'd gone. "My mother acted like nothing she did was wrong. She wouldn't listen. In the end I cast my own spells on her mind. She couldn't prevent it with her own power because I was protected by Edwin's. She couldn't reach me. I finally had the upper hand and used it to restrict my mother's power, making it impossible for her to ever use mind control outside the law again. On anyone. Then I erased her memory of the confrontation. I wanted to walk away and live my life."

"We'd all abandoned the rules by then," Edwin added, as if in defense. "It was safer to leave the judge in the dark about what exactly had happened. She has a knack for turning knowledge into power."

"I can't say I'd have done any different," I admitted. They'd been in an impossible situation. "But there has to be a better way."

"Oh, and how would that go?" Bickel gave me a snide look.

"I'm not saying there is a better way. I'm saying it shouldn't be like this. Someone like Judge Herrera shouldn't be able to escape accountability because of her position or magical ability. There should have been a way to take her to trial."

"I don't disagree. But there wasn't a better way. Wishing doesn't solve anything." Bickel acted as if my observations were pointless and barely worth his time to acknowledge.

Juliet looked like she was getting frustrated, maybe with both of us. "It doesn't matter. Even if there had been a way, I don't think I could've have taken a trial. I couldn't even take everyday life. And I didn't want everyone to know. I just wanted to get on with my life without everyone knowing the worst things that had ever happened to me. And that's exactly what I did. It worked fine up until now."

I wanted to assure Juliet that things could be okay, even when they hadn't been for her in the past. But I had no answers to go with my convictions, only a hope that this situation with the disappearances wouldn't end the same way, with her having to protect herself from everyone around her. "Not everyone would know. Personal details are kept private. And if you're worried about that now—having to explain what you think your mother is doing and why—I'm sure there's something we can do to protect you. Only those who need to know for the case would—"

"Please, Mea," Bickel interrupted at his most harsh. "Tell me you're not so deluded by the Authority to think they handle things with care. You work there after all."

"I'm not delusional," I snapped at him. I appreciated all he'd done here, but he was so abrasive and I didn't have the energy to deal with it gracefully.

"That's not what I said. Never mind—you're what, naïve then?" He sneered at me. "Confidentiality is crap on big cases. People always talk. Can you honestly tell me you haven't ever noticed? Juliet has the right to protect herself from that. There's more than one problem at play here."

I felt like he was chastising me incredibly unfairly. "I know the problem of accountability at the Authority is complex, especially in this particular situation."

"Honestly Mea, I wish everyone was like you." Bitterness seemed to creep into Bickel's eyes. "But some of us know better. Successfully getting through a trial is only half the battle. I'm not inclined to trust the court after how it treated me. There's a lot more to fix before we reach your ideal world where there's a better way."

"You?" I couldn't help being caught off guard. "What does this have to do with you?"

"Now that, I'm not going to tell you." Bickel adjusted his

already perfect bow tie. "However, I'm sure you can find out if you tune into office gossip. Especially with anyone on the East Coast who's been at the Authority for more than thirty years. As I say, the organization has a confidentiality problem."

"I'm not going to ask around about you." I scowled, resenting that he thought I would pry. "But I feel like we're getting off track. I'm not trying to argue. Or say things are fine the way they are, or that there isn't more than one issue. I'm just trying to find a way forward. Regardless of the past, we have to find a way now to sort this out. After her showing up today, you have to be thinking Judge Herrera has something to do with the disappearances, right?" I looked to Juliet.

"Yes, but we have no proof the judge is involved." She sounded surprisingly diplomatic.

"But we need to look into it." I didn't quite see the connection as to why the judge would be involved in the current mess, but her using the disappearances to manipulate me into arranging a meeting with Juliet was too coincidental for her involvement in the rest not to be a possibility, especially when considering the judge's history with her daughter.

"Yes, I've been trying." Bickel looked frustrated, so I figured there was no need to ask if that had been going well. "It's hard when it's only me against the rest of them."

"And who do you think I am?" I sounded as frustrated as he did. "I'm going to help, and I'm sure others would too. I mean, you work at the Authority, Mr. Bickel. You can't sit there and be so cynical, acting like you don't trust us when you're one of us. Even after all this, you chose to work with us; what changed your mind? Something had to have swayed you."

Bickel made very intense eye contact with me, but I refused to back down. A cold sweat broke out on the back of my neck as he tried to work his intimidation on me. He didn't have to tell me his life story, but I refused to accept things that didn't add up.

Abruptly, Bickel seemed to reconsider. He got up from the armchair and stalked off to a fully stocked bar in the corner of the room. "I may work at the Authority, but my trust has remained limited, Mea. I didn't change my mind. I'm trying to make a difference."

Bickel giving in to my stubbornness was almost as shocking as his apparent motivations, and it was annoying to learn that he might actually be a good person deep down. This threatened to make me feel bad for disliking him. Except he'd still treated my similar hopes for a better way with derision.

The man began making himself a drink. "Regardless of my past career choices—*now* we must remain quiet and not be liberal with our trust. Yes, others might help, it's not an organization staffed purely by monsters, but we can't count on people not to talk. How can we be sure that anyone we go to won't—even accidentally—tell someone who's on the judge's side? We have to be careful who knows what we're doing before we have evidence."

He paused, sipping his whiskey. "Judge Herrera has already used her status to interject herself into the case. It would be easy for her to discount any accusations that arise against her before we have solid proof. No one will take our side over hers. And after she discredits us, no one will take us seriously, making it much harder to find anything out." The man got out a second glass and Juliet got up to join him.

I followed suit but decided to pace in front of the windows instead of grabbing a drink. "You're right, accusing her of too much too soon could blow everything. We need to find out exactly what's going on before we take this conflict to the wider Authority."

I hated that that was the reality. We shouldn't have been reduced to secrecy and mistrust, but I saw no other way.

Juliet cradled a whiskey in her hands. "Once we know, I suppose it'll be time for me to tell my story to whoever needs to hear it. The things I couldn't handle before, I think maybe I can now, and if there is a way to take my mother down I'm not letting secrets stop me."

19

JULIET

That night Edwin deposited Mea and me back at my house. I settled in the living room to organize the displaced contents of my office.

"Juliet?" Mea hovered near the entry. She wore a look that told me she wanted to talk.

I picked up a random pile of papers. "I just need some space, Mea."

She hesitated and I swore she was about to say something. I turned away, needing to be busy. Now wasn't the time to stop and think. My energy was drained. I wanted to be ready to face my past and put it to rest, but I was feeling less confident than I had been while drinking in Edwin's living room.

When I looked up, Mea had gone.

I stayed up half the night filing.

ARIA ARRIVED at the house at eight thirty the following morning and I showed her to the place I'd cleared for her at my dining table. I'd been up early, anxiously awaiting Mea's departure from the guest room, but for some reason I hadn't seen her yet.

"Oh, wow. You brought the office home." Aria sounded bemused as she examined the neat stacks of papers surrounding the laptop.

I sat myself beside her. "Since we're closed, there won't actually be much for you to do other than field new email enquiries. So feel free to—um—browse the books."

It wasn't fair for Aria to go without pay while my business was on hold, so I'd told her I'd keep paying her wage regardless. Aria had insisted she come over and find something to do in exchange and I hadn't been able to come up with a way to refuse.

I was glad to have her here, but feared Aria would resort to tidying my house like she'd done with the office if she wasn't suitably occupied.

Aria switched on the laptop, accepting all the odd changes to her job without batting an eye. "So what are you up to today? Reading?"

"No. It's a long story."

Aria looked intrigued.

I'd deliberated about this most of the night, but in the end I concluded I'd have to tell Aria what I'd told Mea. Though I'd rather not have shared, Aria was a member of my team and nothing but helpful. I didn't distrust her and if there was a chance the whole story was coming out, maybe it was better to bite the bullet now.

I outlined the key points for her and it was fine. I didn't die of discomfort and Aria didn't appear to be passing any judgments, on me anyway.

The outrage pouring off Aria as she heard what my mother had done was almost tangible.

No matter how I tried, I couldn't escape the realization that

Aria knowing everything would prevent my mother using her as she'd done with Mea. In this case letting people in—just enough —could leave me more insulated than icing everyone out. On that front, Mea had been right. Not that I'd told her so.

Besides, talking to Aria was different. The young Witch and I were friends with clear boundaries. She wouldn't ask questions I was uncomfortable answering. Mea, on the other hand—I feared she wanted to know me with exposing depth, and would ask all the questions I couldn't face. Telling Mea the facts was hard enough, how was I supposed to respond when she asked me how I felt about it all?

"Why would your mom be sending notes and snatching your associates?" Aria asked after she'd digested my closest kept secret. "I don't doubt that she would. She sounds like the absolute worst kind of person, but what's she trying to accomplish?"

I rubbed my temple for so long the action became counterproductive. "I'm not sure. Going after other people seems random. That's why I discounted my mother being behind it from the start. I imagine she wants me to reverse the spells I cast on her mind, restricting her own mind-altering ability. Maybe it all boils down to intimidation. A way to force my hand."

Aria considered. "So she's all—*I'm going to abduct everyone around you until you give me what I want?* No offense, but it seems easier just to go after you directly."

I smiled humorlessly. "She can't get to me. I'm protected, the house is protected. I really screwed her over the day I met Edwin."

Aria grimaced. "Yeah, we're lucky he's on our side."

"Thank you, Aria—"

She gasped in surprise, a hand over her heart, as Edwin stepped out from behind the entry wall.

"—but I hoped you'd known me long enough to realize I'd

never be on the villain's side." Edwin scowled at us from beneath the brim of his expertly tilted hat.

I *humphed* at him. "If you didn't do things like purposely sneak up on people, they wouldn't take you for such a devious jerk."

"But being a devious jerk is my thing, Juliet. If people liked me, I'd have to talk to them." He joined us at the table, setting down his hat and handing out drinks from the Coffee Cat Cafe.

"Yes, a classic jerk move—bringing everyone coffee." Aria accepted a cold brew. "You must have got there right after I left. You know, I could start doing the coffee run. Save you the trouble."

"It's no trouble," Edwin mumbled, fiddling with the lid to his tiny espresso cup. "Where's Mea?"

"She's giving me space." I tried to ignore the fourth coffee in the tray along with my growing guilty conscience. I wasn't pleased with a lot of the things I'd said to Mea yesterday. Between lashing out and everything I'd admitted, I was trying not to think about any of it.

Edwin and Aria both looked at me keenly, like they were making speculations.

"What?" I said more defensively than necessary.

Edwin narrowed his eyes at me. "I've missed something. What's exactly happened between you two?"

"Nothing." My voice came out even, but my face heated like a damned traitor. It was pointless to be thinking about the shift in Mea's and my relationship, given everything that had happened since.

Edwin didn't miss my embarrassment. He raised his brows in question and I gave him a tiny nod, feeling even more red-faced than before.

Aria pretended to be doing something on the computer to give us a moment, but I caught her tiny smile.

Edwin's own grin was sly and teasing, like he was oblivious to the fact I'd already blown it with Mea. "In that case, it's not a good sign if she's hiding. What did you do to her?"

I feared my blood was boiling. "She's not hiding, and especially not because of *that*."

"I'm sure it's fine, Juliet. Don't panic." Edwin put his hand briefly on my shoulder.

I wasn't panicking, was I?

Should I be?

Maybe Mea was avoiding me and not just giving me space. Maybe I wasn't the person she thought I was, a possibility that made me suddenly sad.

I'd been busy fearing what Mea would think of the real me, or that there was no real me for her to see. But I'd shown her my true self when I'd assumed the worst in her, said unkind things and not apologized or even acknowledged how any of my actions were a problem. I'd been too focused on myself to think about Mea, even after I'd calmed down and realized she hadn't meant any treachery. Maybe Mea didn't need to compare me to the ghost she first met to find me lacking. All she had to do was look at who I was when backed into a corner.

I was someone who fought mind control with invasive spells of my own. I lashed out to protect myself first, and assumed the worst without exception.

But I didn't want to assume the worst with Mea.

I was considering getting up and knocking on Mea's door—with no clue what I'd say—when she popped into the living room.

"Oh good, there's coffee." Mea grabbed the last cup and leaned up against the doorway to the kitchen.

She seemed fine. The same. Maybe. Me on the other hand—I was staring, almost transfixed. Trying to telepathically figure out what she was thinking.

"I've done some digging on Jasper Suarez," Edwin announced, likely thinking he was saving me from an awkward moment. "Nothing noteworthy has come up. He was seen at work during the time of the first two disappearances, but I haven't been able to catch up with his friend Ben Shaw. Ben's work partner said he was away sick. When he's recovered I'll hopefully succeed in confirming Jasper's reason for seeking out Juliet."

"And is Jasper back at work, as per usual?" Mea asked from behind her coffee cup.

Edwin nodded. "He's assigned to Judge Geer for the week."

"That's good." Mea looked somewhat indifferent.

"Yes. All very unsurprising and unhelpful," Edwin agreed.

There was a coffee-sipping-filled silence. Jasper was never much of a lead, especially now we had my mother to consider, but it would have been silly not to check. Besides, there wasn't a lot else to go on. Judge Herrera wasn't an easy Witch to investigate. Edwin had already been sniffing around and found nothing.

"So what's the plan?" Mea pushed off the wall and came over to the table.

We all took turns looking at one another. Unfortunately, it didn't seem like anyone had any bright ideas hidden up their sleeves.

"Why not follow your mother around until she does something incriminating," Aria suggested. "Mr. B could cast a diffusion spell strong enough to render you near-invisible."

"You're forgetting the law, Aria." Edwin's impatient tone gave away some of his frustration, though I suspected with the situation rather than with Aria. "Officials can't just follow Witches around willy-nilly and then enter what they discover into court as evidence. That kind of cloaked spying isn't legally justifiable based on suspicions someone is up to no good. We'd need solid evidence the judge is currently breaking a law before we could surveil her. Even then, we couldn't follow her unrestricted, we'd need a clear aim."

Aria frowned at her coffee. "Fine, kill my idea. But I mean, I suppose that's all reasonable."

Edwin's expression was twin to Aria's. "You'd think it was more than reasonable if someone was trying to follow you around unseen without cause."

Aria agreed and set about chewing on her straw in thought.

Coffee consumption took our attention once again. My mind kept drifting back to Mea, preventing me from entertaining any useful thoughts. Should I not have told her I needed space? But I had—

Aria put her cold brew down and turned to me. "Does your mom have an assistant?"

"Yes, I believe so. Why?"

"Why don't you talk to them? See if Judge Herrera has been flying out to California a lot. That would be proof, right?"

"I suppose an assistant is well placed to know those kinds of details." I directed a questioning look at Edwin.

"It would be a start." He ran the silk of his bow tie absently between his fingers as he spoke. "But I think it would raise too many alarm bells if I went asking questions. I'm not exactly social at work. It's not like I could rock up to the break room and ask Mr. Abbott how the judge's calendar was looking without him reporting back to her on my strange change in behavior. And I doubt he'd give me an answer as to where Judge Herrera's been over the last few weeks, no matter how I phrased my questions."

Mea put her coffee down. "So what if the assistant reports back? The judge has to know we'll be looking into things after yesterday's disappearing act. I know we have to keep what we're doing quiet, but how are we going to get anything done if secrecy is restricting us?"

Edwin assessed Mea like he was questioning her agreement to be on our side. "Secrecy isn't the problem. The judge's assistant isn't going to talk to me without checking with her first. It'll be a dead end."

"Well, you could have just said that plainly."

Even if I wasn't sure what was happening between us, I was sure Mea would support Edwin and me in looking into my mother however we thought best. In that respect I trusted her. She'd been understanding yesterday even when I hadn't extended the same courtesy to her.

A thought struck me, an idea of how to use some of the recent events in our favor.

I took a hold of Edwin's wrist and he looked at me. "Maybe I could talk to her assistant. If my mother has been coming out here to kidnap people, it's not like she's telling anyone what she's really doing. If she's made anyone aware of her movements, what's the bet she said she's been visiting me."

I NURSED A SECOND COFFEE, sitting at a table in a busy New York cafe. According to Edwin, my mother's assistant Mr. Abbott bought lunch here almost every day.

Mea was at the back of the shop. At first I'd feared she'd try to talk to me now the others weren't with us—I kept oscillating between wanting her to say something and fearing she would— but she'd only taken up her position as discreet back up without a word.

I found myself disappointed.

Aria was back at the house with instructions to call if anyone came to see Mea or me. That way Edwin could quickly pop us back over, to keep up the facade I was at home. Edwin himself had gone to work. Apparently he had tasks to accomplish.

A few factors worked in my favor when it came to approaching Abbott. Almost no one knew of my complete estrangement from my family. I didn't tell anyone, obviously, and my mother wouldn't ever volunteer personal information that made her look bad, so it was highly unlikely Abbott would see anything strange in me asking after my mother.

It would be best if Abbott didn't mention my run-in with him to the judge—and I was hoping he wouldn't if I asked, in the same way Mea didn't mention the fateful meeting to me prior—but my mother finding out I was poking around wasn't the end of the world.

She'd expect nothing less of me.

The judge knowing I was asking after her movements wasn't the same as word getting around the Authority that she was suspected of the disappearances. That was something she could counteract. As long as the conflict remained between us Herreras—hidden from everyone but Edwin, Mea—I had a chance to get ahead of her.

A tall, gray-haired Witch in a black suit entered the cafe and settled at the back of the line.

I waited for him to collect his coffee and bagel before standing from my chair. "Mr. Abbott?"

He blinked at me. "Yes?"

"Oh, great. This is perfect. Excuse me for interrupting your break, I'm Juliet Herrera. Can I talk to you for a moment?" I gestured toward my table, smiling warmly.

Abbott sat down in a manner that suggested he was inconvenienced but trying to hide it. "Juliet, yes. I recognize you from the photograph. Nice to meet you at last. I trust you arrived with the judge last night? She mentioned the second ticket was for you this time."

Photograph? Did my mother keep one on her desk? The idea almost pushed me off balance.

I swallowed, my throat feeling dry. "I arrived this morning, actually."

"Oh. I'm sorry to hear about the nastiness in your neck of the woods." The Witch sipped his coffee. "Hopefully the judge's visit was helpful?"

"Yes, very. Thank you for arranging all her flights."

Mr. Abbott looked flustered. "It's my job."

"Still, I know she's been doing a lot of last-minute travel recently." I tried not to hold my breath, hoping I was right and that he would follow my suggestion.

Abbott glanced at the door. "Fitting all her personal trips around court isn't easy."

"I can't imagine it would be. I mean, how many times has she gone across the country lately? I'm almost losing track." I gave him a fake laugh.

He didn't join in and instead looked at his watch. "Too many times. I'm sorry, did you come here to find me or—?"

"Sorry. No, it was good to run into you though. I was hoping to surprise my mother for lunch. Do you know when she's free?" I second guessed the wisdom of this lie. What if she was free? This was the kind of thing Abbott might ask the judge about later, to see if I caught up with her.

Even if it wouldn't ruin things, I'd still rather my mother not know exactly how I was poking around.

Abbott gave me an apologetic frown. "Not today, I'm afraid. The judge arranged a last-minute working-lunch with one of the clerks."

I tried to act disappointed. "Never mind, then."

"Would you like me to pass on a message?" He picked up his bagel, probably in anticipation of departing my company.

"No, need. I'd still like to surprise her, if you wouldn't mind not mentioning this." I gestured between us.

"I'll forget we even spoke." He looked glad to.

After Abbott left, Mea approached. "Shall we go for a walk?"

I followed her out, relaying the conversation as we headed in the opposite direction from the Authority building, which was only around the block.

Mea looked at me sideways. "Was that enough to be sure?"

I wasn't disappointed that she was being nothing but professional. I wasn't. "It's a start. I'd say there's little doubt the judge is directly involved in the disappearances. If she were only trying to use this situation to manipulate me, it's extremely unlikely she'd have been out West before yesterday's visit."

Mea nodded as we walked, no longer looking at me. "I agree it's looking like she's directly involved. But I'm surprised Mr. Abbott knows about her trips, and that she hasn't hidden absolutely everything."

"Traveling isn't enough proof on its own, so it's not that much of a risk."

We walked in silence for a block and I tried to think of the next best move.

Mea glanced at me in a way that almost looked nervous. "I can't help wondering: why did your mother bother to meet with you? Why call attention to what she might be doing? She lost any element of surprise, put herself in a riskier position, and didn't seem to accomplish anything with what she said to you yesterday."

It was odd to have to explain this to Mea. For me this sort of sly chess match of secrets and guessing felt, if not normal, then familiar. "The uncertainty she left me with was probably her aim. In that sense my mother accomplished exactly what I'd guess she meant to. If she didn't want me suspecting her, she'd have stayed away. Therefor she wants me to know she's up to something."

Mea had taken us toward the park, not that I was surprised given her love of outdoor space, but I hadn't realized I'd allow her to lead or that I'd been blindly following.

Mea paused to look at me once we'd turned off the street. "Are you all right?"

"Yeah, I'm fine." I glanced at her quickly, trying to give her a reassuring face before continuing.

A flock of pigeons scattered before me. It took a moment to realize Mea wasn't following.

She was standing there, staring like she was trying to think about too many things at once.

"What?" I called from several feet away.

Mea slowly made her way forward. I found myself nervous, wanting to fix whatever was going wrong between us. She seemed disappointed, though I wasn't sure why.

"I'm sorry about yesterday." I wasn't able to meet Mea's eyes. "About what I said. I know you wouldn't sell me out, I just wasn't thinking. But that's no excuse. And you're not clueless or too trusting—" I faltered. This was sounding like the worst apology. All I was doing was bringing my insults back up.

Mea waited for me to go on before filling in the rest herself. "And I'd never sleep with you as some sort of diversion, or with deceitful intentions."

"No." Shame made my face hot. "I know that."

"In a sense I get why you went straight there. You don't trust people, and for good reason. You've had to look out for yourself and I get that's what you were doing." Mea's look of understanding should have been a comfort.

But her statement implied that she was just the same to me as *people*. When I wanted her to be different. I'd lumped her in with everyone I didn't trust without even thinking and I couldn't just undo that by saying sorry. If I wanted Mea to know she was more to me than anyone else, I'd have to show her, and I feared that meant letting her in even more than I had. Trusting her with more than facts and the investigation.

And I'd already failed. Pushing her away last night and again just now, saying I was fine when she could probably tell that I wasn't.

"I'm not going to hold on to the things you said in fear yesterday." Mea put a platonic hand on my shoulder. "I just hope next time you know whose side I'm on."

I'd never make that mistake again but I didn't think that was enough to rebuild something between us. I didn't know if I could stop pushing Mea away, even if it was the only way to save what we'd started.

I just wanted to be back in the world of two days ago, where we'd had something simple. Maybe my instinct was right yesterday and whatever that new beginning had been was over and not coming back.

Maybe this was the end of us, not because I'd had to open up and tell Mea about my past, but because I'd treated her just like anyone else when I could have chosen to trust her.

20

MEA

The next morning Bickel showed up before I emerged from my room. Seeing as the coast he actually lived on was three hours ahead, his early arrival wasn't as objectionable as I wanted it to be. It just would have been nice to have a moment with Juliet before he arrived.

Not that we hadn't had an opportunity last night that we'd both shied away from. Bickel's annoying presence wasn't the thing coming between us, I just didn't know where we were going from here, or what I wanted from Juliet, and it was easier to blame him than figure the rest out.

I found Bickel and Juliet in the kitchen, having coffee out of the pot rather than from the cafe that was starting to feel like an extra member of the group.

"Oh good, Mea, join us." Bickel gestured to a third mug.

Juliet handed me the cream.

As I fixed my coffee, Bickel filled the silence. "I had a strange interaction at the office this morning, regarding Ben Shaw."

Juliet narrowed her eyes, which were done up as impeccably as ever, her demeanor reminding me of how she'd been the morning after the attack on her house.

I'd thought the two of us were beginning to connect and that she was starting to show me what affected her. Yes, I understood a lot about Juliet now, and that acting okay was probably her coping mechanism, but she was keeping herself distant rather than letting us build on what we'd started. It made me unsure about everything going on between us.

Juliet's suspicious gaze fixed on Bickel. "Strange how? Is Ben not feeling better?"

He put his empty mug in the sink. "That's the thing, apparently he was never sick. His work partner came to find me, apologizing. Said he'd been mistaken. He thought Ben was sick, but got word this morning that the man was on paid leave, taking a vacation. Ben's partner wanted to correct his inadvertent mistake in telling me the wrong information. It was a bit much, but I suppose I appreciate it."

"He's probably worried about getting on your bad side." Juliet poked Edwin in the shoulder.

He huffed, as if it was an unreasonable worry.

Bickel wasn't as much of an asshole as he liked to pretend to be, but I didn't get why he bothered. Both of them, actually. If you had people thinking you hated them and colleagues scared to get on your bad side, but didn't actually care that they found you intimidating, what was the point?

I drank my coffee, but it didn't help with clarity on any account.

Juliet was staring at my mug, then looked up and realized I'd caught her. She turned toward the other Witch in a hurry. "I don't know if I'd call that strange, Edwin."

"Mixing up being sick with going on vacation is weird," Bickel insisted. "Who texts their work partner to say they're on leave, but doesn't mention the trip prior? Given we're dealing with disappearing Witches, I'd like to check."

"It wouldn't hurt. It'd be nice to wrap up this Jasper lead, at the very least." A sinking sensation settled over me. It was either worry about the case and that we were only stuck on Jasper because we had nothing else, or it was the realization that I'd started to fall for another person who shut me out.

I didn't know which was worse.

I COULDN'T HELP FEELING like we were on a pointless run around as the three of us stood on the street, braced against a chill wind while Bickel rang the buzzer to Ben's apartment.

"Hello?" came a faint voice from the intercom.

"Yes, we're looking for Mr. Shaw," Bickel replied, holding on to his hat so it wouldn't blow away.

"He's not here, sorry."

"I'm a work colleague, may we come up and talk to you?"

There was an extended pause before the person buzzed us in.

After climbing five flights of stairs, we knocked on Ben's door.

A short woman—Witch—with red hair answered. Music throbbed faintly in the background. "What's up?" She put her hand on her hip as she eyed us.

Bickel introduced himself and me, ignoring Juliet as she wasn't from the Authority. "Do you know where Ben might be, or when he'll be back?"

The woman straightened her posture. "I don't know. I haven't seen him since Friday."

I tried discreetly to get a look at the apartment behind her, but an easel and canvas blocked much of my view. "Is that usual?"

"Not totally," the Witch said, in a less than helpful manner.

There was an awkward silence.

"His partner thought he might be sick," Edwin prompted.

"No. Ben texted me this morning saying he was out of town, taking a break. Though I thought he was over at his mom's for the weekend." She pulled out her phone and turned it to face us. Sure enough, there was a text exchange to from this morning where Ben said he was out of town.

"So he's been gone since Friday but only now telling you he's away on a trip?" Edwin sounded skeptical.

"Yeah. Is something wrong?" The woman pocketed her phone, looking concerned for the first time since we'd arrived.

"Not as far as we know. I'm sorry, you are—?" I gave her a politely interested smile.

The woman ran a hand threw her hair. "Carli, Ben's housemate. He didn't take his big suitcase, so I can't imagine he'll be gone long." She looked over her shoulder and surveyed the room behind her as if looking for anything helpful.

I followed her gaze. "Are spontaneous trips Ben's style?"

"No. He's actually kind of boring. I mean, no offense, since you all work for the Authority. But you know what I mean." Carli looked at us as if daring us to disagree. "I'm an Artist," she added with an air of youthful superiority.

"Lovely." Bickel didn't make an effort to sound like he cared. "Does Ben have a romantic partner, a close friend, or family member who might know more about where he's gone on vacation?"

Carli frowned. "I don't think Ben's seeing anyone. He spends most of his time at work. And I don't really know his friends. They never come over. Like I said, boring. But he's a good housemate. He was a bit low-energy last time I saw him, that's why he went to his mom's. She makes good chicken soup."

I shared a glance with Bickel. "I thought you said he wasn't sick."

Carli shrugged. "Maybe he was, I don't know. He never

mentioned it, is all I meant before. Either way, he's obviously doing better if he's off on a trip now."

"Would you mind letting us know when you next hear from him?" Bickel took a business card out of his pocket and I did the same.

"Sure." Carli took them and slipped the cards into her phone case. "Why don't I give you Ben's number? Calling him would probably be easier than waiting. Oh, I'll give you his mom's too. She might know more than me."

As I took down the numbers, a thought occurred. "Have you talked to him on the phone, or just texted?"

"Just text." The Witch looked at me like the idea of a phone conversation was horrific.

On that note, we bid our farewell.

Halfway down the hall, Juliet said, "So both his housemate and his work partner only received word Ben was on vacation this morning?"

"With only text communication, there's no way of knowing if Ben even sent the messages." Bickel opened the door to the stairs and waited for Juliet and me to proceed downward. "It's like someone is sloppily trying to cover for his absence."

"But it sounds like he might have actually been sick." I wasn't convinced the change in story, or lack of phone calls, were evidence of any sort of cover up.

"We should check with his mother," Bickel suggested. "Though going home because you have a cold seems a bit extreme."

I could imagine Juliet rolling her eyes in agreement, but couldn't actually see more than the back of her head.

I turned to look at Bickel on the stair behind me. "Let's just try to call him."

Ben's phone went directly to voicemail. After leaving a quick message I tried his mom. She was easy enough to reach and after a short conversation I hung up. "Ben was with her this weekend but left on Monday, still feeling under the weather. She was unaware of any travel plans. She'd assumed he'd gone back to his apartment and hasn't talked to Ben since she saw him midmorning Monday."

"And no one at work has seen or talked to him, other than by text, since Friday?" Juliet said from a few steps ahead.

I continued down the stairs after her. "I mean, it doesn't add up neatly. But being sick wasn't incorrect, so maybe he really is on a trip he told no one about."

"He decided to go away before he got better?" Edwin sounded dissatisfied with the reasoning. "Ben didn't request the leave in advance, I checked. Why not continue on sick days and save the PTO?"

I stared at my feet as we progressed downward. "That is weird, but it's still not clear that he's missing. Even if Ben's been detained against his will for the last day, it doesn't fit the other disappearances. There was no effort made to hide the fact that Sarah or Lana were gone, and no one's scrubbed the magic from Ben's apartment."

"They couldn't take him from home like the others if he didn't live alone," Juliet called over her shoulder.

"But we didn't even think Jasper was involved." I leaned against the wall at the bottom of the stairs feeling a frustrated sort of denial down to my bones.

"True." Bickel reached the ground floor last. "But Mr. Suarez's story has become increasingly hard to corroborate. And it shouldn't be that difficult to figure out if a man is sick or on a holiday."

We exited onto the cold street.

I pulled my sweater more tightly against me. "Let's circle back to Jasper. Maybe ask if he's heard from Ben since they're friends. He might even know about the trip."

Even though Ben's absence had a few too many mysterious elements, I still felt we were heading in the wrong direction. What did this have to do with Judge Herrera? Why start taking victims who weren't directly linked to Juliet if her aim was to intimidate her daughter? Maybe none of it was actually connected at all.

If we suspected the judge was up to something, why waste time looking into this when proof lay with her? Only, now we suspected something might not be right, we couldn't ignore Ben entirely until we tracked him down. The whole ordeal becoming exhausting.

A much deeper frustration had settled over me in the last day. We had to figure out what the judge was doing and where the missing people had gone, but beyond that I didn't want to be a part of the Authority anymore. My hopes that the expansion was an opportunity for positive change seemed almost naïve now. I'd been fine to give the Authority another chance, but why? What I'd been hoping to do at a new branch wouldn't solve any of the organization's huge problems.

I could no longer go on as I had been, trying to get away from the things I didn't like and committing to do what small things I could. It wasn't enough. I had no power to instigate significant change, but staying and doing next to nothing was no longer an option I was comfortable with.

I didn't know where that left me.

I had to get out of LA, but without the Authority there was no reason to move closer to Juliet. In a sense that was disappointing. Or maybe it was a blessing in disguise.

Juliet—I just didn't know what to do about her. I understood why she was an accuse-first-ask-questions-later trust-no-one type of person, but felt like that understanding brought us no closer together.

Juliet and I would never work if she pushed me away first

and everything else came second. Not to mention, I didn't know if she wanted us to work. Maybe our one night together was all the woman wanted from me. Looking at her now, it was hard to tell if she'd given me a second thought. Juliet looked completely focused on the case as she stared at Ben's building in deep contemplation.

Bickel checked his watch. "Judge Geer should be out of court soon. I'll hover around and catch Mr. Suarez as he's heading home for the day."

Juliet nodded her agreement. "Should we go back to your apartment and wait?"

Bickel considered. "Why don't I drop you off at Coffee Cat? They'll be open another two hours. I'll be back as soon as I can."

Teleporting had gotten better, but was still far from a comfortable experience. I looked up and down the street. "There aren't coffee shops closer by?"

For some reason Bickel blushed faintly. "There are indeed local coffee shops—" He paused like he was searching for his own reasoning. "But you can't stay here. Don't you need people thinking you're sitting around in California?"

I shrugged. Honestly, what did it matter?

Bickel glared at me, cheeks no longer pink. "Just go sit."

JULIET and I were deposited back at her house and from there Aria drove us all over to the coffee shop I'd heard so much about but hadn't yet visited.

The place was cute, small, brightly decorated and apparently owned by Aria's boyfriend. We received an enthusiastic greeting from a bubbly Mortal man working the register. He was a friend of Aria's and the two of them started chatting immediately. They didn't stop as we waited for our drinks, apparently carrying on some earlier conversation. Juliet and I left them to it and went to select one of the few remaining tables.

Juliet sat stiffly across from me, looking down at her macchiato. "Should we—um—talk?"

Not going to lie, I was stunned.

"What?" Juliet was blushing but also frowning, like maybe she regretted her suggestion.

"Nothing—I just—what do you want to talk about?"

Juliet flicked her wrist. "What a fucking mess I've made of everything."

"Oh—" So maybe she'd given me a second thought after all. I waited for her to go on. The longer she was silent the more I wondered if she was hoping I'd contradict her and say everything was fine.

Juliet somehow looked like she was squirming in discomfort even though she wasn't moving, like her anxious uncomfortable energy was a living thing, but I waited. Wanting to talk had to be a good thing. It was something she'd never have suggested a week ago, but she couldn't seem to find her words.

The charged mood spread to me. I wasn't sure what to say. I hadn't yet figured out what I wanted from us. Three nights ago, I'd have said I was happily on a path to a relationship. Now I had too many second thoughts.

And on top of us, I had no idea what I was doing with my life. I couldn't stay with the Authority but didn't want the huge change leaving would impose on me. I didn't know what to about anything.

The silence filled the air until Aria sat down next to me.

"Sorry, did something kill the conversation?" Aria looked between us. "I can go back to talking to Tristan if you two need a minute."

We were saved having to answer by Bickel's arrival. The man gave us an acknowledging nod and strode purposefully to the register. For some reason both Aria and Juliet found his manner of ordering coffee fascinating.

"What are you staring at?" I asked, mostly to distract myself from the conversation that wasn't happening, and the life plans I wasn't making.

At my words the two of them looked quickly away from Bickel, almost guiltily. Neither said anything. Whatever this secret was, I didn't have the energy to care. It could hardly be relevant either to the case or my personal conflicts.

"Bad news," Bickel said as he joined us, smoothie in hand rather than a coffee. "Jasper wasn't in court."

I wanted to whine *come on* at him. This was ridiculous. "But Jasper was at work yesterday. Don't tell me he's sick."

"Judge Geer confirmed Mr. Suarez was doing his job as per usual yesterday. But this morning he was a no-show. Geer tried to call and check on him but didn't get an answer or a call back." Bickel took a grave sip of his green drink.

Juliet looked like she was taking this new development as a personal offense. "His and Ben's disappearances can't be a coincidence."

Are they disappearances, though?

I ran through the few details we had in my head. "The two instances don't quite match. If someone took Ben and was using his phone to try and cover it up via text, why not do the same with Jasper and respond to Geer? And neither case is anything like what happened to the Witches out here."

Juliet made a *tutting* sound. "So we've come across an entirely separate set of disappearances?"

"*If* they are disappearances." Everyone looked at me. I may have been a bit loud, like the stress of everything was getting to me. "We should stop by Jasper's house. If his housemate has some dodgy story, then yeah, okay. But we might just find him at home."

"Wait." Juliet grabbed my arm, the gesture surprising me. "Abbott said my mother was having a working lunch yesterday, with a clerk. It could have been Jasper."

"But why?" I looked at where she gripped me and wanted to twine our fingers together, possibly against my better judgment. "What does this have to do with snatching your local associates and showing up to your office to shove it under your nose? Why—"

An unexpectedly strong breeze interrupted me, rattling the window we were sitting next to and stealing all our attention momentarily. Juliet's hand disappeared from my arm. She hid it in her lap.

"My mother having lunch with a clerk is strange." Juliet was talking fast, even more confident than before. "If she had to talk about work, she'd just summon the clerk to her office, or send a message through her assistant. I should have picked up on it yesterday but was too focused on the flights and—everything else."

"From what I've experienced of her," Edwin cut in as if he could sense my coming objection. "Judge Herrera wouldn't bother to meet anyone low level for lunch."

"So Jasper is *maybe* missing after *maybe* having lunch with the judge. That's too many maybes." I crunched an empty sugar packet, knowing we'd have to look into it but not seeing how any of it could add up.

The wind outside picked up. The next gust let out an ominous howl, loud enough that everyone in the cafe hushed as all the windows rattled and the door blew halfway open.

There was a crack of thunder.

"I don't remember seeing any storm clouds outside." Aria peered out the window, her thought process apparently following mine.

The second booming sound shook the whole cafe. It

sounded just like what had happened at Juliet's house several nights ago. Some of the customers looked around nervously. There was another tremor and someone muttered about earthquakes.

I turned to Juliet. "Is the cafe protected?"

When we'd arrived I hadn't examined the pace like I'd done when first entering Juliet's house. But why would I? Checking for protective spells wasn't something I did wherever I went. Before Juliet answered, I reached out with my magic and, sure enough, the building was buzzing with the same intensity as Juliet's property.

"After what happened to Aria, we didn't want to take any risks. She lives upstairs." Juliet looked at Bickel, who nodded.

Aria had mentioned the extra protection to me, but I hadn't but it together with the cafe until now. At least her living upstairs made more sense than a Witch trying to get into a Mortal business.

The wind continued to howl and there was a slight disturbance in the air at the table. Bickel shifted abruptly in his seat.

"Damn it," he growled, looking almost winded.

"Did you just stop time?" I tried not to sound awed by the fact that such power was almost unnoticeable.

Bickel took a grateful sip of his smoothie. "Yes, and searched the area. Whoever is casting the ill-advised attack isn't here. I also checked the Herrera home in New York—from outside Mea, don't worry—as well as the Authority building. The judge isn't in either location, and no one was casting this kind of spell from there either."

"Too bad you can't search the whole country," I joked even though both Juliet and Aria looked concerned at the man's news.

"I don't think it's advisable to have things frozen for that long," Bickel answered seriously. "Besides, I don't have the mental fortitude to walk around alone, searching for what would equate to years on end. The last 'hours' were more than enough."

Another boom sounded and a few customers left the cafe to investigate outside. Even though the wind was relentless, the palm trees off in the distance showed no signs of disturbance, giving away the fact that the wind only bore down on the cafe.

"What the hell is going on with the weather?" The Mortal from the register came over to our table to peer out the window beside us.

"Gale force winds," Aria said without missing a beat.

"Huh." The guy looked skeptically outside. "What, is this place made of straw? Wind doesn't shake a two-story building."

Everything vibrated around us.

Another man came out from the cafe's kitchen to join our table. He placed a hand on Aria's shoulder. "What's up guys?" From the meaningful look he directed at each Witch, I assumed this was Aria's boyfriend who Knew about magic. "I hope I don't need to be worried about the cafe. Again."

"Can't you make it stop?" Aria hissed at Bickel. "Or are we going to risk all these Mortals catching on?"

"Oh—right. Sorry." Bickel jumped up and rushed off to the bathroom where I assumed he'd hide to do a counter spell to fend off the attack.

If we couldn't find the person while they were making their move, there was no reason to let the disturbance go on.

After one final violent shudder, everything stopped. Most of the cafe patrons had ducked under their tables or hurried outside. They cautiously returned to their seats.

"Come on, Tristan," Aria's boyfriend said to the other Mortal. "Let's go—um—check nothing fell off the shelves in the kitchen."

"I'll help." Aria got up to follow, and they departed, leaving Juliet and me briefly alone.

Juliet didn't seem as shaken as during the attack on her house, but she wasn't looking as confident as before.

No matter how confused I was getting about us, I still cared. "Are you okay?"

"I don't want anything to happen to Aria. Not because of me." Juliet sounded hollow and regretful.

A mingle of compassion and affection for her cut through all the other feelings that had been plaguing me. "First of all, it's not because of you. Your mother implying that was victim blame-y and manipulative. Second, nothing's going to happen to Aria if her home is as protected as yours."

Juliet didn't relax but seemed grateful for the reassurance. "Thank you, Mea. I'm starting to wonder where I'd be without you."

I wanted to tell her she'd be fine without me—that was the truth—but perhaps she didn't want to be.

21

JULIET

"How could my mother have known I was at Coffee Cat?"

"She might not have," Mea assured me the next morning over coffee at my kitchen counter. "Maybe she was going after Aria again. Everyone else got a note days before they disappeared. Um, not that that's better."

I scowled at my cup. "At least she'll be disappointed not to have gotten through."

Mea was adding more than her usual amount of sugar to her cup. She frowned. "What if she wasn't? Your mother could have detected the protection when I accidentally sent her there on Sunday."

"So what? That would make yesterday a show of intimidation?"

Mea shrugged.

I abandoned my coffee. "I guess that's what she was doing when she made the attempt on my house. She had to know she couldn't get me here."

"Knock, knock." Edwin's voice drifted in from just outside

the kitchen. He poked his head around the door frame. "Didn't want to be accused of sneaking up on people."

"Just come in." I let my frustration out, knowing Edwin wouldn't read into it.

He entered the kitchen unbothered and deposited his hat on the counter before helping himself to the last of the coffee. "I managed to get a personal item from Ben's desk. It was harder than I'd thought. The man is respectably averse to clutter."

Since there was nothing useful we could do about the Coffee Cat incident, we were at least trying to track down our other loose ends.

Mea went about setting up a location tracking spell, placing two bowls, candles and herbs around my kitchen floor. Edwin withdrew a plastic bag containing a pair of used-looking socks from his pocket. He shook the bag over the empty bowl, careful not to touch the socks as they fell.

Edwin wrinkled his nose. "If anyone finds out I was snooping in Ben's office—stealing articles of clothing out of his gym bag—I'm never helping you again, Juliet."

"What do you care if your colleagues find out? It's not like you want them to like you." I lit the candles with a flick of my wrist.

"There's a difference between being intimidating and unapproachable, and considered a total creep," Edwin said gravely.

Mea and I bypassed Edwin's complaints and got straight into the spell. To our dismay it revealed nothing. Any hope Ben was actually on vacation dwindled. We still couldn't find anyone who'd had knowledge of the supposed trip, or who had talked to him since he'd 'left,' and Mea's attempts to call him had gone unanswered.

To be sure nothing could be gained from the location spell Edwin had a turn, but the bowl of water showed nothing more than my ceiling.

"It's one similarity with the others, at least." Mea helped me put the items away, looking displeased with the observation. "Ben is as well-hidden as Sarah or Lana. I just can't imagine why he'd be pulled into all this."

Edwin drained his coffee and bent to return the socks to the plastic bag, employing a method that reminded me of how dog owners pick up after their pets, complete with a slight look of discomfort on his face. After returning the bundle to his pocket, Edwin held out his hands to us. "Never mind. On to the next."

We disappeared.

BACK IN NEW YORK EDWIN let go of our hands. "Your tolerance for teleporting is much improved, Mea."

She looked only slightly nauseous. "Oh, goodie."

"I could always leave you at home," he teased.

"No—don't you dare." Mea seemed playful rather than serious, and I was glad the two of them were starting to get along.

I wanted to include Mea in my life, if she still had any interest in that. The desire terrified me, leaving me sure I wanted something that wasn't going to work, but I'd take Mea's growing tolerance for Edwin as a good sign. There might be hope for me yet.

I pressed the buzzer to Jasper's apartment. No one answered.

He'd been absent from work again today and hadn't called in sick or responded to attempts to reach him. As far as Edwin knew, no one had seen or heard from Jasper since the day before yesterday.

"Do we know if he lives alone?" Mea asked after several more attempts at the buzzer.

"No idea." Edwin stepped back on the sidewalk and looked up the building, trying to see in the windows.

"We should go in, knock on his door just in case," I said when it was clear the buzzer was either broken or no one was home.

The other two agreed so I laid my hand on the door handle and muttered an unlocking spell. We slipped inside, relocking the door behind us, and climbed the stairs to the third floor of the small building, passing only one apartment per floor.

There was no need to knock to see something was wrong. As soon as we got to the correct landing, I could sense magic leaking out of the Witch's apartment in sharp, almost static waves.

Edwin, being thorough, knocked anyway. "Jasper—?"

No one answered.

I laid my hands against the door to examine the magic, straining to hear anything inside, and was greeted with silence.

Diagnostic spells were like sifting through sand and looking for a specific grain if you weren't used to them. All magic felt the same unless you could pick out the components and examine each fine piece as its own element. After years of training and practice I could unpick what a spell did, how it was cast, and who cast it—unless the Witch had concealed themselves. From there it was possible to reverse engineer a way of undoing it, assuming I had enough power.

The spell coming from the apartment had a hard, opaque quality pointing to confinement, tinged with a disorienting undercurrent.

"It's trapping someone, or something, inside," I said, even though the others were both sifting through their own analysis and likely had already figured that out.

Edwin drummed his fingers on the door. "It's also locking us out."

"And—" I paused, trying to measure the spell's strength. "I don't think this is a spell I could undo by myself."

Jasper, being a slightly younger Witch and not possessing any particular magical gifts, wouldn't have the ability to cast something this strong. At least not on his own. But none of us really thought he'd been the one to cast it.

"I doubt we could even break it together," Mea said to me before turning to Edwin. "You can get through it."

"Of course, but aren't you usually worried about me trespassing?" Edwin looked bemused. "I shouldn't have to remind you, Mea, we need to get approval to break magic keeping us out of someone's home—search and trespass laws being what they are. We don't know for certain that this magic isn't here at Jasper's request."

"Yes, I'm aware. I wasn't saying you should bust down the door here and now." Mea sounded impatient with Edwin's teasing manner. She turned to me. "So, who do we trust enough to go to for approval? Because having to get a judge's signature when trying to covertly investigate a judge seems like yet another flaw in this whole damn system."

AFTER A BRIEF PHONE call Edwin teleported Mea and me directly into a large wood paneled room in the New York City Authority building. We were here to see Judge Geer, who was—not a friend—but the only one of Edwin's superiors he seemed to like.

"What's all this about an urgent warrant?" a wild-haired, older white man asked from his seat behind a formidable wooden desk.

Edwin took a seat and balanced his hat on his knee. "It's about Mr. Suarez, Charles."

"The clerk?" Geer looked completely baffled and yet delighted for no reason I could deduce.

"Yes, the clerk. As you know, he's been unaccounted for at

work. I went to his apartment and found it's been placed under a strong confinement spell."

Judge Geer—who was proving to be a very animated person —made a show of shock, his considerable gray eyebrows rising to impressive heights. "Oh, that can't be good. Please sit." He flapped a hand in Mea's and my direction. "Who've you got with you, Edwin?"

Edwin made introductions. The older Witch smiled distract-edly at the three of us as Mea and I settled ourselves in the remaining chairs.

Being here made me uneasy, even if no one else knew we were in the building. I tried to push the discomfort away and focus.

"It's nice to meet you, Ms. Herrera. Are you finally going to join us?" Geer seemed to be genuinely interested in my answer, leaning forward in his seat with his eyes fixed on me.

It was the last thing I wanted to hear. I indicated I wasn't here for that, hoping I managed to sound polite as my gut churned with something like anxiety.

The older Witch looked disappointed. "So why are you here? Not that I'm not glad to meet you, but—" He turned a ques-tioning look on Edwin.

"It's a long, loosely connected story."

"One that has you teaming up with all sorts of people." Geer took a turn regarding Mea. "I'm surprised, Edwin. Given your preference for solo work. I'm also intrigued—though concerned for the clerk." He added quickly, expression grave.

Edwin hesitated. "Before I get into it, I'd appreciate if you kept this meeting confidential."

"Naturally." Geer sat up, suddenly at attention as if he were offended by the comment.

"I mean just between us, Charles," Edwin said in his most

understanding tone. "It's best no one else knows about this just yet, colleagues included."

The wild-haired man looked riveted. "I see. You know I'm good for keeping things quiet."

After a short pause, Edwin explained about Jasper, though not exactly why we first tried to get in touch with him. "We think this could be related to the disappearances out West. We don't have any actual evidence of that, just suspicions, so I don't want to say too much more—but it isn't looking good for a certain member of the Authority. Someone potentially involved in the case."

"Really?" Some of the delight faded from Geer's face.

Edwin leaned forward in his chair. "We won't know exactly what's going on with Jasper until we find him. I admit, his situation could be completely disconnected from the case Mea has been assigned to, but if it isn't, I wanted to alert you to potential —uh—trouble within the agency."

Geer considered, deep in thought. He ran his hands through his gray hair, making it an even more tangled mess. "Regardless of the bigger picture, you have enough to search Mr. Suarez's home, seeing as he's been missing from work and suspicious magic is present at his place. I'll sign that off now. But given what you've implied, I'm going to have to ask that you keep me updated."

We agreed to keep Geer informed from here on out. The judge didn't seem bothered that we hadn't told anyone else, and agreed our suspicions shouldn't be spread around without something solid to back it up.

Edwin and Geer turned their attention to the paperwork, organizing the warrant.

Even though we hadn't told Geer much, at least someone beyond our trio knew the direction this mess might head in. It wouldn't be a complete shock to link the disappearances back to an official. I could only hope Geer would remain accepting if we presented evidence it wasn't just someone at the Authority at fault, but a close colleague he'd sat on the Judicial Committee with for decades.

As we departed back to Jasper's, a weight seemed to lift off my chest. Maybe it was hope, or I was just glad to get out of the Authority building.

22

JULIET

Back in Jasper's doorway, Edwin countered the spell locking us out of the apartment and we stepped cautiously inside.

We found Jasper in his room, lying in bed. For a split second it looked like he was dead, but a quick analysis of the magic in the room told me he was only suspended in a dreamless sleep. He was completely immobilized and confined in such a way that no one would be able to pick him up and carry him off without first breaking the spell.

Mea moved around the rest of the room, searching for other spells. "Trapping him at home wasn't exactly a pro-move. It's the first place you'd go to look for someone."

"You're right, this was sloppy." I didn't need to add that finding Jasper here didn't fit the carefully planned abductions we'd seen so far, or the strange situation with Ben. I put my hand on Jasper's ankle to get a better feel for the magic subduing him and picked through the grains of power. "The caster went through a decent amount of trouble to keep all trace of their identity from the spell work. So they weren't totally careless."

That matched the other incidents at least.

Edwin came to stand next to me. "Shall we wake him up and see what he's got to say?"

We all laid a hand on Jasper—Mea from the opposite side of the bed—and went through the counter magic.

Jasper's eyes snapped open; he sucked in a breath, possibly about to scream.

"Hey—" Mea put her arms up in surrender. "We're here to help."

Not comforted, Jasper let out a loud swear and crab-walked frantically away from us until he hit his headboard. "What the hell are you doing here? How did I get home?"

I tried to project calming energy. "We don't know how you got here. It's what we're trying to figure out."

"*Juliet?*" Jasper looked at me like he'd seen a ghost. "Are you following me? Fuck. R-really—I'm sorry for bothering you. Please just leave me alone."

"Jasper," Edwin snapped, capturing the guy's attention. "You recognize me from work, yes?"

"Fucking, shit." Jasper's eyes grew impossibly wider. "I mean, yeah—uh—s-sorry Mr.—"

Edwin waved Jasper's stammers away in annoyance. "We found you trapped in your home. You've missed work. Geer sent us to look for you. Now, can you tell us the last thing you remember?"

The clerk looked around at all of us and then down at the bed he was on. "I don't know. I only remember being at work Monday morning."

"It's Wednesday," I informed him.

Jasper shook his head. "Why are *you* here? You don't even work for the Authority."

I wasn't sure what to say, not having expected him to act as if he were afraid of me. He had no reason to be.

"Let's try to focus." Edwin gently put his hand on my elbow

and I stepped back. "Jasper, can you please recount your Monday for me? It's important. We don't know how you got here, or who did this to you, but we're trying to figure it out."

He took a breath and his tense posture eased. "Um—I woke up, went to work. Everything was the same as usual. Took my time catching up on email after a few days off. Then got to my paperwork for Geer's court sessions. Then went out for lunch—" He strained, trying to remember.

Mea gave me an *I-can't-believe-it* look across Jasper's bed—possibly remembering who else we knew had lunch with a clerk on Monday—before turning to him. "Where did you get lunch?"

He scrunched his face. "I don't remember getting anywhere, just leaving the building. Why does it matter where I was going?"

Edwin caught my eye. "Do you usually meet with anyone for lunch? Or have a regular place you go?"

"No. And I wasn't meeting anyone on Monday."

"Okay, that's good to know. We just wanted to check." Mea gave the guy a smile. "Is there anyone you can think of who'd want to hurt you? Have you had any problems with anyone?"

"Not problems, no." Jasper gave me an embarrassed look. He had a terrible poker face.

"What?" I didn't really know what Jasper's problem with me was, other than my presence here being a bit unorthodox.

Jasper swallowed. "I'm sure it has nothing to do with this." He gestured to his current position. "Um, so never mind. Forget it."

"Humor us," Edwin said without any levity.

Jasper grimaced and tried to sit up in a less vulnerable position. Edwin and I shifted away, giving him room to put his legs over the edge of the mattress and stand if he wanted.

The clerk only put his head in his hands, elbows on his

knees. "It's just so weird you're here, Juliet." He looked up at me with what I could only interpret as a guilty expression. "You know—after I tried to contact you. And. Well. About that. It's stupid, but um, I lied. Ben never told me to look you up. We aren't even friends. Actually, your mother, you know the judge, asked me to go see you." Jasper averted his eyes.

I couldn't find my voice. I looked at Mea, who was almost as shocked as Jasper had been to see us in his bedroom.

"Why would the judge do that?" Edwin asked for me.

Jasper looked at Edwin in defeat. "I don't know, man. It was a while back. Months. When I first emailed you about lunch, Juliet. The judge asked me to meet with you and—uh—report back."

"Like spy on me?" I found myself less surprised than I should have been. Was he the only one to ever attempt this? Or was the reason my mother had stayed away because she'd sent others in her place?

"Yeah." Jasper sounded miserable and maybe regretful. "But I swear I wasn't doing anything against the law. Not like stalking you, or anything. I was just supposed to befriend you and tell the judge what I learned."

My stomach churned. "That's why you approached me at the bar? Did you know I'd be there, or was it a coincidence?"

"Not a coincidence. I um, followed you from your office. Then I had my cousin meet me at the bar. I really was spending time with him too. But you weren't interested in talking to me. After that and the previous failure, I told the judge it seemed pointless."

"Why would you agree to spy on me?" My mother's motivations were less mysterious, but I didn't see how she'd convinced this guy to go along with her. Surely this hadn't happened before, if only because finding spies had to be tricky.

"Well, I didn't see much harm in it," Jasper mumbled.

"Excuse me?" Mea's tone was harsh.

Jasper twisted awkwardly where he sat on the opposite side of the bed to look at her. "I mean, it wasn't like I was trading state secrets, only everyday stuff. She just seemed interested in what you were up to. And now I say it, it sounds bad. I know—and I'm sorry. Um. I was supposed to get a promotion out of it." He blushed at the feeble justification.

Edwin ground his teeth. "And what did the judge think about your lack of success as a spy?"

Jasper didn't seem to want to look at Edwin and so chose me instead. "After my first failed attempt she was disappointed and didn't mention trying again. But when I was out your way last week—legitimately visiting my cousin—I decided to try one more time. You know, I was still keen on the promotion. When I told the judge about it on Monday after I got back, she was mad I'd acted without checking with her first. She made it seem like I'd done something out of line. Which wasn't fair, she never told me the deal was off."

"Yes, how unfair," I said in my most dry tone.

Jasper cringed. "I made an excuse to get off the phone after that. Told her I had to rush to something to eat while I had time between meetings. And I mean, it was that time of day, so I went to get a sandwich."

"And leaving the building for lunch is the last thing you remember?" Edwin asked.

Jasper nodded emphatically, then paused. "Oh my god, do you think it was her?" His mouth remained open in disbelief. "She trapped me here? Why? Because I suck at spying?"

Mea caught my eye again and I didn't know whether to laugh or cry. Jasper wasn't the sharpest; normally I'd say my mother was smarter than to involve him, but his obliviousness probably kept him from questioning her intentions too closely.

Jasper had first contacted me—well, Aria, considering she

did the emails—what felt like ages ago. Long before the disappearances. Was he the first step in some plan, or did his failure prompt my mother to be more aggressive?

"So—um—what happens now?" Jasper asked.

The three of us looked at one another, ignoring the clerk's question. We had to tell Geer, but exhaustion was beginning to creep up on me.

I closed my eyes briefly. "Can we deal with this tomorrow?"

Edwin put a hand on my shoulder. "Sure, why don't we all head back to my place."

"You're not counting me in, are you?" Jasper looked reluctantly hopeful.

But we were in fact, counting him in.

Edwin and Mea closed up the apartment, leaving it exactly as we found it, confinement spells and all. Now the only thing magically trapped on Jasper's bed was a spare pillow, but you couldn't tell the difference when examining the magic from the outside.

Edwin took all of us back to his place, where he immediately conjured a bucket for Jasper. The clerk curled up on the living room floor, making a bigger deal out of his nausea than seemed necessary.

"Am I going to be fired?" whined a despondent Jasper as he lay on his back, bucket balanced on his chest.

Mea helped him up, being kinder than Edwin or me.

Edwin huffed. "Your employment status isn't our problem, but I guess you'll find out when we see Geer tomorrow. For now you're stuck here with me."

Jasper clung to the bucket. "What, why? Not that I'm not glad you rescued me, but I can't be trapped here. How is that okay? I don't get why you couldn't leave me at home."

Edwin turned abruptly and walked away as if he'd reached the end of his rope and couldn't do another second of Jasper.

Mea clenched a fist at her side, betraying her own loss of patience. "Jasper, it's looking extremely likely that Judge Herrera did this to you after your deal went awry. It's best if she doesn't know we've freed you. So you can't go to work or be seen coming and going from your apartment. We re-sealed your place as a temporary ruse, but if the judge or whoever trapped you goes back and sees you gone, we don't want them to be able to find you and attempt anything else. So you'll have to stay here until we can present our case, with you as a witness."

"Case? *Witness?* But what we did wasn't illegal." Jasper took a few steps back and bumped into Edwin's couch. "You can't hold me here."

Edwin returned holding a glass of water. "We could go see Judge Geer now, rather than in the morning. You could ask to stay with him instead."

"Wait—" Jasper waved his hands in a calm down motion.

"Trying to befriend Juliet under false pretenses wasn't technically illegal, but what happened to you is," Edwin said in the condescending tone that gave him his unfriendly reputation. He then undermined this by handing Jasper the water. "It's possible there might be something else going on here. Unless you really think your deal with the judge was about nothing more than learning *everyday stuff.*"

"Oh." Jasper gave us a look of dismay. "Something else, like what? Like she used me for more than she was telling me?" He sipped the water gratefully.

"She just might have, Jasper. Now let me show you to the guest room." Edwin led the way down the hall.

23

MEA

*J*uliet ordered take out for dinner. Her disinterest in cooking wasn't a great sign, not that one was needed. Who would be in good spirits after finding out a family member asked a random person to pose as a friend to spy on you?

We were picking at our food in silence when the doorbell rang.

"Want me—"

"No." Juliet rose from her seat. "It's fine. I'll go."

With all the protection on the place it couldn't be anyone dire, but I found myself straining to listen to the muffled voices, just in case.

Juliet returned with Easton. My low spirits sank.

The Witch surveyed our half-eaten food. "Do you mind giving us a moment, Juliet?"

She made a huffing sound, picked up her plate and walked off toward the living room, heels clicking.

"It's her house. We could have stepped out." I didn't get up or offer Easton a seat at the table.

He joined me anyway. "This is fine—I needed to check in. I heard your meeting wasn't the most productive on Sunday."

What had he heard? It didn't seem like Judge Herrera told anyone Juliet and I disappeared on her. I was sure I'd have been questioned about that right away, not three days later. "It wasn't as productive as I'd hoped either. The judge didn't offer more than her concern for Juliet. It was a more personal call than anything else."

Easton scowled. "Of course she's concerned. The judge also said you were less than cooperative, and didn't make an attempt to get Juliet to engage with our efforts."

"What efforts? Judge Herrera made no concrete offer to do anything. And the rest of the Authority—what are you actually doing to solve this?" My voice was close to being raised but I didn't care.

"Excuse me? We're doing plenty. What are *you* doing? Other than palling around with a potential suspect." Easton picked up a chip and popped it into his mouth.

It was outrageous that he wasn't joking. Twisting things back on me when all I was doing was asking straightforward, relevant questions. Pointing out that just because the judge said she was helping didn't mean she was actually doing anything. But, as always, the Witches in charge had the last say and there was no room to disagree. How had I ever thought getting away from particular people would make a difference, or affect how things in any part of the Authority were run?

I ground my teeth. "You told me to stay here with Juliet. Don't act like I'm doing something wrong. I've done everything you've asked."

Easton cocked his head. "So you don't deny she's still a suspect? Interesting."

"What? No. Of course she's not. There have been two attempts to get through magical protections around Juliet. She's obviously a target." *Is he serious?* I stared at Easton, trying to assess his every movement.

The Witch didn't look convinced by my adamant denial. "Juliet is the only *target*"—Easton made air quotes with his fingers—"who hasn't been successfully whisked away. Not to mention, there's no sign of a motive for anyone other than Juliet to go after the three victims."

"And what's Juliet's motive?" I had the distinct feeling trying to point out logical holes in Easton's argument wouldn't matter. He'd never liked Juliet and was counting that as evidence in itself when it was nothing of the sort.

Easton picked up another chip. "Breakdown of working relationships, revenge, attention seeking."

I looked at him in what should have been disbelief but was more like predictable outrage. "None of that is supported by facts."

The man took a moment to chew before saying, "I've heard Juliet has a history of making unsubstantiated claims and trying to paint herself as a victim to gain others' trust. That seems to fit this scenario."

"Where did you even hear that?" Not that I needed an answer. Who else would spread something like that, and have enough sway to get the likes of Easton to listen, other than Juliet's mother? "That sounds like a bunch of bullshit."

"Language." Easton glared at me. "I don't need to justify my sources to you, Ms. Dubois. Maybe we shouldn't have had you on this. I thought your history with Juliet was defined by a mutual dislike. Some sort of petty rivalry. I never thought you'd be biased in her favor. Just know we're looking into all possibilities, no matter what you think the completely useless *attacks*"—more air quotes—"on Juliet mean."

What it looked like was the judge seeding doubt before Juliet could expose her. Had she told Easton her 'concerned' visit was out of worry Juliet was involved? I wasn't shocked Easton had fallen for vague suggestions against Juliet. He talked about bias when he was fine with it, as long as it aligned with his own.

I was afraid that even if Easton knew the truth—all Juliet's history, Jasper's weird deal—he'd still dismiss it all and side with the judge. That's what the Authority did, it looked after itself, kept people like Easton around even though there'd been complaints about how he handled things.

"Is there anything else?" I asked coldly. There was no point continuing this chat. Juliet, Bickel, and I were on our own and might be running out of time from the sound of things.

Easton scowled. "No. Just don't forget which of us is in charge here, Ms. Dubois."

24

MEA

My appetite had disappeared so I didn't bother returning to the kitchen after I'd escorted Easton out. I slipped quietly into the now-familiar living room, the towering books calming me unexpectedly.

Juliet sat on the couch, shoes off and feet curled beneath her. Her dinner was abandoned on a side table. She looked at me and I wondered if she'd been rubbing her eyes—they were red.

"I was listening," she said without emotion.

I sat down beside Juliet. "Good. Easton probably assumed you were. Though I don't know what he thinks broadcasting his unjustifiable suspicions will accomplish."

Juliet shrugged like she thought my colleague's actions were normal. "At least Edwin has faith in Geer."

"Yeah—but it shouldn't come down to Bickel's personal connections." I dropped my head back against the couch in defeat.

"I wish it hadn't come down to that either. It would be nice if people were as good and reasonable as you expected them to be, Mea." Juliet looked even wearier than I felt, like she was tired and no amount of sleep would help.

"Yeah, but I shouldn't expect so much of people like Easton who've already made it clear where they stand and how they see things." I should have learned this lesson before now, and not just with this one Witch. All the evidence had been there.

I'd always known what the Authority was like, that I couldn't solve the organization's problems and didn't want to be there if nothing changed. And I'd rationalized it away, practically ignored my gut feelings. I'd been determined to give the Authority chance after chance, not just because I tried to see the good in everyone and hoped things would improve, but because it was easier than the alternative. I didn't like change and sometimes, instead of being honest about what I wanted and figuring out how to best achieve it, I focused on how to preserve what I had, latching on to any small possibility of improvement. Making the best out of a bad situation that I didn't need to be in.

Like my engagement. If I'd been honest with myself I'd never have proposed. I'd known the relationship wasn't working, but instead of acknowledging that I needed something different I fought to preserve it despite my doubts.

Juliet put her hand on mine. "I don't like seeing you so dejected."

I picked my head off the couch and sat up. "Me? You're the one who's had a bad day."

"I don't want to say I'm used to it, because I'm really not." Juliet's hand remained unmoved. "But I've never expected better of anyone."

"Still, what your mom and Jasper were doing would be a shock. Easton—not so much—but sending someone to inform on you like that is terrible."

"It's shocking, and it isn't." Juliet gave an alarmingly casual flick of her wrist, hand disappearing from mine. "I can't say it gives me confidence in spreading my friend circle much further than Edwin. It's like my mother knew I was considering it and had to ruin it, even though I know that's not true. But I'd never have guessed it from Jasper, talking to him at the bar. That worries me. The whole thing doesn't make me inclined to trust new people."

"No, it wouldn't." I leaned in closer in a way I hoped wasn't too eager given the nature of what we were discussing. "But you want to?"

"Sure." Juliet picked up a book from one of the many piles, considered it, and moved it to another stack. "I seem to be failing at it though."

"No—"

Juliet cut me off. "You don't need to protest, Mea. I'm not saying this in a woe-is-me way, looking for comfort. I should have trusted you, even when I was caught off guard and afraid. I'm sorry. I'm really trying to be more open, and not fool you like I do everyone else. I just don't know if it's working, or if I'm actually getting anywhere."

She looked at me as if she'd asked a question. My gut reaction was to reassure her—*yes, everything's fine*—but I had to be honest, not pretend things worked for me as is.

"Opening up isn't going to happen overnight," I offered, needing to know if Juliet was willing to try and continue to open up, meet me halfway. That was when it was worth giving people the benefit of the doubt and sticking it out for a second chance. However, I couldn't make it happen on my own.

Juliet nodded, not otherwise reacting. She ran her fingers up and down the spine of a book.

I was trying to keep us in a cautiously optimistic space, but didn't know if her comment was quite enough, and she didn't offer more.

Sitting here, I couldn't ignore the last time we'd been on this couch together. The memory made me fluttery. There was no denying the spark between us. If only chemistry was all that was required. I knew it wasn't, and wouldn't fall into being the one doing all the emotional work in a relationship again, holding on to something that didn't work when no one else cared to fix it but me.

Getting closer to Juliet still felt like a risk. I could see her pushing me away when things were hard, if not turning on me outright and even if I understood why, that didn't mean I wanted a relationship like that.

Not really knowing what Juliet wanted was another challenge. To an extent she wanted me—as evidenced by the last time we'd been sitting here together—and she wanted a friend. She'd just said as much. But that sounded like friends with benefits more than anything. Given her challenges with trust, I didn't know if Juliet was ready for a relationship, and it would be a mistake to push for one.

Juliet turned away from the books and undid the silk scarf around her neck. She folded it and set it aside. "Things not happening overnight isn't necessarily a bad thing." She looked at me sideways from beneath her dark lashes, sounding optimistic for the first time this evening.

"Oh?" I'd assumed we'd left the conversation behind.

"You're still planning on moving here right? That hasn't changed?" Juliet gave me a sly look, maybe like she was trying to hide her interest.

"I think I'm coming around to your view of the Authority's expansion, actually." I hesitated, not wanting to say too much before I had a new plan.

"Huh. Is that so?" Juliet had a thoughtfully smug air about her as she fiddled with the edge of her skirt. "I'm not suddenly arguing in favor of expanding, but it would be good to see each other around more."

"Yeah, for sure." My optimism remained muted. Juliet's comment might only be in reference to expanding her friend circle. Which was good. I wanted that too, but it wasn't everything I hoped for.

Juliet smiled and for a moment it softened her whole face, like she was thinking about something wholly great. Then she frowned. It wasn't any less beautiful. I liked the severity and intensity, but had no idea what had triggered the change in her.

"I didn't like what Easton was saying to you."

Ah. Right. It wasn't the change in subject I wanted. I shifted in my seat, turning sideways and crossing my legs on the cushion so I could look directly at Juliet. "I know, I'm sorry. I can't believe he thinks you'd do any of this."

"What—no, that's not what I meant." Juliet made a dismissive gesture. "I don't like that he's spinning this in a way that implies you aren't doing your job. Easton should be on your side. I get why he's not on mine—but I worry that I'm ruining things for you."

She took me aback. "What?"

"No one at the Authority likes me. And hopefully we'll come through this case with proof I'm not a kidnapper, but I'm still not going to be popular. I don't like that my reputation is rubbing off on you. Even if everything goes as we hope, being buddies with me might not look good for you, Mea."

"We're buddies now?" I really didn't know what else to say. I'd never have thought about how others would see my friendship with Juliet, and it all felt irrelevant now. I didn't want to work with people who would take that kind of judgmental view.

Juliet looked like she wanted to laugh at my words, an almost-smile turning into good natured exasperation. "Oh, you know what I mean. Stop deflecting. I just don't want friendship between us to blow back on you. That's all." She averted her eyes, getting up and moving around the couch to the bookshelf.

I tracked her movement, twisting around where I sat.

Her words were touching, in a way. I could see what Juliet

was trying to do. She was trying to look out for me, save me from things going badly. Yes, she was going about it in a very Juliet way, but it was still kind. It seemed like she'd offer to distance herself, or pretend to for public perception if that was what I wanted.

I got up and joined Juliet at the bookshelf. She looked over her shoulder at me as she ran a hand idly along a some of the spines.

I shoved my hands in my pockets. "It's just a job, and definitely not one worth pushing you away over. Even for show." I could have said I was done with the damn job regardless, but I wanted this moment to be about us, not me coming to terms with a life change I hadn't been planning on.

I liked Juliet on my side. She was supportive when she wasn't thrown into defensive mode and had time to think things out. I just didn't know if the space we were in now—working together—would last, or if we'd always fall back into conflict. If stress would always prompt her to push me away.

I wanted to be on Juliet's team. This dynamic felt like something worth giving a second chance, even a third chance. It was worth persistence and working on when it sounded like both of us were on board. It almost made me want to say I'd do anything for Juliet, and that freaked me out, but maybe she'd offer the same for me.

"Thank you for saying that." Juliet sounded bashful, or maybe like she hadn't expected me to turn down her offer to save my public face. "I'm glad you're here with me."

I shifted closer to her. She raised her eyebrows and I blushed. "I'm glad I'm here with you too, but I wish there wasn't so much going on."

Juliet half chuckled, leaning back against the bookshelf. "I'm open to distractions."

It was all the suggestion I needed. I leaned in.

Was this a good idea? I had a flash of doubt. Shouldn't we figure out where we stood with each other first? But that felt too complicated. I couldn't settle on any one thing I wanted, so how could I expect Juliet to?

Maybe this dance back and forth was a necessary part of figuring out what we were to each other. Slowly opening up and clashing.

It was easier to lean into Juliet than to try and find the right words. I didn't need to be sure of her yet. Or know where my life was going. We were feeling each other out, and I knew without a doubt that right now I wanted the exhilaration of her touch. Maybe we'd be friends who slept together sometimes, maybe we'd turn into more if we could ever trust one another.

Maybe we'd be nothing more than this—bouncing from conflict to comfort and back again—and that wasn't necessarily bad.

I ran a hand through Juliet's curls and she closed her eyes at the touch, one of her hands bracing herself on a lower shelf.

"I feel good when I'm with you, Mea," she whispered.

Knowing that was a thrill. The last of my hesitation disappeared.

I kissed Juliet's dark red lips, pressing against her and gripping the shelf on either side of us. When we were like this, I felt good too.

She could frustrate and baffle me to no end but then be the most comforting person out of nowhere. I craved those polarizing feelings. Her soft lips, her sharp words. I didn't know if that was enough to create something lasting, but right now that didn't matter.

Only good mysteries and secrets lay between us as we kissed.

I didn't always have to worry about the bigger picture. Juliet might not be. I suspected she worried a lot, but with us it seemed like she was able to switch off and just be with me. We had the best moments together. No one's hands had ever felt so right on my hips. If we could be good for each other when we most needed it, did we have to always work?

I could accept this thing between us for what it was. Perfect, right now. I wanted this comforting feeling so badly amidst everything else. Part of me liked not knowing what would happen with us next. It kept me hooked in a good way, when in the rest of my life the unknown terrified me.

"Take me to bed?" I breathed between kisses.

Juliet pushed me back with a gentle hand, then reached out to cup my face. I felt like she was searching for something and I tried to give it to her. I didn't look away, and if such a thing were possible to convey, I told her how much I needed her with my eyes and body language. I didn't shy away from feeling desperate or letting her know it.

I liked giving Juliet my unfiltered emotions and seeing what they did to her.

One of Juliet's hands tightened in my hair. She leaned in to kiss me on the cheek and down my neck. I let out a breathy sound and felt her smile.

"Come on, Mea." Juliet slipped out from between me and the books and held out a hand.

I let her lead me to her bedroom. As we reached the bed she let go of my hand and stepped back from me. I made an involuntary sound.

Juliet smiled, bringing that sharp beauty back to her face. "I'm not going anywhere."

I knew that, but still liked her saying it.

Juliet put her hand on her hip and looked into my eyes. I'd rather her hands were on me, but I waited, feeling the tension grow between us. Juliet's hand moved along her hip and up to her waist, where she undid her belt and let it fall to the floor.

She shimmied out of her skirt and let it pool around her ankles. The hem of her white button up blouse fell beyond her hips, not quite hiding the black fabric of her panties.

"God, you're hot." My need intensified. I moved closer to Juliet and rested my hands on her hips, under the shirt.

Juliet took a strand of my hair between her fingers. "And you're just a little bit desperate for me, aren't you?"

I sucked in a breath. "More than a little."

I loved her confidence. It felt different here than out in the wider world. That confidence was part show and part defense, this felt closer to who Juliet was: a woman who knew her body and her wants and didn't pretend to apologize for them.

I'd have thought Juliet would have given me one of her wicked grins next, but she treated me to a look of such warmth that it made me all fluttery inside.

Juliet slowly unbuttoned my shirt and let it fall, followed by my bra. She ran her hands over me, the silver of her rings catching the low light in the room as her fingers teased me. She kissed along my collarbone and between my breasts, her fingers circling my nipples. She was gentle and caring, but not giving me the kind of firm touches I wanted most.

She got down on one knee and kissed my stomach and hips as she undid my pants. Juliet peeled all my clothes away until I was naked, but she didn't touch between my legs, only caressed my thighs as she looked up my body.

I waited in strained anticipation of what she'd do next. I could have made a few requests and had no doubt she'd happily grant them, but I liked putting my pleasure in Juliet's hands.

She nudged my hip with her manicured fingers, not quite pushing me but letting me know what she wanted me to do. I stepped back and sat on the end of the bed. Juliet spread my legs, putting herself between them. She gave me one of those wicked looks then and I blushed.

She kissed up my thigh before putting my leg over her shoulder. I gasped in expectation, but she didn't put her lips where I needed them. Juliet teased me until I was panting, and I tried to be patient.

Slowly losing control and no longer able to stay upright, I leaned back on an elbow, burying my other hand in my hair, overcome by pleasurable frustration.

Juliet took that moment to move her mouth and licked my clit in a slow, firm motion. My moan filled the whole room. I hadn't even realized I'd closed my eyes, but when I opened them, I found Juliet looking up at me. She sucked and my hips jerked before I collapsed backward onto the bed completely.

My thoughts became less coherent as Juliet continued to tease me, letting me get close and then changing what she was doing until the only thing I was aware of was building tension.

When I begged, Juliet pulled back and said, "Not yet."

I let out a protesting whine.

"Don't worry, Mea. I'll give you everything soon." Juliet's voice was husky with desire, but I was too boneless to pick my head up and look at her.

I told her I trusted her and meant it completely.

I wasn't sure if Juliet said anything in response, I had the impression she'd started to say something and then she was back to distracting me from thoughts with her mouth. When her lips closed around my most sensitive spot, I came in a dizzying wave.

I drifted in a content cloud, relaxed but not sleepy, just in my own head and enjoying everything.

"Come up here, Mea."

I blinked and turned to Juliet where she was now lying on the bed, propped up on an arm amongst the pillows. She patted the pillow next to her. I still had my legs dangling off the edge and slowly turned over to crawl towards her. On my way up I paused and pulled Juliet's panties down and tossed them away, then undid the buttons of her blouse, kissing her soft exposed skin as I went.

Juliet pulled me to meet her mouth. She tasted like lipstick and me.

We kissed almost lazily, touching each other in soft strokes. My fingers trailed over Juliet's belly button and she gasped like she was ticklish.

"I trust you too, Mea," Juliet whispered.

My heart skipped. Was Juliet only trusting me to give her what she needed sexually? Or did her feelings extend beyond what we were doing right now?

Would she show me if they did?

Not that the question was going to be resolved here in bed. However, I'd still relish this time together. Not being sure we'd ever be all in didn't make this meaningless.

Juliet was already pulling me into a kiss, not waiting for me to respond to her words, and that was okay. I hadn't known what to say, so perhaps it wasn't the time to say anything.

Instead I trailed my fingers over Juliet's hip and down to her thigh. She let her legs fall open and I followed the invitation and touched her, making her sigh.

Juliet rocked into my touch and murmured against my lips. She was telling me how wonderful I was—as a whole or at getting her off, I wasn't sure. Not having it clarified only meant it might be both. I thought Juliet was wonderful too, in any context, and I murmured this back to her, leaving no need for her to wonder exactly what I meant.

Juliet kissed me hard and pushed me all the way onto my back. She focused on my face like she'd come out of a trance and sat up, shifting so she was straddling me.

"How's this?" she asked.

I ran my hand up her thigh and slipped my fingers between her legs, moving them in tight circles. "Perfect."

She looked radiant, her dark hair tousled, curls falling every which way. The crumpled blouse was open and half off one shoulder, exposing her nude lace bra and full breasts.

Juliet could have anything she wanted from me and I needed her to know it. Could she already tell? Maybe I should say it. But we were both breathless and I lost my train of thought as Juliet's orgasm unraveled her, leaving us both panting. She collapsed onto me and I wrapped my arms around her.

Juliet murmured my name in my ear.

It felt like a request, almost a plea. Not quite knowing what it was for didn't stop me from whispering back, telling Juliet yes, I was here.

25

JULIET

It was morning. I could tell by the light but didn't want to get out of bed. Mea had left some time ago and I'd promised to meet her in the shower, only to drift back to sleep.

The water was still running in the bathroom but that wasn't what had roused me. Groggily I realized my phone was buzzing on the bedside table. Cursing the device, I picked it up without looking at the caller, just wanting to make it stop. "Yes?"

"Juliet," came my mother's crisp voice.

I sat up in bed, my pleasant drowsiness instantly replaced by a dull headache. "What?"

She made an unhappy sound. "No good morning—how are you?" She paused pointlessly. "I'm calling to try again, Juliet. After the disappointment of the other day. Can't we talk?"

I narrowed my eyes at the empty bedroom. "Sure. What about? The real reason you came to see me?"

"Yes. If we must." Admitting she had veiled reasons wasn't the response I'd expected. My mother let the silence stretch and I held my breath in anticipation. "I want to discuss the future, find a way forward that works for both of us. You know what I need from you. So come home, and we'll work out our differences. I mean—there's no way you want to stay where you are, not knowing who's working against you."

I was suddenly too warm in bed even though I was mostly out of the covers. Yes, I knew what my mother needed from me, but I wasn't removing the restrictions I'd placed on her. "Who's to say I don't already know who's working against me."

"Oh? Have the investigators figured out who's behind it? Has an arrest been made that I'm not aware of? Wait—" The judge made a dramatic breathy sound that almost sounded like a gasp. "I have heard something—there's really only one person of interest."

I ground my teeth in response to my mother's over-the-top sweet tone and didn't take the bait. The only person of interest was me, if Easton were to be believed. I glanced toward the bathroom, the shower still running. "I have to get going, if that was all you wanted to say."

My mother didn't hesitate this time. Maybe I'd surprised her with the dismissal. "What if I said I knew who was behind all your trouble, Juliet? That maybe I could do something about it."

"That wouldn't be a surprise," I grumbled, throwing back the rest of the covers and getting out of bed. Now if only she would admit it was her instead of circling endlessly around what we both weren't saying.

It's you and we both know the other knows it.

The sound of a creaking door shutting came over the phone line and my mother dropped her friendly demeanor, her voice echoing as if she'd just walked into a parking garage. "Yes, of course *you* know who's behind the disappearances, Juliet. Don't be so sure you'll get away with it. You might think that the attempts on your home and the coffee shop clear you of blame, but it's not impossible for you to have orchestrated those attacks yourself."

Technically she was right, magic could be set up to run while the casting Witch did other things. I'd like to think no one would believe it of me, but I knew better than that.

My mother was still talking. "Come home and help me out, Juliet. I'll make sure none of this points back to you. You'll need all the help you can get if any more evidence against you turns up."

Any more? There was none to start with. But was she implying there would be? Were things about to get a lot more solid?

I stopped in front of my dresser, dropping the clean pair of underwear I was holding. My heart rate picked up despite my innocence. As the Authority member behind the disappearances, my mother was perfectly placed to frame me in a much more conclusive way than had been done so far. But I held my ground. "There is no evidence against me. Only one man's suspicions and your whispers."

She *tutted*. "You sound very sure. Almost as if you've bought into your own delusions."

Delusions? Was she serious?

I didn't bother countering her comment. Challenge didn't serve any purpose in this game. My mother wouldn't back down from her insults or accusations regardless of their inaccuracy or irrelevance. Trying to argue against her only made me feel helpless, so I tried to focus on what mattered. "Have you forgotten the Authority has an agent watching me? Anything from the third disappearance onward, they know I haven't done."

My mother's voice turned cold and unfeeling. "That logic assumes you're working alone. Loner that you are, some might suspect that. But you have one very notable companion. I doubt anyone can account for his whereabouts." She cut the call before I could reply.

I set the phone down and leaned against the dresser. This was an angle I hadn't considered. Telling Easton and whoever else that I was behind the disappearances was one thing, but implying Edwin was involved along with me was quite another.

Panic flared in me. How dare my mother involve more people than she had already. Wasn't it bad enough to kidnap innocents? No, she had to go after my only friend. She knew first-hand what even the whiff of involvement in criminal activity would do to Edwin. It wouldn't matter if my mother's claims were baseless, and proven false—rumors could ruin Edwin just the same.

I'd never let her do that to him, not after all he'd been through.

He could escape the shadow of doubt once, but twice would be pushing fate. Witches' memories were too long, and Edwin's power had always put people on edge, their fear making them quick to believe the worst.

Me on the other hand—I didn't care if everyone thought I did it, as long as I proved otherwise to the Witches that mattered. I spent a lot of time worrying what people thought of me, but that was all rooted in my personality and fearing I didn't know myself. This was different and didn't scare me in the same way. The stigma of these accusations could follow me around forever and I'd only turn it into armor. But not so for Edwin. And Mea—regardless of what she'd said last night, she'd have to distance herself from me soon, if it wasn't already too late.

Neither of them needed to be involved in this feud. But my mother had come for me thoroughly. She knew I'd never free her power to save myself; I'd let spite bolster me to my grave. Only for others would I feel trapped into considering desperate actions.

I tried to cling to confidence that, in the end, we would prove who was behind this mess. But what if revealing everything now was too late? *What if we can't prove it was my mother after all?*

Jasper wasn't enough, he hadn't proved anything worthwhile and we had nothing else.

Confessing to my own illegal magic use could be part of the proof; it revealed my mother's motive, but wasn't enough either. There was too much room for doubt, even with psychics. We had to find the rest of the Witches and with them solid facts not dependent on anyone's word, or account of personal history. Things that reputation couldn't obscure or confuse. I needed to tell Geer everything, and should have done so yesterday. What if, even now, my mother was telling him and the other judges her version of events?

Fear of not being believed had contributed to me keeping this quiet in the first place, and now that decision might come back and give everyone reason to cast doubt on me. It felt like backward logic and a slap in the face.

The shower continued to run, the faint sounds of Mea singing drifting through the air. I tried not to feel the things she stirred in me. Whatever was starting with us felt impossible now.

Last night Mea didn't seem concerned about any lingering effects this case might have on her, but what if my mother found a way to cast suspicion on Mea too? More than her career, or transfer to a new city could be at risk. The best-case scenario was Mea escaping my shadow before it became damning, worst case this ruined everything for her too. There was no room for a relationship anywhere. I could only be glad my mother didn't know what Mea meant to me, and hoped it would stay that way.

I'd sensed a change in the woman, even though I'd only spoken to her twice. My mother wasn't the same person as the one I'd known. In the past she never would have involve someone from outside the family in our conflict. Growing up, the secret that things were not okay was kept without exception. Involving others now felt like a significant step.

How far would my mother go? Setting up innocent people could be the extent of her plan, or maybe just the start. The missing Witches were still alive, as evidenced by the failed location tracking spells, but for how long?

What might have become of Jasper if we hadn't found him when we did? Why had he been at home? Was he supposed to be found? I couldn't see why unless we'd gotten there a bit too soon. Maybe another scene was supposed to have awaited discovery.

My mother might find it more compelling to threaten me and my friends with murder charges than kidnapping. If Judge Herrera succeeded in putting Edwin and me away as murderers, no one would believe anything we said again. My history would be assumed to be nothing but lies and Edwin's would be used as proof he'd always been heading toward a bad end. Was that the next move if I didn't give in? Or was I blowing things out of proportion, determined to see the absolute worst in everything?

The shower clicked off at last. I felt a pang for disappointing Mea and not going to her. But it was for the best. There was no need for either of us to get more attached when everything was about to go to shit.

I sent Edwin a quick text, asking him to meet me as soon as he could.

Mea was making sounds in the bathroom, moving around and opening draws. I dressed quickly and hurried out of my room. I should have waited for her to emerge, but I was a coward and needed more time to organize myself.

I went to brew some coffee. The sound of the grinder crushing the beans screamed in my ears, my head pounding even worse than before. I longed to crawl back in bed.

The sound of the front door jarred me out of a daze.

"Hi," Aria called out from the dining room.

"Morning," I called back, my voice sounding the same as

ever. But of course it did, I'd spent more time learning how to pretend to be fine than figuring out how to genuinely get there. And with that thought came other revelations I didn't care to look at.

I poured myself a coffee.

"Any chance I can snag some?" Aria poked her head into the kitchen.

"Sure, help yourself."

She selected a mug and looked at me closely, seeming unsure what to say.

"I'll take one too." Mea was as bubbly as ever as she entered the kitchen. She was dressed in different clothes than yesterday, meaning she'd slipped by to her room without me noticing. For some reason that made me feel lost.

Aria looked between us, her attention lingering on me once again. "I'll just be in the other room if you need me." She slipped through the doorway and out of sight.

"What's up, Juliet?" Mea came close and reached out, touching my hand.

I pulled Mea against me and let out a sigh. "I'm sorry I abandoned you in the shower." Suddenly apologizing felt incredibly important. I should have gone and found her instead of running out here.

Mea brushed a bit of hair out of my face. "That's all right. We'll make up for it. But what's going on? You look pale."

I looked into Mea's hazel eyes like I was trying to memorize them. I wasn't avoiding talking to her, that wasn't why I was quiet. I was stuck, like my mind had stalled out. I didn't want to have to give up this new thing blooming between us.

A muffled footstep followed by the sound of Aria gasping came from just beyond the kitchen.

"I seem to have scared Aria, but it was unintentional this

time." Edwin came into view. "I fear I'll soon be forced to knock on the front door."

Seeing the mischievous look on Edwin's face made my heart twist. I wanted to tell him I'd never do such a thing, he was always welcome to barge into my home, but that assurance was insignificant compared to everything else.

Edwin lost his levity at the sight of me. "What's wrong?"

I looked between him and Mea and didn't know what to do. Maybe I could stand here, just for a second and hope it helped. Mea was still holding me and I leaned in, smelling my shampoo in her wet hair.

Eventually I turned back to Edwin. "Where's Jasper?"

He paused like he was considering insisting I tell him what was wrong. "Mr. Suarez is sitting in Judge Geer's office. I've just come from there. The judge wants to talk to you, Juliet. I didn't mention anything about your history but he has questions about Jasper's arrangement with your mother."

I nodded. "Did Geer say anything about our delay in seeing him after finding Jasper last night?"

Edwin frowned. "No. Why?"

Mea cocked her head beside me. I could feel her gaze on me.

Not dealing with Jasper immediately had been a mistake. If my mother made accusations against Edwin, could him keeping Jasper overnight be taken as evidence of Edwin's involvement? Would it make it seem like Edwin had set the whole thing up, and thus wasn't worried about reporting what we found right away?

"Who else has Geer seen this morning?" I asked instead of answering Edwin's question.

"I don't know." Edwin studied me as if he were waiting for me to expand on the question.

Mea turned me to face her. "What are we missing, Juliet?"

Looking at her, I told myself I could do this, braced myself and recounted the conversation with my mother. "What if she's already seen Geer this morning?"

Edwin didn't appear as worried as he should be. "If so, he didn't give anything away when Jasper told his side of the story. Charles doesn't have the best poker face. It didn't look like he was holding anything back, or like he was drawing nefarious conclusions about my involvement in things. He seemed surprised to hear your mother's name at all."

That was missing the point. I tried frantically to explain. "Geer's surprise might just be because he can't believe his colleague would collude with Jasper like that. Maybe Geer was surprised to hear her name again, after she came to him to spread her theories about us."

"We can't know either way." Mea's steady voice interrupting my anxiety spiral. "We need to go talk to Geer now, fill in everything we held back yesterday and see what he says. There's no point worrying what else he's already heard. All we can do is move forward."

"And then what?" Edwin was still examining me, eyes narrowed. He knew me better than Mea, and his mind worked like mine. He'd likely guessed what I was about to say and didn't look pleased.

"I need to do what my mother is asking."

Mea stiffened at my side. I should have pulled away but only pressed tighter against her.

"No." Edwin's expression hardened, and not in the way it did when he was hiding his thoughts. It was a look I'd never seen, some mixture of determination, fear, and something like betrayal.

"She's going to frame us, Edwin. We can tell Geer everything, but we've run out of time to get proof to back it up."

Edwin started pacing back and forth, shoes clicking on the kitchen tile. "Let her try. We already knew things were heading in this direction. Easton has been suspicious of you from the start. Not much has actually changed. There's no need to be rash."

I felt a flash of annoyance. "Everything has changed. I just—I'm not letting her fuck you over, Edwin. Not again."

He was calmer than he had any right to be. "How is she going to frame me, Juliet?"

"I don't know, but come on. You know the advantages that come with her position. And she's clever. She'll find a way—not that I'll let her. All I need to do is make her believe I'm going to undo the spells. I'll go home, do what I have to in order to stop this going any further. I'll demand she free the Witches before I free her power."

"Will she go for that?" Mea sounded skeptical.

I turned away from Edwin to find Mea looking deeply conflicted. I didn't know what she was torn between. "My mother will have to go for it. I'll make it seem like the only way to get what she wants."

Edwin put a hand on my shoulder, pulling my attention and making me feel like a pinball between them. "What do you think Judge Herrera will do when you don't hold up your end of the deal, Juliet? What's to stop her from doing something even worse when she finds out you lied?"

As long as worse didn't put him, Mea, or anyone else in harm's way, I didn't care. This was between her and me, and I'd make sure it stayed that way from here on out. "I'm hoping freeing the Witches will be enough to pin this on her. There will be proof there, you just have to find it. That way we don't have to worry about what she'll do when she realizes I've lied. She'll have bigger problems."

Mea shook her head. "What if the captured Witches are all as clueless as Jasper? What if they have no idea what's happened to them?"

She was right. This flimsy plan wouldn't work. My mother wouldn't leave anyone able to point to her, unless she'd always planned to kill them. Even then, it would be smarter to cover her trail as she went. There might be no solid proof, short of catching her in the act of releasing the Witches.

But as long as they were freed and no one other than me faced consequences— "We'll go to Geer. Now, before I make a move. Tell him everything. If he knows our plan in advance, hopefully he'll back us up when the time comes."

"Juliet." Edwin's hand hadn't left me. He squeezed my shoulder, almost too tight. "One out of seven isn't good odds. Geer is only one judge, sitting on the same committee as your mother. The way the other five will fall, we can't be sure."

Edwin was right but I wouldn't back down. His blue eyes fixed me as if trying to drill into my soul, but Edwin's stare wouldn't work on me. He couldn't change my mind when I was doing this for him. One of us deserved to move on from our pasts. I hadn't dealt with mine and now it was time. He couldn't do this for me or use his power to stop it, any more than I could let it take him down alongside me.

"She'll never release the Witches if they can point back to her. You know that," Edwin said.

"But they have to be found. I need to at least try to get them freed. Then, either way it will all be over."

"*Either way?*" Edwin took off his hat and crunched it in frustration. He was seething, cheeks going red. "Can I have a private word, Juliet? Mea, do you mind?"

Mea checked to see what I wanted with a questioning look, like she didn't mind giving us space but only if I didn't need her by my side. I gave her a slight nod and she grabbed her coffee before slipping out the back door.

I didn't want her to go and hoped she didn't feel like I was pushing her away. In this case, it wasn't fully my choice if she got to hear this conversation. I didn't know what Edwin needed to say. It wasn't just about me.

At the soft click of the sliding glass door, Edwin exploded. "What the *hell,* Juliet?"

"Aria is still here," I said, keeping my calm.

He stalked out of the room. "Put on some noise cancelling headphones or go outside, Little Witch." Aria grumbled a response and then Edwin was back. "Juliet—you don't need to let your mother frame you to save me."

"I'm not," I all but lied. "I'm forcing this mess to end. This is about me and her. It's my decision if other people get dragged in. And I refuse to let this happen to you."

"You don't have to do that. I can handle it." The red had spread all the way to Edwin's ears. "I'm not broken."

"Of course you're not. I've never once thought that. I know you can handle anything, Edwin. I'm not treating you like you're fragile because of your past. It's not that at all. You just shouldn't *have* to handle it, not as collateral in someone else's fight. Okay?"

He stepped closer, none of the determination leaving his eyes. "Fine, Juliet. You care about me and that's—good. But you're acting like this is all your fault. Her actions aren't your responsibility."

I met his assertive stance with one of my own. We were practically chest to chest. "I can't control what she does, but I also can't sit back and let my mother hurt others. We tried to find evidence pointing back to her and got nowhere. If I don't take some form of action to resolve this, I won't be able to live with myself."

For a moment I thought he'd argue, but Edwin's posture relaxed like the snapping of a string, his tension gone as he leaned back against the counter. "Okay, I understand where you're coming from. Just don't worry about me, please. We'll go to Geer and get everything in order, as much as we're able, and pray for the best." He looked as if he detested the thought of placing so much on hope.

I reached out and cupped his elbow gently. "Thank you, Edwin. Honestly, it's overdue."

Frustration lined his face. "How do you mean?"

"I haven't dealt with—anything—for decades. I need to confront this now." Exhaustion almost overwhelmed me and I wished I'd never gotten out of bed.

I sipped the dregs of my coffee in search of any form of energy, feeling I'd held back from too much, for too long. And not only with my mother. The ominous *thing* I hadn't been looking at for years was creeping from the corner of my vision to the center, and in my worn down state I wasn't able to avert my eyes.

I'd held myself back this whole time, all these twenty-six years, but I hadn't only been holding back from the likes of Mea and casual acquaintances. I'd held back from myself. That was the problem. The reason everything felt wrong. I hadn't been open with myself in so long I didn't know what it was truly like. My lies weren't for others, or for protection from my past, but a crutch to keep myself from looking within.

Of course I hadn't moved on from what happened with my mother, the effect of her spells or how she treated me. I'd tried my best to ignore it all. I wasn't really afraid of opening up to Mea, or anyone. That was only a partial truth I told myself so I didn't have to take a real look at me. It was how I avoided dealing with anything.

Edwin shook his head, like he was worried I was losing my grip. "We did deal with things, Juliet. We confronted her. You made sure she could never mess with someone's mind again."

I almost laughed. "Really? Because she's messing with me pretty thoroughly right now."

He scowled. "You know what I mean."

"Yes, but what we did wasn't actually dealing with it. Or not fully. I mean on a personal level. I need to be upfront with myself, and not hide behind my own lies. I need to accept what those spells did to me and heal. Try to resolve what's between my mother and me instead of ignoring it, and if not—I have to stop holding on to the whole ordeal as my defining feature. Find a resolution for myself."

"But you have healed Juliet. You don't need to confront her again. There's nothing to prove. She's only manipulating you." Edwin looked pained and little bit worried, maybe uncomfortable not knowing what to do.

"Of course she's manipulating me. I know that. But I also haven't healed. I haven't processed any of my emotions or trauma or whatever, only run away from it and pretended everything was fine."

I wanted to open up without having to worry it was a risk. I wanted my life to be shaped by things I did rather than what I avoided. But I didn't think now was the right time to tell Edwin that. I knew he'd object because he had lived his last decades in almost the exact same way I had, and probably couldn't see any need for change in his own context. But I was ready for mine now.

Edwin blinked, as if taken aback. "I had no idea you felt that way. I thought we'd supported each other, and helped each other move on. I mean—look at the lives we've built."

"I know—I'm not saying you and I have made no progress over the last decades, or that we didn't help each other significantly. But maybe we both stalled out a while back and forgot to keep pushing forward. I didn't even know I felt this way until recently, or maybe I did and ignored it. You're my dearest friend." I grabbed his arm. "And you did support me. I couldn't have gotten anywhere without you, and not just because of magic. I'm just afraid that in many ways we helped each other not move on as much as we could have."

"But—" Edwin said hesitantly.

"No but. I needed your understanding back then exactly as you gave it. I still do. I'm not saying I'd change anything about our friendship. Only—there are more personal things I've ignored. I couldn't live without your unwavering support, but I think I needed a bit of a kick and a change of perspective."

"And we're too similar for that." Edwin looked hurt and resistant, but seemed to understand the core of it. "We're good for each other in some ways, but not others. I suppose I can see that."

"It's not that we aren't good for each other. I don't think it's that simple." I gave his arm another squeeze. "It's just good to see and try things different ways sometimes."

"How balanced of you." Edwin's tone was stiff, but he smiled. "So, Mea got you unstuck, did she?"

I returned his smiled and wondered if it looked hollow. "I don't know. Maybe she's forced me to confront thing without actually asking me to. This whole situation has been a kick in the teeth, and now I need to do something about it."

26

MEA

*J*uliet pulled me aside in the entryway before we left her house.

Bickel gave us a considering look and wandered off, the muffled sound of him talking to Aria floating over the entryway wall.

"I didn't mean to exclude you back there," Juliet murmured. She looked stricken, almost ill, like she was running a fever.

"Don't worry about it, really. I get that I don't need to be a part of you and Bickel's private conversations."

I didn't expect the guy to open up to me. Bickel had been involved in Juliet's problems with her mother for so long it made sense if there was a personal aspect for him in all this. This wasn't Juliet pushing me away when things got hard. I was glad to take a step back and let them deal with their disagreement.

"Right, okay." Juliet didn't appear relieved. She looked nervously toward the front door and back. "Are you sure you want to come with us?"

"To see Geer? Of course."

For Juliet it seemed like everything had changed this morning, though I couldn't help agreeing with Mr. Powerful-Witch;

we'd known accusations were heading Juliet's way before. I wanted to reassure her it wasn't too late, things weren't so dire she had to give in, but now might not be the opportune time to be looking on the bright side. I didn't want any assurances I made to come across as if I was discounting Juliet's feelings or reactions to what was happening. She could handle this. She was strong and resilient, not to mention innocent. We'd prove it.

But Juliet was more on edge than I'd ever seen her, and I hoped she wasn't about to tell me she didn't need me because that would be pushing me away. Surely not after her previous comment. Right?

Juliet took my hand in hers and rubbed circles with her thumb. "It might be best for you not to come to New York in case this goes badly. If you aren't a part of what Edwin and I are up to, then it can't hurt you. We won't contradict any story you want to spin."

I looked down at our hands.

There was no doubt they'd back me up if I wanted to claim I'd never been helping them. That wasn't what mattered here or had me worried. "Would you like me to go? Leave you and Bickel to sort this out by yourselves?" I asked as casually as I could.

Juliet took a shuddering breath and I tried not to hold mine. She looked me straight in the face, not hiding her emotions at all. "No, I don't want you to walk away from this. Maybe that's selfish, because it would be a safer bet for you to cut yourself off from me and go back to Terra and the rest of your team. But I think it would be better if we would do this together."

The mood wasn't right for smiling but I felt weirdly light inside. "It's not selfish of you to give me the choice, or tell me how you feel. If you think it would help, of course I'll come. Do whatever I can. I want to be here for you. It's nice to know you want me there too."

"Oh." Juliet's deep brown eyes were wide, her lashes almost fluttering in surprise. "That's—well. Thank you." She gave me a quick smile. "Just don't blame me if this ends up ruining your career."

"You're worth so much more than a job." I responded seriously even though I suspected she was trying to make light of things. "And even if you'd told me to leave, rather than give me the choice, I wouldn't be going back to Terra and the others. I'm done."

There was a charged silence.

All the tension returned to Juliet's face. "Done like leaving your job at the Authority? Because of me?"

"Not because of you, or even this case. It's the culmination of a lot of small things."

"So what will you do?" Juliet's brows were crinkled above an unsure gaze as if a thousand questions were passing through her mind.

"I have no idea." I shrugged, and even though not knowing twisted my insides, it was the most manageable problem we were facing right now. "Maybe we can talk about it later."

"I'd like that." Juliet's features relaxed with relief. Maybe she'd feared my abandoning my job and possible move also meant I was done with her. Before I could say anything, she gave me a little yank, pulling me forward. Juliet's forehead was hot against mine and we kissed in a brief meeting of closed lips.

Bickel cleared his throat.

Juliet pulled back, rolling her eyes at him and looking a lot less ghostly. "Let's go." She held out an expectant hand to the dapper Witch.

"That took longer than expected," Geer said the moment we appeared in his office. "I've been fending off meetings waiting for your return, Edwin."

"Apologies." Bickel surveyed the room. It looked unchanged from yesterday. "Where's Mr. Suarez?"

"I've sent him to have tea with my wife, at our home. She'll keep him out of trouble for the time being." The judge frowned as Juliet, Bickel, and I sat in the chairs arranged in front of his desk. "If I may be frank—I'm not sure what to make of his story, or your theory."

Bickel quirked a brow. "The theory that Judge Herrera trapped Jasper after he took their deal further than she'd intended?"

"Is there another theory I could have confused it with?" Geer sounded short of patience. "It seems very—extreme. No matter how harsh someone's personality, taking the leap to unlawful confinement is a lot. Not that I approve of either of them reaching out to you under false pretenses, Juliet."

Juliet looked deeply uncomfortable. "Yes. Well—there's a few things I've left out that will make the apparent leap seem more like a logical slide. Remember when Edwin mentioned the disappearances in my area might connect back to someone working here—"

As Juliet outlined everything from the beginning, her attention wandered my way, like she'd rather focus on me than Geer. I tried to project supportive vibes, and maybe it worked. The longer Juliet spoke the more she seemed to unwind.

Geer, on the other hand, became more and more frazzled the longer Juliet went on. "You're admitting to casting illegal spells of your own?" he squeaked when Juliet got to that part.

I wished he hadn't chosen that moment to speak up. Juliet faltered, probably worried Geer would get sidetracked and rather focus on her admitted wrongdoing than the rest, but she pressed on with Bickel's and my occasional interjections about current events.

"Blackmail? Framing? I don't want to believe it. How could this have been happening?" The judge pulled at his hair. It was no wonder it stood on end.

"It's not a question of want," Bickel reminded him.

"I know." The frown lines on Geer's face deepened. "I'm not saying I doubt you, Juliet. We'll have to validate your testimony psychically, but making such a serious confession of your own lends a certain credibility. We'll have to see what's to be done about that—but if it's all true, honestly I'm at a loss."

"I wanted better proof of what my mother was doing now, before explaining." Juliet was serious but didn't seem worried, glossing over Geer's implication she was in trouble herself more easily than I'd have been able to.

"I understand. But it's better I know—" Geer waved his hand at Juliet in reference to all she'd just told him. "If Judge Herrera has been acting this way for so long while keeping the rest of us easily fooled, she isn't likely to leave an obvious trail or make any overt threats. Waiting for something solid isn't the best way to deal with this. I mean, it sounds like everything she's said to you so far can be interpreted more than one way, and can thus be explained away."

"I know." Juliet's voice was tight with suppressed emotion. "But maybe that's why she trapped Jasper. He was a loose end connecting her, not to the kidnapping plot directly, but to less than reputable behavior in relation to me."

Geer's expression was distant, like he was lost in thought. "I'd always wondered why I never saw you around, Juliet. Given your career choice, your absence from certain circles didn't make sense. But now, I suppose there are a lot of small inconsistencies with your mother's comments about you that fall into question."

There was a long uncomfortable pause. Juliet looked like she wished painfully to be elsewhere.

"But this whole thing," Geer went on, waving his hands without restraint. "Edwin, Juliet, you really shouldn't have handled things the way you did all those years ago—"

"Yes, but—" Bickel jumped in defensively.

"But at least you were able to help Juliet, with the spells I mean. I'm not discounting that." The judge looked genuinely relieved for a second. "It's just a fucking mess, that's all."

My phone vibrated in my pocket. I held back a groan, hoping it wasn't Easton or even Terra. I unlocked it and looked at the message. It was from Carli, Ben Shaw's roommate.

Carli had messaged me yesterday as well, to check if I'd reached Ben. When I admitted we couldn't get through to him, she seemed to catch on to the fact that everything was less than fine. Carli had promised to forward me any messages she got from Ben, and this morning, her worry seemed to have intensified.

Her message read: *Look at this! Nothing can be wrong with Ben if he's chilling on the beach right?? Everything seems ok, please tell me you're able to catch up with him now!?*

Attached were two photos and a forward of the text Carli had apparently received from Ben. His message said: *Sorry Carli, service is so spotty here! But the beach is worth being offline haha. Not that I'm totally free, look I'm working on vacation *cry face emoji**

The attached pictures were a selfie of Ben on a white sand beach and a close-up of a folder that looked like it had an Authority label on it. The beach seemed like it could be remote, and thus possibly out of reliable cell-range. From what the shot showed, it looked like no one else was on the long stretch of sand behind Ben.

"Mea, what do you think?" Juliet's question pulled me away

from the messages. She was looking at me with intense concentration.

"Sorry, what?"

"Is something wrong?" Juliet glanced down at my phone.

"No—I just got a message from Ben, by way of Carli." I passed it to her.

"Who the hell is Ben?" the judge asked in exasperation.

Bickel peered over Juliet's shoulder at my phone. "He's an investigator here who we haven't been able to locate and who no one has seen, or received more than texts from, since Monday."

"An investigator? *Here?* Tell me you don't think that means he's missing." When no one contradicted him, Geer moaned. "Where does this end?"

Judge Geer really should have been able to handle this better, what with so many decades of experience. Maybe finding out Judge Herrera, whom he probably thought he knew well, was implicated in more than a few crimes was a personal breaking point.

I outlined what we knew and didn't know about Ben for Geer's benefit, trying my best not to get distracted by his theatrical facial expressions.

"If Jasper was confined because of his deal, has Ben done something similar?" Judge Geer pointed at my phone accusatorially. "Was he snooping around you too, Juliet?"

"No." Juliet was still looking at the texts. "The only reason I can think Ben's vanished is his ability to contradict Jasper's story about why he was trying to see me."

"That feels like a stretch." Geer raised a skeptical brow. "Maybe Ben has concealed his own whereabouts, and that's why your location spell failed. He could have a jealous ex or any number of people he wants to avoid. Some Witches like their privacy, you know. What if the texts really are from him?"

"But the sheer strength of the concealment spell means Ben didn't cast it. Not alone," I reminded everyone.

"He could have hired someone," Geer insisted. "Maybe he just doesn't want to answer his phone."

"But we can't assume these messages are from Ben with everything else we know is going on." Juliet zoomed in on a photo, scrutinizing it. "These images might have been sent from his phone to Carli, but it feels like too much proof. Like including work files screams see-it's-really-me even more than a selfie, which could be old for all we know. I mean, who'd bring work on a beach vacation?"

"You," I joked and Juliet flashed me a grin, like she knew I was right.

"Wait—he's sending pictures of Authority documents?" Geer seemed almost more alarmed than he'd been at anything else he'd heard today.

"It's just a folder. I wonder if it's even real, or if the number corresponds to a current case." Juliet passed my phone over to the frazzled judge.

He put on a pair of reading glasses and examined the picture. "That's a genuine file, I'd say. Nothing sensitive in the picture, but still. Not good practice." Geer made a *humphing* sound. "Why don't I look up the case number listed? Then when it matches, we can stop wondering if it's manufactured evidence he's working on the beach."

Geer tapped away on his computer as the rest of us shared a look. It seemed we were in agreement that the file being real didn't disprove that the photo was manufactured.

"See, this case is indeed assigned to Mr. Ben Shaw. Actually —I'd like to call him and ask him if he got approval to take materials out of the office. I know it seems small compared to everything else, but you can't let the little things slide." Geer set my phone down. I grabbed it off his desk as he picked up his landline.

After two tries the judge hung up in annoyance. "It's ringing, so he's not out of range."

I pulled up the photo of the work folder again. "You can't actually see the beach in this one. How do we know someone here didn't just photograph a file?"

"Yes, if Ben's been abducted by someone working here—" Bickel gave Geer a hard look. "The file isn't proof he sent the message himself."

"But he's on the beach!" Geer's voice rose. Maybe he really didn't want to believe it was Judge Herrera after all. "Why are you so convinced the texts are fake? He might not even be missing! The motive you gave is even weaker than the one regarding Jasper. Look—" He appeared to be trying to calm down and ran his hands through his wild hair. "Check the photo's what's-it-data. Meta data. My niece was telling me just last week how easy it is for Mortals to stalk people these days. She made me turn off my phone location, or something."

It was actually a good idea, though it didn't fit Geer's theory that Ben was concealing himself via magic. Surely he'd have his phone locked down if he was that worried about someone finding him.

Possibly, Geer only wished Ben weren't missing and was trying as hard to convince himself as us. He'd said he didn't want to believe any of it, and seemed determined to try.

I saved the pictures to my camera roll and opened them up. The one of Ben on the beach had no location or camera data attached, just today's date. Maybe he'd turned his location services off after all.

The next photo had more details, including the model of smartphone used to take it, which matched the phone we knew Ben owned. There was a timestamp from less than an hour ago, around the time we'd arrived here at Geer's office, and a location. But it wasn't a beach.

"This photo was taken in New York City."

"At the Authority building?" Juliet put out her hand excitedly for the phone.

I passed it over. "No. I don't recognize the streets."

"Well it's certainly *not* a tropical getaway." Juliet sounded triumphant. "Authority files shouldn't be loose in the city. That's not an address I recognize either."

Bickel leaned over to have a look. "*Hell—*" He snatched the phone from Juliet.

"What?" Geer and I asked as one.

"This isn't just somewhere in the city. That's—it's *my* building." Bickel gave Juliet a look of complete alarm, the vulnerability making him seem much too young.

Juliet reached out and placed a hand on his wrist, turning it slightly to look at the phone again, but I suspected she was actually aiming to comfort him with the touch. "No it's not, Edwin. What are you talking about? Your apartment is near the park. I don't even know that particular neighborhood."

"This obviously isn't my apartment. I own more than one building." Bickel's face turned to stone, re-aging him and making him look almost cruel. He passed the phone to the judge and Juliet's hand fell back to her lap. "That one in particular is a warehouse I've owned since the mid-eighties."

The atmosphere was tense. Geer seemed to have calmed down but in a way that made me miss his frantic mannerisms, as if seriousness didn't bode well.

"What are you using the warehouse for?" I held off on asking the obvious; how the hell could a photo taken and sent from Ben's phone have come from there?

"Nothing." Bickel was very still, looking at Geer unblinking. "It's rented out, as far as I know."

"Tell me it's not the same—well, you know—" Geer was almost pleading with Bickel. Of the two of them, it was impossible to tell which was more uncomfortable.

"Of course it is," Bickel said cryptically. "I haven't been there in over thirty years. The property is managed by a broker. I intended to sell—but didn't get around to dealing with it."

Juliet sat at attention. If her narrowed eyes were any indication, she was piecing together the fragmented bits of conversation. I was missing a lot more context here than she was.

Geer handed me back my phone but his focus remained on Bickel. "I'll need a record of who has access to the building, who manages it, and any spells cast on the property."

"Wait." Juliet stood up, her chair scraping back on the wood floor. "I just told you, Judge Herrera implied she'd frame Edwin this morning. That's all that's happening here. You don't seriously think Edwin has anything to do with this?"

"No—granted a minute ago I wasn't sure Mr. Shaw wasn't on vacation." Geer took a moment to look wildly between the three of us. "But pictures of Authority files taken in a building owned by Edwin, to set up fake I'm-okay-texts, seem like perfect evidence against Edwin himself." The judge held up a hand for us to be patient. "Evidence, which could be easily manufactured by a culprit who sits on our Judicial Committee."

"But how would Judge Herrera know about this warehouse? How would she know Bickel owned it?" I didn't want to poke holes in the theory now Geer was on board, but still needed clarity.

Everyone in the room looked at me. The atmosphere was so grim I almost didn't want to be let in on whatever I was missing.

Bickel didn't look at me. "It's a matter of Authority record, from my trial. The Judicial Committee in 1980's New York had the same members as it does today."

"Oh." I tried not to let my surprise show. He'd mentioned a trial, but I hadn't realized he was a defendant, not a witness.

"You know I'm not involved in this," Bickel said to Geer, his composure slipping, a note of pleading in his voice.

Juliet looked pained and I felt frustratingly out of my depth. I wasn't Bickel's biggest fan, or even a lukewarm fan, but I didn't doubt he was on our side.

"I know, Edwin." Geer slumped in his chair and it felt like we all relaxed a fraction. "And not just because I'm pretty sure you were in my office at that timestamp. I trust you. I'm only surprised you didn't sell the place."

Bickel took off his hat and put it on again, his hands clumsy. "I wish I had, but I put it off and forgot about it. For the most part."

"So you say." Geer's words made Bickel flinch. The judge hastened on, warning in his tone. "All I mean is—I know there's nothing to read into here, but others won't see it that way. They'll think you held onto more than the property."

Well that was ominous. Geer must have meant the other judges. What had Bickel said—one out of seven wasn't good odds?

"Okay." I slapped my hand on the desk a little too hard and Geer jumped. "Plan time. What are we going to do about this?"

"Yes, Mea. Thank you." The judge seemed to collect himself. "We need to take a look at the warehouse. Finding this hint pointing to Edwin's property seems almost too timely, given the apparent threat of framing only occurred this morning. No one would reasonably assume we'd be checking the location data of these messages. At least not immediately—this may have become a damning detail if it was discovered later, once accusations were officially made and investigators were combing through all sorts of records— But then, does that mean more conclusive evidence is at the warehouse? The missing Ben's phone, perhaps?"

"Or more than his phone," I suggested.

"What if we find the worst?" Juliet sounded nervous. "Whatever's there might make it harder to prove Edwin and I aren't involved, not easier."

"But if we weren't supposed to find this connection to Bickel yet, then it might be the perfect timing," I said, following a hunch. "Geer's right, it's a detail that may have been discovered eventually, when Ben was officially declared missing—and we know our kidnapper is thorough—but no one knows that Carli is forwarding Ben's messages. Hell, no one else knows we suspect Ben is missing. What if we go to the warehouse now, and like finding Jasper at home, we get there before—whatever is being set up eventualizes? We might find something useful, evidence your mother has been to the warehouse. Anything."

"I think Mea's right." Geer stood up and buttoned his suit jacket. "We should move quickly. See if we can get ahead of this framing plot. I feel that's better than trying to pretend to give into blackmail, Juliet." He turned to Bickel. "I do trust you Edwin, hopefully you believe that."

Bickel made an unintelligible noise.

Geer nodded. "Right. Can we have your permission to search your warehouse?"

The dapper Witch sighed and just the sound of it made me tired on his behalf. "Yes fine, I have nothing to hide. But that doesn't mean we'll find nothing there."

27

MEA

Juliet, Judge Geer, and I stood on a quiet street lined with warehouses waiting as Bickel talked on the phone. All the buildings in the area had seen better days, but our destination was by far the most neglected on the block.

My companions were distracted. Bickel uncharacteristically so, probably by whatever being here dredged up, and his uneasiness seemed to have captured most of Juliet's attention. Geer, I had the impression, was scattered more often than not, leaving me feeling like I had to be on alert.

Bickel hung up and shoved the phone into his pocket. "The property manager wasn't happy to hear from me. He says the building hasn't had a tenant in the last few years. And please don't ask me why I didn't know that. I paid the man so I didn't have to be bothered with this place. From the look of it, no one's been making use of the maintenance fee."

I tried to catch his eye. "And the protective magic? I know you haven't been here recently, but anything from before that's still in place could be helpful."

"There is no protective magic," Bickel grumbled, not looking at me

That was too bad. I'd have thought his distrustful personality meant everything down to his last sock was protected. It wasn't like spells expired. Surely this place didn't have bad connotations from the moment he'd bought it, and even the most basic protective spell, no matter how old, would help us now. It might not keep a powerful Witch out, but if someone broke through a spell to get in that would be evidence we could use. However, hindsight was rarely fair. He couldn't have seen this framing plot coming.

Bickel glanced at us, his stance becoming more defensive. "There were spells cast on this place once. The Authority ordered their removal. Undoing them was the last time I was here, and my broker is a Mortal. I could hardly ask him to cast protections."

A regretful silence followed his words.

"Ah well, nothing for it then, gang." Geer clapped his hands as if he were trying to bolster us. "Let's go in." The judge led the way across the street with a confidence he hadn't shown back in his office.

We ignored the large loading dock out front and entered through a side door into a small office lined with grimy windows looking out onto the open warehouse beyond. Everything was covered with a layer of dust, shelves and desk otherwise bare.

Bickel's usually pale face turned ashen, his blue eyes blazing with a mix of emotions I couldn't interpret. Geer seemed not to notice the other man's unease as he quickly scanned the room before exiting out a second door whose hinges protested loudly as he pushed it open.

Juliet stepped in front of Bickel. "You don't have to come with us."

"Don't be absurd," he snapped.

"Don't you dare call me absurd," she shot back with equal venom.

I wanted to tell her to give him a break, the guy looked ill. But Juliet knew better than me. Her reaction jarred Bickel out of the worst of his daze.

"Sorry, Juliet. I never thought I'd be back here. But it's just a place—my reaction is the only absurdity, not you looking out for me. Come on." Bickel marched after Geer, looking more like his usual self.

Juliet and I shared an apprehensive look and followed into the large open space that made up the warehouse. The only light came from windows high up along the wall behind us, casting long hazy shadows. A small stack of musty crates stood along the far wall but other than that the place was empty.

At the far end of the cavernous room stood a narrow staircase leading to a loft and a mezzanine floor that housed what looked like more offices or small storage rooms, all with windows facing out onto the warehouse floor. The only sound was our shoes on the cement floor as we made our way to the stairs. No hint of magic crackled in the air and it wasn't hard to imagine we were the first ones to set foot in here in years.

Maybe this was another dead end, staged as nothing more than a damning detail to work against Bickel. Even if we found Ben's phone, then what? We wouldn't be able to prove how it got here.

Geer and I ascended the stairs first. "It's been a long time since I've worked in the field," the older Witch said conversationally.

"Miss it?"

He looked back over his shoulder. "Not particularly."

Behind us Bickel snorted.

We turned down the hall and came to the first room. The door was shut, but turning the handle, I found it unlocked. Dust and stale air greeted me as I stepped inside a space as empty as the downstairs office. We moved on.

The second room held only overturned boxes and broken glass.

I reached for the last door handle and received a painful jolt as I tried to turn the knob. I pulled my hand away with a confused cry. I couldn't sense any magic, but my palm was sore enough to discount static electricity. I reached out for the handle again but didn't touch it. Heat was emanating from the metal, so hot I could feel it even with my hand hovering an inch away.

I turned to the others, who'd been watching closely.

Juliet looked like she was concentrating, eyes narrowed. "I can't sense anything."

"Me either, that's the problem. Whatever is in that room is hidden much better than Jasper was." Maybe we weren't getting here ahead of the game. Maybe whatever we were supposed to find was waiting exactly as it was intended to be.

"Could be dangerous." Geer said, as if his thoughts had followed mine. He beckoned Bickel forward. "It's a good thing we've got you with us, Edwin. Look sharp my man, and freeze things if anything dire jumps out."

No one made a move to deal with the door's hidden magic.

"We didn't come down here to stand outside." Geer nudged me out of the way and laid his hands on the door, crystal rings flashing as he muttered a counter spell to avoid being burned. He took his time analyzing the hidden magic, muttering and making animated faces as he pieced it all together. Once he seemed to have it figured out, Geer carefully unraveled the spell sealing the door.

A rush of magic burst forth, setting the air in the hallway alight with energy.

Geer gasped and pulled his hands back. He caught my eye, brushing his hands off on his jacket. "No harm done."

Now that I could inspect the spell properly, it felt familiar, reminding me of what we'd found at Jasper's apartment.

Geer threw the door open. Nothing jumped out. The room looked empty from where I stood.

The judge peeked in more thoroughly before entering. I followed closely with Juliet at my heels while Bickel waited outside. It looked as unhelpfully bare as the first two rooms. Dust covered everything from the floor to the empty shelves but there was enough magic bouncing around to hide any number of things.

I knelt down and placed a hand on the dusty floor to take a look. The spell's strength seemed to be about the same as the one we found at Jasper's apartment, and its purpose was similar.

One look at Juliet told me she was probably hoping the same thing I was.

I stood up and together Juliet, Geer, and I unraveled the spells. The magic dissipated and a shriek came from the corner of the room where four people were suddenly huddling, arms around one another.

Relief overwhelmed me. I recognized Sarah and Lana from photographs, and Ben was there too, looking largely unchanged since I'd known him in college. Except for the terrified look on his face. The fourth person must have been our third missing California Witch, whose identity Easton hadn't ever revealed. She looked as upset as the others, but at a glance they all seemed relatively unharmed.

The Witches clung together like frightened children, barely sparing a glance for me or Geer. Their eyes were fixed on Juliet, almost eerily focused and unblinking.

"Lana, Sarah, Ben, we're here to help." I took a step forward, arms outstretched in a non-threatening manner.

Sarah's attention snapped to me as if she truly hadn't noticed me until I'd spoken. "Please leave us alone!" She tried to back further away, leaving the safety of the group's arms, but the back wall trapped her. There was nowhere to go but she kept trying to back up, as if she didn't realize what she was doing.

"We're getting you out of here. Taking you home," I said as calmly as I could.

Ben looked around the room as if he hadn't seen it before. "Where are we?"

They were frightened and disoriented, and unlike Jasper, seemed to be having serious trouble getting their bearings.

"It's a trick," Lana whispered to the other captives. "Why else would she be here?"

All four of them glared at Juliet.

"She's the reason we're here." Ben pointed at her.

Juliet took a half-step back, worry lining her face.

"What do you mean?" Geer asked in a soothing voice, probably meant to sound understanding.

Ben glanced from Geer to me, like it was hard to focus. His gaze quickly flicked back to Juliet. "It's her fault."

"Perhaps it's best if you step outside, Juliet." Judge Geer put a hand on her shoulder.

Juliet shifted away from him. "I didn't have anything to do with this."

"Liar!" Lana yelled, making us all jump.

Juliet looked at me pleadingly, fear in her eyes. "You know I didn't."

I grabbed her by the shoulders and leaned forward until our foreheads almost touched. "Yes. We all believe you. But Geer's right, we need to talk to the Witches without you here. Something's not right. We need them to stop being distracted by you so we can figure it out."

Juliet nodded, her moment of panic gone like she trusted me completely. She left the room without further protest, something Juliet never would have done a week ago. I spared a second to appreciate what that meant, even though this was so not the time.

"You're letting her get away," Ben yelled as Juliet disappeared into the hall. He launched himself forward, arms outstretched like he meant to grab her.

Geer intercepted him with a firm hold around the guy's waist. "Steady on. Let's talk, Mr. Shaw."

Ben wiggled and thrashed until Geer let go. Ben didn't continue after Juliet, choosing instead to round on Geer. "Who the hell are you, old man?"

Geer's eyes went wide in shock. "*Excuse me*—that is completely uncalled—wait—you don't recognize me?"

Ben hesitated, anger still apparent, but uncertainty crept into his belligerent demeanor. He glanced back at the door where Juliet had disappeared as if Geer hadn't spoken and then back at the other three Witches still huddling in the corner. "Where are we?" He seemed like he'd only just remembered he was some-where strange.

"He already asked that. Something must be seriously wrong with his memory," Geer muttered to me before readdressing Ben. "Mr. Shaw, can you tell me where you work?"

Ben looked even more unsure than when he'd questioned his surroundings. "The Authority?"

Geer gave the guy a smile. "Yes, good. And I am—who? Have you seen me before?"

"No—" Ben's eyebrows drew together in confusion like he was trying to solve a particularly tough math problem and didn't want to.

There was no way Ben, an investigator for the New York branch of the Authority, didn't know Geer. We all knew the judges in our districts and presented to them in court as a regular part of our jobs.

"I thought Juliet said her mother could no longer alter minds outside the law," Geer whispered to me.

"She can't."

"Then who did this to him?" He pointed to Ben blatantly, but the befuddled man didn't react at all to our discussion.

"It must not be true mind-magic. Maybe it's a curse," I whispered. "If we can calm him down and analyze whatever spell he's under I bet you could break it."

Geer shrugged. "Let's hope so. Curses like that are dangerous and unreliable. Something might have gone wrong given he's acting so obviously strange. But one thing at a time." Geer turned to the man. "Do you know who did this to you, Ben?"

He perked up at the sound of his name, full of confidence once more. "It was Juliet."

Geer turned away from Ben. "And you're sure Juliet's whereabouts have been accounted for since late last week?"

"Yes. Of course." I knew he had to ask but couldn't help being afraid Geer was changing his mind. "Why would Juliet alter Ben's mind in such a sloppy way, letting him remember she was the one behind his confinement? She could have done a real alteration to his mind, one that would have been near impossible to detect."

"That may be, but it's still best for her to have the backing of a solid alibi, in case we can't free Ben from whatever compulsion he's under. We need to get these Witches back to the Authority. They'll need medical attention. If they've been left cursed like this for days, that's not good." Geer turned to the Witches, standing straight and looking more official than a moment before. "Can anyone tell me how long you've been here? Have you seen anyone else?"

"We're here now," Ben said with the kind of blind confidence that usually came with intoxication.

"I was at home yesterday," Sarah offered, seeming to genuinely believe what she said despite it being incorrect.

"What a damn mess," Geer grumbled, striding to the door and poking his head into the hall. "Edwin, can you please come here?"

Bickel appeared in the doorway looking no more lively than before.

"Help me take these four back to my office. We'll sort everything out from there."

Bickel scanned the room. "I can't take everyone at once, seven is too many."

Ben crossed his arms. "I'm not going anywhere."

"Would you rather stay here?" I was losing patience even though I knew the way he was acting wasn't his fault.

Ben glared at me. "I just—I demand to know what's going on. How do we know you aren't taking us off to kill us?"

Geer approached Ben in alarm. "Why on earth do you think we'd do that?"

Behind Ben the other three Witches were beginning to panic, looking around frantically and huddling as close together as possible.

Lana fixed her attention on Geer. "We'll go with you. Don't leave us here."

"I might as well take the willing ones first." Bickel made his way over to Lana and the others as if he were as keen to get out of here as the captives. "Link arms and we'll be on our way—be aware of the nausea." Half a second later they were gone.

Ben looked at the now empty corner of the room like he'd never seen magic before. "Who are you people?"

"Someone's really messed with your head, son." Geer moved closer. "Here, let me see—" He reached out a cautious hand.

Ben almost tripped over himself in his effort to get away from the judge.

With a subtle pop, Bickel was back.

"You're some sort of unnatural freak. Bet you're in on it too!" Ben snarled at the reappeared Witch.

"Just grab him," Geer shouted as he tried to capture Ben.

Ben threw a punch connecting with Geer's shoulder, then spun around to have a go at Bickel. Between the two of them, they managed to take hold of the distressed man. All three disappeared just as Ben's hands closed around Bickel's throat.

I could imagine the scuffle continuing in Geer's office.

"Mea—" Juliet rushed into the room. "I think someone else is here."

28

JULIET

"What? Who?" Mea rushed up to me and grabbed my shoulders.

I looked back toward the hall even though I couldn't see anything. "My mother. Probably—I don't know for sure. I only heard the creaking of the downstairs office door."

The room's windows looking down onto the warehouse were shuttered with blinds so we couldn't see from where we were. But we also couldn't be seen.

"No one knows we're here." Mea's hazel eyes were sharp and focused. "We can hide in one of the other rooms and, if it's your mother, see what she does when she finds the room's magic gone. We've as good as caught her. There's no reason for her to be here, other than the captives. She can't explain this away."

I wanted to believe Mea; her logic was sound. Knowing that didn't stop the feeling of dread growing inside me. If my mother was just here, sending Ben's texts, then why was she back so soon? Had she followed us somehow? Had we walked into her trap despite everything?

Mea and I crept into the hall and moved quietly toward the next room.

"Edwin will be back soon," I whispered. "If only Geer were still here." I wanted as many witnesses as possible, and preferably ones that weren't being framed for kidnapping.

Mea slowly opened the door to the middle room. There was a creak on the stairs as we slipped inside and Mea closed the door swiftly behind us. She didn't shut it completely, likely wanting to avoid the sound of the latch clicking.

Unhurried footsteps sounded in the hall outside.

Then the person stopped. We'd left the door to the captives' room open, but that didn't matter now all the magic was gone. There was a long silence, during which Mea and I barely breathed.

"Is there any point in hiding, Juliet?" My mother called.

A spike of anxiety gripped my chest. It mingled with a disconcerting level of surprise. But why was that? I'd known it was her all along.

Mea leaned in to whisper in my ear. "Juliet, you've got this. I'll be right here. You can end this now, confront her, say what you need to say, or I can go out and handle it. Either way, the others will be back any second. You're not alone." She grabbed my hand and squeezed.

I looked at Mea, unable to form my own words. The mess of emotions I'd been feeling were joined by something else, a contradictory feeling of stability and almost safeness. I wanted to tell Mea how much she meant to me, but the sound of my mother walking around the room beside us drew my attention.

I led Mea out of the room, my heart pounding and resolve strengthening, but I froze just out of sight of my mother, experiencing the most unpleasant kind of déjà vu.

I looked at Mea. She cocked her head in question, eyes darting toward the room, apparently not wondering what I needed but seeming to ask if she should go ahead, like she knew I required more time to collect myself. I nodded.

Mea leaned up against the doorframe of the captive's room, casual as can be. "Judge Herrera."

My mother's voice floated out into the hall. "Ms. Dubois. I wish I was surprised to see you here, but after running out on me the other day, I can't say I'd expected any better."

Mea ignored the judge's words. "What are you doing here?"

"I could ask you two the same."

My stomach roiled but I ignored it. After years of feeling one way and acting another, I could face her and pretend it didn't affect me. Otherwise, what was the point of it all?

Gritting my teeth, I took up a spot in the doorway opposite Mea. "We're here with the owner's permission. So—what are you doing? Breaking and entering?"

Judge Herrera looked delighted by something I couldn't quite identify. "Here at the owner's permission? What about the tenant? I don't know that unannounced inspections are allowable."

"What, are we nit-picking over Mortal laws now?" Mea's frustration was evident in her tone. "There is no tenant, and either way, *you* shouldn't be here."

My mother cast her gaze around the room. "Why should I have to explain my presence? I'm only taking part in the investigation, looking for those poor missing Witches. Is there any evidence I've done anything wrong?"

Yes. Her presence here was damning. Wasn't it?

Mea didn't lose her focus. "What led you to this place in particular, if you're investigating?"

The judge ignored her, folding her hands behind her back and looking at me instead. "You and Mr. Bickel are in a tight spot, Juliet."

I narrowed my eyes. "Why? There's nothing here."

"Then shall we go?" My mother gestured toward the doorway Mea and I were blocking. "No?" She asked when neither of us moved. "That's fine. We need to figure out how to proceed, Juliet. There may be nothing here now, but I can sense all the broken spells. It seems the Witches were moved before I could get here."

I narrowed my eyes. "You can't know the Witches were here just from the residual magic."

"But you've just confirmed they were here. Teleported away, no doubt. What are you going to do now that your only notable friend has been found to be abducting those around you? Will it come to light that it was your plan he was enacting, or will you accept my help in proving he was acting alone?"

I was sick of dancing around things and having veiled conversations, so I asked one of the questions that had been on my mind for years. "How long did it take you to figure out something was wrong?"

"Excuse me?" My mother gave me a bemused look like I was being ridiculous.

"How long did it take you to figure out I'd restricted your power? How long did it take you to realize you had memories missing? Not twenty-some years, surely."

My mother's demeanor changed instantly. She glared, whether mad at what I'd done to her, or mad I wasn't letting her control the conversation, I didn't know. "I can't believe you'd admit that, Juliet. That's a serious crime."

I pushed off the wall and stalked toward her. "Is it? Then I'll just have to face that, won't I? And what about you? Your crimes? What about the reason I did such a thing in the first place?"

My mother let out a laugh. "I've never done anything to you, Juliet. It's hardly my fault if your youthful rebellion led you to attack me. Was it his idea? Now that I can understand. If I'd known you'd met Mr. Bickel, I'd have been able to warn you and *this* might have never happened."

Was she still trying to bring everything back on Edwin?

Why? Because she thought he'd gotten away with something more than thirty years ago? Because she was still mad the committee's majority hadn't gone her way in his trial?

More likely, she didn't care about Edwin one way or another, only knew that I did. She'd use him any way she could. But didn't she know me better than to believe I'd throw him under the bus to win her favor?

"So are you over this *phase* then?" The Judge narrowed her eyes at me.

"My life isn't a rebellious phase. Edwin didn't influence me—"

"He helped you attack me. And don't think I won't see you both punished for it."

"Edwin never did anything other than break the spells you cast on me and stand by my side. The rest was all me. I went to talk to you and you tried to shut me up with another spell. You were never going to stop, so I did it for you."

My mother turned away from me and began pacing the room. "That's always Bickel's story isn't it? He's a bystander to others' bad deeds but never at fault. How many times will that tale be believed?"

I would not let it hurt that she was continuing to focus on Edwin rather than address anything that had happened between the two of us. Did she really have no emotions about what I'd just said? It was as if my mother believed nothing bad had ever happened, and yet this whole conflict was about us and our toxic relationship.

I reminded myself I didn't need her acknowledgment to deal with this myself. The power to wrap this up and move on didn't lie with her. Honestly, I didn't even need to be having this conversation now. It was a chance to clear things up she probably didn't deserve, and she didn't even want to take it.

I took a breath and focused on the matter at hand. "I'm not

going to undo the spells I cast on you, mother. You won't be able to pin these kidnapping on me any more than you can blame my past actions on Edwin. So stop trying."

She pursed her lips in dissatisfaction. "You'd rather take the fall with him, than reconcile with me?"

"Reconcile what? We aren't even talking about what happened between you and me. Not even close. Besides, I've already admitted to Geer what I did to you. And I told him why. You can't hold my illegal magic use over me. It's not a secret."

"No, you didn't." My mother looked rattled for the first time, her eyes going wide like she couldn't imagine I'd confess. "You're lying," she said more strongly, as if she thought believing a lie turned it into truth.

It seemed as if her whole plan had hinged on the fact that I couldn't bring her down without hurting myself, and she'd assumed I'd never put others before me.

There was a subtle pop and Edwin was suddenly standing between my mother and me. For half a second I was relieved to see his confused face as he tried to take in what was happening around him. Then there was a flash of light and Edwin crumpled to the ground.

A trickle of blood leaked out from the back of his head and onto the floor.

I cried out and fell forward to grab him. Mea was at my side in an instant.

"What did you do?" Mea growled at the judge.

"Relax, he's only magically incapacitated." My mother sounded genuinely annoyed. "Couldn't have him freezing things before we finished our chat, Juliet."

"He hit his head," I said in a choked voice.

Edwin's blood was on my fingers. This wasn't right. This wasn't how it went.

Mea stood and approached my mother. "You're under arrest for assault."

"Try me," my mother sneered. "The other judges will believe Bickel made the first move. I was only defending myself. And against someone like him, there's no room to be delicate."

"I wouldn't be so sure." Mea pulled out her phone and was already dialing. "Didn't you hear Juliet? Geer knows everything. He was just here with us. Where do you think the captive Witches went?"

The phone flew out of Mea's hand and crashed into the opposite wall.

"If you call, you'll be sending Juliet and the man on the floor to jail."

"You don't have as much influence as you think," Mea shot back. "This set-up is far from a done deal. And you know it. That's why you're panicking."

"You're wrong." My mother was standing almost chest to chest with Mea, doing her best to tower over the blue haired woman when she was barely an inch taller. "I had no reason to abduct these people and no one can prove beyond doubt that I did it. Even if the victims in New York don't match the others in their association with my daughter, it doesn't point to me. Why would *I* go after Ben Shaw? Juliet on the other hand was mad that Ben had sent Jasper to see her. She couldn't stand them meddling in her life, harassing her, so she got rid of them. That's what Juliet does, she deals with people she doesn't like with force. Admitting she attacked me and erased my memory will only prove the point. It's a pattern." She turned away from Mea and focused on me, cold and calculating. "The only way to escape this mess is to restore my command of my power. Then we can all walk away. Well, maybe not Bickel. Consider him a lesson learned. There's no one I can't reach. Even without magic."

"Except that's not true," I said from the floor. The bleeding at the back of Edwin's head had mostly stopped under the pressure of my hand, but I couldn't let go of him. "Ben never told Jasper to see me. They aren't even friends. We talked to Jasper last night. He's currently having tea with Geer's wife."

"No." My mother blinked in shock, the frown lines around her mouth deepening. It didn't look like she'd realized we found Jasper yet. She tried to school her face back into neutrality, but I could see the sharp anger in her eyes. "It doesn't matter. Jasper is a fool. Besides, you *thought* Ben sent him. It will be easy to convince people of that. The reality isn't relevant to your motives. You were acting on what you knew."

"There's no scenario where you and I walk away from this without consequences." I looked away from my mother and muttered a quick spell to check Edwin really was only magically subdued and not concussed.

Magic tickled my sense and with it came the beginning of relief. Edwin was okay, I could wake him with a counter spell.

"You aren't walking away from this at all then, if that your choice," my mother said.

I tore my eyes away from Edwin again. "Everything between us is out in the open. Mea, Geer, and I all know about your deal with Jasper. It's obvious you tried to cover it up. And that's not all. I bet Geer's talking to Abbott about your suspicious personal travel as we speak." I had no clue if this was true, but someone would talk to Abbott before too long. I took a steadying breath, feeling calmer. "You need to accept that your plan didn't work, mother. I'm not letting you walk away free to place people's minds under your influence. And now that Geer—and soon everyone you've worked with—knows what you've done, you'll have to face it."

There was a ringing silence. I could only imagine the thoughts swirling through my mother's mind.

Her resolve broke, twisting her face in anger. "Can't you see how similar we are?" She sneered before taking a heaving breath. "You used your power on me. You couldn't resist. Don't fool yourself into thinking that will be overlooked just because I did it first. Especially when your claim that I did such horrible things to you is wrong. I was only trying to help. Make you into the best you could be. It wasn't malicious, not like what you did."

But I'd heard this before—how her spells were for the best. Done with good intentions. Last time we'd talked, she'd refused to acknowledge my perspective or the pain she'd caused. She didn't see what she'd done as a big deal—maybe she didn't want it to be because then she'd have to accept what she'd done—and nothing I said would ever change her mind. She would never choose to see herself at fault. It was always my reaction that was unreasonable, my unhappiness that was the problem. I should have welcomed all her little restrictions and adjustments, forgiven her cruelty and ignored myself.

I didn't need to have that conversation again.

My eyes found Mea, where she seemed to be waiting for my cue. She stepped toward my mother as I pulled out my phone.

29

MEA

wo weeks later.

"Shall we go get coffee?" Bickel asked as he, Juliet, and I exited the Authority building onto the crowded street.

Juliet's eyes sparked with amusement. "At Coffee Cat?"

"I—we don't have to." Bickel paused, glaring back at his place of employment. "But let's at least get out of this neighborhood."

Neither Juliet nor I had any objections. If the others were anywhere near as exhausted as me, coffee and distance from official Witches were necessities right about now.

We'd each been in individual interviews for the past fortnight. It felt like I'd recounted everything to half the organization's upper management by now, and I was the lucky one. My questioning had actually ended a couple days ago, but I'd been sitting around in various Authority waiting rooms while these two got through the rest of theirs.

Terra, Easton, and Reyes had flown out with our boss last

week for what was an extremely uncomfortable afternoon. If I hadn't already been planning to leave the Authority, I'd have quit out of protest due to Easton's latest bullshit. He'd somehow turned the whole thing into a personal offense, like I'd been out to make him look bad this entire time. Really, why Bickel had the reputation for being a jerk when so many Witches were way worse, I'd never know.

But I'd had the last laugh, so to speak. I still couldn't believe how things had turned out with the Authority.

"Let's go to Coffee Cat." I shivered from the combination of the late afternoon shadows and wind. "I'm ready for some unseasonably warm weather."

Bickel nodded in approval. He'd recovered from our trip to the warehouse seamlessly and was back to his usual self. Maybe he'd carefully tucked his past away again, or the shock of that day hadn't rattled him as deeply as it initially appeared. Either way, I hadn't heard any more about his previous troubles.

Both Bickel and Juliet were in the clear for the kidnappings —obviously since we were out here making coffee plans. I won't say it wasn't tense, especially in those first few days when none of us were allowed to leave the Authority building, but we'd managed to pull through. Geer did a good job of presenting our side of the story to the other judges, so the case was seen as an attempted set-up from the start, rather than accusations Juliet or Bickel had to defend against outright. I had a feeling that framing made all the difference.

The curses had been successfully removed from the captive Witches, who were now recuperating in their respective homes. Ben was much more himself and seemed almost embarrassed about his belligerent behavior, not that it was in any way his fault.

He and Jasper had been hanging out with me for the last day and actually seemed like they might become friends.

"After this is all wrapped up, I'm booking a vacation for real," Ben had said just this morning.

I'd wholeheartedly agreed, though not enough to join in a group trip as Jasper had suggested. I'd never be able to overlook his attempted spying and would be fine never crossing paths with him again.

Judge Herrera had been suspended, detained, and was awaiting a trial date. She hadn't counted on anyone finding out about her deal with Jasper, which made it much harder for her to continue to present herself as someone of flawless good-character, and when everything was set out at once it looked quite damning. There were too many lies, and she was in no longer in a position to refuse a psychic interview.

My favorite detail—if I could have such a thing—was how flying across the country caught her out. The judge had her assistant book tickets for her and her husband, but there was proof that Mr. Herrera had never left New York. He seemed unaware of his wife's scheming, and though she'd requested he lay low while she was away, he'd instead attended several dinners out with friends.

The second plane tickets had been used to get the abducted and cursed Witches back to New York. Juliet's mother had tried to cover this risky transportation with masking spells used to confuse airport security footage so there would be no seeing who was actually with her. Her justification was that as a high-profile couple, she and her husband always travelled with extreme privacy precautions, but when he admitted to not going with her it was harder to explain a second masked person's presence.

If the judge had left everyone in California, we might not have been able to directly connect the initial missing Witches to what was happening in New York, but she was almost as hell-bent on framing Bickel as blackmailing her daughter. I got the impression Judge Herrera's hatred of our teleporting friend came in large part from the fact he'd been accepted into the Authority as an employee against her recommendation. Rather than let that go over the intervening decades, she'd apparently grown resentful. Who knows, maybe Judge Herrera really did blame Bickel for what Juliet did to her.

Juliet's alterations to her mother's mind hadn't been overlooked in all this. There was no need for a trial since Juliet had admitted everything and she'd come to an agreement with the remaining judges. The court would restrict Juliet's own ability to alter minds, effectively removing the power from her with their own court-approved mind alterations, which Juliet consented to. Then in twenty years, Juliet could apply to have the restriction lifted if she wished.

She'd been very blasé about the whole thing, and barely mentioned it more than to let Bickel and me know a decision had been reached. I wondered if she would ever ask for the power back. She seemed happy to let it go.

The three of us arrived at Coffee Cat and I breathed in the warm air in relief.

Juliet held back as Bickel went to open the cafe's door. "Do you mind ordering for us, Edwin? I'd like to talk to Mea for a moment."

"Not a problem." He disappeared inside.

I turned to Juliet. "Is everything all right?"

"Oh. Yes. I mean—after the last month, maybe *all right* isn't the most accurate descriptor, but things are as good as can be expected. Better even."

"Okay—" I couldn't help smiling as Juliet tried to hide her obviously flustered mood with bland look. The affect was ruined by the blush heating her cheeks.

"I was wondering if you'd want to go out on a date sometime?" Juliet ran a nervous hand through her hair. "Not right now. I can't say I'm in the right mindset, but—I thought it best to let you know I was intending to get around to a date. So that there's no confusion. If you're interested. Um. And I know you probably aren't moving to town now that you're leaving the Authority, but I can drive. I mean I can meet you in LA or wherever."

I reached out and put a hand on Juliet's arm. "I'd love to go on a date with you."

"That's a relief," Juliet said with a straight face, making us both laugh.

"As far as moving—I had an unexpected meeting with my boss's boss this morning." A meeting I'd almost declined. My resignation had been sent in a week and a half ago, but I'd been curious what they wanted.

I shoved my hands in my pockets. "Management wanted to talk to me about my reason for resigning. I didn't hold back in my letter and at first I thought they were going to be mad at me, but they only wanted to discuss it."

I'd outlined all the problems that had led me to leaving and, despite expecting an argument, management had agreed with many of my points. They also made it clear they didn't think it would look good for the organization if the investigator who found the missing Witches and brought the judge in quit immediately. I'd said I didn't really care how it looked, but this only prompted them to ask what it would take for me to stay.

My demands had been steep and I'd assumed none of them would be met. I'd said there needed to be a way to complain about the Authority, both about individuals like Easton and about the handling of cases or trials as a whole, and that people outside the organization needed somewhere to go if the Authority was the problem to begin with.

That was about when they'd asked if I wanted to be the one to set up such a system.

So we'd created a new position. I'd oversee a team who would be in charge of keeping an eye on Authority operations in the Southern California region. We'd decided to base it outside of LA to enforce a separation from the rest of the Authority. The idea was that I'd be working alongside them, rather than within the organization itself.

It wasn't part of the expansion but a pilot program—a specific outpost that didn't just assign bodies to cases and enforce law, but checked how things were going, during and after cases, and checked directly with the people involved, not just the Authority agents. I wouldn't be working as an investigator in the same way I had been, but that was fine with me. If this new team proved effective, I'd get the opportunity to request the program be expanded throughout the country.

I explained all this to Juliet and she looked just as surprised as I'm sure I had when it was first discussed.

"It's a kind of accountability system, and I'm not sure if it's the right solution, but it's something I can actually do. A way to use this weird new-found favor management has decided to bestow upon me. But watching the Authority seems like very *Authority* response. you know?" I was being upfront about my doubts this time. Not ignoring them.

"Surveillance is a big thing of theirs, and I get what you mean." Juliet smiled at me. "But you're right, it's still worth a shot."

"And hopefully better than nothing." This wasn't me giving the Authority another chance as I'd been doing all these years, or as I'd been trying to do with moving. This wasn't avoidance, and it wasn't me trying, alone, despite everything stacked against me—it was a collaboration.

Maybe it would work, or have some positive impact, lead us toward a better, more well-rounded solution in the future.

Juliet crossed her arms. "So where is this taking place?"

I glanced around. "Here, actually."

She raised her brows.

"I know." I shifted uncomfortably. "But I swear I didn't pick the location because I was hoping to date you. That would be so irresponsible given I'm trying to set up a way to reduce inappropriate uses of power. I actually suggested we start in New York, but it was the LA management I was talking to and they didn't think we could swing that just yet. We had to start in our district and so they suggested here for the same reasons this town would have been good for a new branch. The high Witch population and the position relative to the rest of the district."

Juliet laughed. "It does make sense. If you're keeping tabs on Authority activity, you have to be within reach."

"But not so close people think we're interchangeable with the rest of the organization. Ideally this job wouldn't be part of the Authority at all but it kind of has to be at the start to get anything done." A twinge of discomfort still gripped me. "It's weird it's me leading this effort, don't you think? I feel like I've been given credit I don't really deserve. You and Bickel did just as much as I did on this case. Maybe more. I didn't do anything noteworthy."

Juliet crossed her arms. "Please, you were great. Edwin and I don't care about credit, especially when you're doing something with it. And I needed you in all this, not just for your professional abilities. You helped me Mea, in ways no one else could have."

"I—" Suddenly it was hard to accept Juliet's honesty. I looked at the ground. "You can always count on me."

She reached out and squeezed my hand. "Maybe we can count on each other?"

I swallowed a surge of emotion. "I'd like that."

"Yes, I thought you might." Juliet grave me a knowing smile.

I cleared my throat. "I'll have to go to LA for a bit to sort out the details and gather a team. I'm thinking of hiring a combination of Authority members and outside lawyers. But I'll be back before you even realize I'm gone."

"Like I wouldn't notice. But it's fine, I'm more than happy to wait. Once our lives have settled down, this"—Juliet gestured between us—"is going to go well. I can feel it."

"You can, can you?" I was teasing but Juliet didn't seem to want to drop her serious mood.

"I wish I hadn't pushed you away for so long, Mea, and I'm not going to pretend that there isn't still a lot I need to deal with. But I'm committed to actually doing it—seeing a therapist and that sort of thing. Whatever I need to do to sort myself and my past out, and that will take time. But as of now, I want to stop holding back so much. I'll still be apprehensive about a lot things and doubt I'm about to start trusting every Witch I meet, but I don't need to fear the worst all the time. I want to take risks with you. I want to sit in my sparkly backyard and laugh with you. And everything in between." Juliet's brown eyes were blazing. "You—you know what I mean?"

"I do." I wrapped Juliet up in a hug and she squeezed me tight. "I want to take risks with you too, Juliet. I have a feeling you're going to keep me on my toes, and I like that."

"I'll make sure I do." Juliet gave me a swift kiss.

When she pulled back I was blushing. My heart went all fluttery and suddenly everything I wanted with Juliet felt like too much to hold inside me. I didn't want to wait. I wanted to be in the future now, where we were a couple, but I also wanted to enjoy getting there. I just wanted it all, even if I couldn't have both at once.

I was excited for us. For all the little moments like this one. I couldn't wait to look back on this day and remember everything from the exhaustion to the hopeful feeling burning inside me. We were ending the day on a perfect note, the cafe a lovely contrast from the bland businesslike halls we'd just left.

"What's the deal with this place, anyway? Best coffee in town?" I asked as I took in the sight of Juliet's sun-kissed face and inhaled the smell of sweet treats and coffee.

Juliet looked over her shoulder like she'd forgotten where we were. "The coffee is good, but that's not why Edwin keeps coming back." Juliet gestured inside to where Bickel was waiting for our drinks and leaned in conspiratorially to whisper, "He's been flirting with that one barista for months."

Inside the same Mortal guy I'd seen before was busy working the espresso machine while Bickel studied the floor.

I looked back at Juliet. "Are you sure? Because it seems like they're ignoring each other."

"I didn't say it was the most effective flirting. Especially at the moment." Juliet shook her head in an affectionate way.

We entered the cafe and sat at a table near the windows. I could imagine Juliet and I coming here, again and again—with Aria and Bickel, just us two, with Terra and other friends.

Juliet arched a brow. "What?"

"Hm? Nothing, I just like it here."

With you.

Four months later.

Juliet was looking out her kitchen window. "Mea, what's going on in the backyard?"

"Huh?" I turned back to the fridge so she couldn't see my suppressed smile.

"Don't huh me. You know what I mean."

When I twisted back around she was pointing a manicured finger outside.

I joined Juliet at the window. "Oh. You mean the ducks."

"Of course I mean the ducks. But what—why are there so many?" Juliet sounded like she couldn't decide if she was horrified or amused.

"There's less than ten," I said reasonably.

"*Less than ten*—" A snort of laughter escaped Juliet despite her efforts to keep it in. "So what, you mean there's nine of them?"

I shrugged. There were indeed nine ducks in the yard, quacking around a bowl of peas.

"Did you tell me we were getting *nine* ducks?" Juliet gave me a mocking stern look. No one was under the impression I had actually informed her how many ducks I was adopting.

I went to open the back door. "They're rescues."

"Uh-huh." Juliet followed me outside and a few of the ducks came to greet us. "Well what if they fly away?"

I knelt down to pat one of them. "Wait. Are you worried they'll get lost? Have you already gotten attached to their feathery little faces?"

Juliet huffed. "Don't be silly. It's just, if they needed rescuing in the first place, it would be bad form for us to lose them. Do you think we should put tracking spells on them?"

The duck I was patting waddled off and I stood. "If you want. But I'm sure they'll be happy to come back. As long as you keep feeding them."

"Like I'd not feed them. What am I, some sort of neglectful monster?" Juliet watched as another duck approached us. "I just think moving pets into my house rather than yours was—an odd choice. Especially as it seems you have doubts about my ability to care for them."

I put my arm around her and Juliet leaned her head on my

shoulder. "I'd never doubt you. But you know, there's not enough room for nine ducks at my studio."

"Maybe you should have started with one."

"But then it would be lonely."

Juliet shook with silent laughter. "Just know I have my limits, Mea. You can't push too many more pets on me. More than a dozen and you have move in as well."

"Is that a hard line in this relationship?"

"If it has to be."

I grinned. "Awesome, I think we should get a miniature donkey."

Juliet startled and pulled away from me. The suggestion was worth it to see the look on her face. She was bewildered, as if she'd never spared a thought for donkeys in her life. Then her features shifted, becoming radiant with delight. Probably not because of the animals but because I'd just implied I wanted to move in with her one day.

"Not right away or anything," I said as my mind swam with more ideas than I could keep track of. "But you might want to be prepared."

"Planning a future with you is no hardship, Mea." Juliet kissed me as a duck pecked at the heel of her shoe.

I set the yard sparkling around us and we smiled as we got lost in the kiss and thoughts of us.

THANK YOU FOR READING
KEEP YOUR WITCHES CLOSE

Please consider leaving a review on your favorite site to help others find magical books they love. 🤍

More from the *Love & Magic* world

ONE WICKED NIGHT
Tristan Taylor Thomás & Edwin Bickel

Would you like a free **bonus scene**? Head over to my website coletterivera.com and subscribe to my author newsletter. I'll send you more of Juliet & Mea!

ACKNOWLEDGMENTS

I would like to thank my editor May Peterson for her work on this book. Without her this story wouldn't have come together quite like it did. I would also like to thank TK for his support of me and his enthusiasm for all my Witches. And thank you to Sam Palencia for her beautiful cover art, especially Juliet's little house.

ONE WICKED NIGHT

After one unforgettable night they were never supposed to see each other again.

Tristan Taylor Tomás finally has the career opportunity he's been waiting for but it means moving across the country and leaving everything behind. A year's worth of flirting with a hot, mysterious man over coffee orders has come to nothing. Unless...

Powerful Witch, Edwin Bickel follows the rules. Especially the ones he sets for himself. His life is carefully constructed, change unwelcome, until sweet Mortal Tristan tempts the misanthropic Witch into abandoning his moratorium on love.

But Edwin's past casts a long shadow and he won't risk getting close to Tristan... so one night is all they have.

When a chance re-encounter has magic of its own, Edwin can't bring himself to walk away any more than he can allow himself to open up. A casual affair seems like the perfect answer, however Edwin isn't the only Witchy influence in Tristan's new life.

Tristan doesn't know magic exists and something sinister is lurking out of sight.

Can Edwin trust Tristan to help stop the biggest magical crime New York has ever seen? And can a Mortal looking for love ever make it work with a Witch who's spent his life guarding his heart?

ABOUT THE AUTHOR

Colette (she/they) is an author of queer paranormal romance novels who lives in New Zealand. Colette loves to write couples who take care of each other and show their soft sides in love, even when they're prickly in other facets of their lives. Sugar, spice, and magic are key ingredients in all of Colette's books.

Colette can be found on Instagram @colette_rivera or on Facebook under Colette Rivera Author and at her website coletterivera.com.

ALSO BY COLETTE RIVERA

Love & Magic

Keep Your Witches Close

One Wicked Night

Witch Boyfriend Wanted

Moonlight Falls

The Fall of Elijah Gray

The Seduction of James Gray

The Cursed Sebastian Storm

The Heart of Moonlight Falls

Lovers of the Damned

Demon's Mate

Demon's Heart

Demon's Desire

Devil's Mate

Shearwater Landing Shorts

I Think I Found a Vampire

Lockwood Coven

Her Ghostly Embrace

Bound In Blood

His Eternal Temptation